PENGUIN B

The Wrong Hand

Jane Jago was born in Sydney Australia in 1961. Originally trained as a printmaker, she began writing whilst raising a family. She has a long-standing interest in exploring the shadow aspect of human nature and in developmental psychology. Passionate about the protection of children and their right to a childhood, *The Wrong Hand* is her first novel.

The Wrong Hand

JANE JAGO

PENGUIN BOOKS

PENGUIN BOOKS

UK | USA | Canada | Ireland | Australia
India | New Zealand | South Africa

Penguin Books is part of the Penguin Random House group of companies
whose addresses can be found at global.penguinrandomhouse.com

Penguin
Random House
UK

First published 2016
001

Copyright © Jane Jago, 2016

The moral right of the author has been asserted

Set in 12.5/16pt Garamond MT Std by Thomson Digital Pvt Ltd, Noida, Delhi

Printed in Great Britain by Clays Ltd, St Ives plc

A CIP catalogue record for this book is available from the British Library

Trade Paperback ISBN: 978–1–405–92042–1
Paperback ISBN: 978–1–405–92041–4

www.greenpenguin.co.uk

MIX
Paper from
responsible sources
FSC® C018179

Penguin Random House is committed to a
sustainable future for our business, our readers
and our planet. This book is made from Forest
Stewardship Council® certified paper.

To my sons

Birth is a lottery. Some children are born into loving, supportive families and are given the best of starts; some inherit a legacy of dysfunction, or worse. *The Wrong Hand* focusses on the aftermath of a terrible tragedy that challenges our very idea of childhood innocence. In an age of social reform, where rehabilitation, redemption and forgiveness are promoted for all but the very worst of adult offenders, violence by children confronts one of our most deeply held taboos, and continues to confound our understanding. Just what influences warp and so desensitise a child's psyche that they can conceive of extreme violence?

It is a sad fact of living that even happy families cannot always protect the children they love. Losing a child under any circumstances is something we all hope we will never have to face. But how does a parent begin to grieve for such a loss when even their sacred memories have been defiled? When they are not left to grieve in private and in peace?

This book is my exploration of these questions: of how such things can happen; of the irrevocable and long-lasting price paid by the victims, and my attempt to comprehend what drives the best and worst in us all. It is my belief that there is no 'them', there is only 'us'.

Jane Jago, 2016

Prologue

It was a Sunday when they found him. Somewhere a truck's brakes shuddered violently; a siren wailed. The woman moved her head instinctively in the direction of the sound, but her eyes registered nothing of the scene outside the window. In the street below, a marked van forged its way from the building's car park across the crawling lanes of city-bound traffic and onto the motorway. Rain on the glass refracted the prisms of coloured light as they bled slowly away into the gathering evening.

The woman looked blankly at the uniformed officer who sat watchfully beside her. The constable's face was white and pinched, but she attempted a weak smile and patted the woman's hand. The woman pulled it away. She gripped her seat and began to rock slowly back and forth, back and forth, back and forth until approaching footsteps on the polished linoleum interrupted her rhythm. She stood up and looked towards the doorway.

Two men hesitated at the threshold, a detective with a bewildered man draped in a grey blanket, whom he gently ushered forward.

The woman scanned his face. 'It's not Benjamin, is it?' She grabbed the man's wrists. 'I know it's not him.'

He was unable to speak.

'Mathew! *Say it's not him!*' She pressed her face against his chest, then slid slowly to her knees.

Choices

'For what has been determined must take place.'

Danny, Holroyd House, Juvenile Corrections, 2001

'Make a list of ten *possible* names you like.'

'Why?'

'Why do you think, Danny?'

'I dunno. Is it a game?'

'No, it's not a game. We've been talking about it for a long time now.'

'A new name? You want me to choose it?'

'We want your ideas.'

'I don't know ten names.'

Dr Harmina Lepik smiled tolerantly. Everyone knew ten names. She slid a slim volume across the desk. 'Take this back with you to your room and have a look through it.'

'*A Thousand Names for Your Baby.*' Danny read the title aloud.

'If you have a particular favourite, put it at the top of the list,' said Dr Lepik. 'You have the chance to reinvent

3

yourself, Danny,' she added, serious now. 'Do you understand?'

He did.

Back in his room, after shutdown, he turned the pages of the little book incredulously. *Aaron, Abbott, Abel, Abner, Abraham, Adam, Addison* . . . What sort of names were these? *Aaron – Hebrew, enlightened. Barry, Beau, Belarmino* . . . Bloody hell. *Benjamin, Bill, Bertrand, Bobby, Barendon, Bradley, Brigham, Byron* . . . No way. *Carl, Cameron, Casey, Chadwick* . . . He was getting bored now. He bored easily. *Dallas, Damon* . . . He continued until his finger slid across the familiar *Daniel – Judged by God. Darcy, David, Dean, Dexter, Dirk, Dudley* . . .

'Dudley Simpson,' he said out loud. *Edward* . . . *Frederick* . . . *Gabriel, Garth, Gavin, Gaylord* – Gaylord! He almost wet himself laughing. *George, Gerald, Glen* . . .

He picked up a pen and began to scribble down names that either amused or interested him. He went through the entire alphabet, until his page was full of names. He tore it off. On the next page he wrote 'Daniel Simpson'. He sorted the letters of his name alphabetically. He tried to come up with an anagram, finally settling on the improbable 'Neil Dimsap'.

Unimpressed with his efforts, he allowed his eyes to wander around the familiar room. He'd only been in it for a week but it was identical to all the rooms he had been in over the last seven years. An unremarkable single

4

bed under a permanently closed window, a built-in ward-robe, a bare desk with drawers and a shelf full of books. The walls were a sickly blue, decorated only with a few sagging football posters and one of a naked girl draped across a surfboard, which 'they' considered healthy – otherwise it wouldn't have survived the move from the last room to this one.

The moves happened without warning, at any time in the daily routine. He might have just finished classes or duties when he was directed by a ward supervisor to a newly allocated room, either close by or in another wing. When he entered it, the new room would be exactly as he had left the other, with all his things in place. He had been told that the moves were a precaution designed to protect him from other boys, who might wish to harm him, but the unspoken reason was that the regular moves enabled his guards to search his room and ensure that he hadn't secreted some means of harming himself. After all these years the silly bastards still thought he meant to do himself in. Suicide had never crossed his mind.

He had once hidden a pair of small blades he had taken out of a plastic pencil-sharpener (stolen from the Centre's library) by unscrewing the wardrobe-door knob and slid-ing the blades behind the chrome collar. He'd done it just in case he wanted something small and sharp during the hours he spent in his room. A few weeks later he was moved again and wouldn't have given the matter another thought, but for his weekly session with Dr Lepik.

From the moment he'd gone in he'd known something was wrong. Usually she was sitting at the table and waited for him to settle into his chair before she started the warm-up questions – 'How are you, Danny? How has your week been?' He would tell her what he had been studying, how he had been feeling, whom he had been interacting with and if he had had any problems. Often he was stirred up so much by the process of communicating that he told her much more than he had planned to. That day she was standing by the window, looking out, not acknowledging his arrival.

He pulled out his chair and sat down. The doctor remained silent, and Danny felt increasingly uncomfortable. In his world other people spoke first and then he could judge where the traps might lie. Harmina Lepik turned around and gazed at him for several seconds. If she didn't greet him, he would sit there for a full hour without speaking. Silence was his one remaining weapon.

'Danny,' she said. 'How are you feeling about things?'

'Things?' asked Danny, unwilling to depart from the routine.

'Life, Danny, the future, what plans do you have?'

This was the stupidest question he'd heard for a while, even from her, so stupid it almost made him angry.

Plans? Future? What future? What did she expect him to fucking say?

'I haven't got any plans. It wouldn't matter if I did. I do what I'm told.'

'We all have plans, Danny, no matter where we find ourselves . . . If we don't like where we are, sometimes we plan how to get out.'

Get out? What was she *on*? Maybe she could get out and go home every night. 'You think I'm going to try and escape from prison?'

'This is not a prison, Danny.'

'Whatever you call it then – juvenile detention centre, secure unit.'

'There are, of course, many ways to escape.'

'Are there?' I wish you'd tell me what they are.

'Danny, you're nearly eighteen. You won't be here for ever. It's very possible you'll be released soon.' He'd heard this line before and regarded it with suspicion. His mother, the lawyer and the doctor seemed to believe it but he wasn't sure he wanted to let himself accept it, or even if he wanted it to happen. The thought of being released made him feel more afraid than he had felt for a long time.

'You must not give up. You did a terrible thing, but you deserve another chance.'

'Okay,' he said, waiting for the punch line.

'Remorse is useful . . .'

Remorse? Who mentioned remorse? He looked back blankly.

'So many people have been hurt by what happened. Harming yourself wouldn't change that, only add to it.'

He said nothing. He had no idea what to say – she was talking crap again.

'Have you thought about harming yourself?'

'No.'

'Do you have hopes for the future? Dreams?'

'What would be the point?'

'Well, that's what I want to talk about. Just imagine for a minute the future you would plan for yourself if there were no obstacles.'

'A future I won't get to have.'

'Put the obstacles aside and just try to imagine . . . Where would you go? What type of work would you do?'

'None.'

The doctor shrugged. 'Keep going. What would you do with yourself?'

Another of her pointless exercises, he thought. 'I'd get a Ferrari and a cool flat in the city, in one of those intercom buildings, or cruise around on a motorbike.'

She looked at him intently, waiting for more.

'I'd go to football on the weekend and maybe do some work, like with computers or something, or be a chauffeur for someone, drive around in a hot car paid for by somebody else.'

'What about other people?'

'Other people?'

'In your future do you have a girlfriend? Are you married?'

'Might have a girlfriend – yeah, one with big tits who likes to fuck a lot.' He wasn't allowed to talk like that anywhere else but you could get away with it in your therapy.

Harmina Lepik barely registered the remark or that Danny was staring directly at her breasts as he spoke. 'How does she feel about you?' she asked.

'Who cares?'

'Well, she might?'

'Then I'd get a new one. I don't know.'

'What about friends?'

'Yeah, until they find out about me.'

'Does that depress you?'

'No, they can get fucked.'

'I'm glad to hear you at least have some thoughts on the future, thoughts not really so different from other teenagers, Danny. Other young people your age, with far fewer obstacles standing in their way, often suffer doubts about themselves, and many normal teenagers go through periods of depression.'

'Yeah? I'm glad I'm not normal, then.'

Harmina reached into her jacket pocket and pulled out something small. 'I believe you were moved again, Danny.'

'They do it just to irritate me.'

'You were upset?'

'No. All the rooms are the same.'

'You don't mind your things being interfered with?'

'They always put them back.'

'Do they?'

'Yeah.'

Dr Lepik opened her hand 'Danny, these were found hidden in your last room.' Two small blades lay in the hand she held out to him.

He recognized them immediately and laughed.

'What were you keeping them for?'

'I don't know.'

'Did you intend to harm yourself?'

He looked at her with contempt.

'Or to harm anyone else?'

'What – with those? They're from a pencil sharpener.'

'Why did you take them?'

'I don't know. I get tired of having to ask for everything. I just hid them for a joke.'

'You wanted us to think you were a danger to yourself.'

'No, I just hid them, so I could sharpen a pencil or cut paper if I felt like it. Big deal! I didn't have a plan.'

She put the objects back into her pocket and sat down. He thought he could tell from the changed expression on her face that she believed him. 'I'm pleased we've had this discussion, Danny, and that we've focused on at least some possibilities for the future.'

Whatever advice Dr Lepik had offered the administrators, the moves had continued. His custodians could not afford to take chances. It was their mission to protect Danny Simpson from the many threats directed against him. Also, a dead juvenile wasn't good for the records. A dead juvenile many *wanted* dead would create a very bad stink indeed.

Back in his room, Danny made his list. In a neat hand he printed a single column of names. He began to enjoy it, scribbling out some of his first selections, then replacing them with new ones until, finally, only ten remained.

Within a week his lawyer had come to the Centre with papers to sign about his release. *Release*: the very word made his palms sweat. The following Wednesday his mother arrived unexpectedly with a letter. Before she had even sat down in the visitors' room, he knew that a day had been named. An ashen-faced Debbie Simpson, hands shaking, read the letter aloud. Gone was all the girlish bravado with which she had reassured him while he had been locked up. 'The lawyers will work something out, Danny, they will, you'll see. You'll be out soon. You'll be able to come home. They won't send you to an adult prison when you turn eighteen. The lawyer's sure of that. Don't you worry, Danny.'

Don't worry. Don't worry because, beneath the surface, she wouldn't. After seven years, he was lucky if she made the journey to visit him three times in a year. When the initial drama of the trial had subsided, and she had discovered the dangerous difference between infamy and fame, she had been horrified by the violence of the public reaction against her.

Sitting across from him, clutching the long-awaited letter, Danny could see she was afraid – afraid for herself. She was barely able to look at him.

Oh, it was all right for Danny! Safely tucked away in custody while she was spat on in the street. He'd ruined her life, might as well have put a knife straight through her heart – all the moves, the hate mail, his brother's suicide . . . He'd fucked them all up. Sure she wasn't a saint, she wasn't the greatest mother in the world, but she'd done her best. It wasn't her fault: he was sick, a psychopath. None of the others had done anything like this . . . barely eleven years old!

He'd never been normal: from the moment they'd given him to her, there had been something unnatural about him, something you couldn't feel for. It wasn't her fault! She hadn't committed the crime! And now he was coming out and it would happen all over again – more moves, more hate mail.

Not this time, not now, not when she'd finally got it together. Not now she finally had a man worth more than a pinch of shit in her life. She couldn't do it. Danny would have to make it alone.

When she said goodbye and kissed him feebly, guilty tears in her eyes, Danny guessed what his mother already knew for certain: he would never set eyes on her again.

Geoffrey, of course, had been *their* idea, like all the rest of it. Sure they had given him 'choices'. No life or *a* life; choices between towns he had never heard of and towns he never wanted to see; choices between *Duncan, Brendan* and *Geoffrey* . . . After a while he realized that when they gave him any choice at all, it was because there really was none.

'*Geoffrey!* Geoffrey wasn't even on my list,' he cried.

'I don't know about that, Danny.'

'Dr Lepik got me to write a list of names.'

'Probably to eliminate any that you might have chosen for yourself. Other people who know something about you might make the same associations as you did.'

Danny was seething. They'd done it to him again – lured him out from cover and ambushed him. *Every fucking time.* 'Why didn't they tell me that?'

'Danny, I think the answer to that is pretty obvious.'

'I don't want to be called *Geoffrey*. What sort of a name is that?'

Jonathan Fisher's smile vanished. He fixed Danny with a hard look. 'I can assure you, *Geoffrey*, that there are a good many more important things for you to worry about than the flavour of your name. Get used to it. We still have to wade through all this,' he said, tapping the substantial pile of documents on the desk between them.

Danny was starting to feel sick. He didn't like the parole officer. So close to his release date, it distressed him to have to open up with someone new.

His nightmares were getting worse with each day that passed. When he woke up from one he wanted to go to Dr Lepik and beg her to stop his release. He wasn't ready. He would never be ready. By the time dawn broke, he knew he wouldn't. He couldn't stay there. Stay inside and die. Leave and be killed.

The dream was always the same: him barely able to breathe, running from something, crashing through the bush, over brittle ferns, fallen limbs and tinder-dry leaves, the smell of hot eucalyptus in his nostrils. Picking his way across sharp stones in his bare feet, stepping into the green ooze of a dribbling creek, then leaping up onto the bank on the other side, not daring to glance behind him. Running along a parched trail between the mottled gumtrees towards the light, and there at the end of the track a little boy, a dark-haired angel, stood staring straight at him. Just as he was drawn to the child, an older boy, with the face of a devil, stepped out of the shadows. 'Come on, baby,' said the older boy, holding out his hand.

'*Noooo!*' screamed Danny, but it was too late. The angel was already clasping the devil's hand.

Night and day, Danny was terrified. Terrified of living, terrified of dying. Terrified of being found out all over again, and terrified most especially of *him*.

The parole officer had assured him it was unlikely their paths would ever cross. It was a condition of his parole that the two never made contact. He could live with that.

'This is your new birth certificate, Geoffrey Roland Wickham.' Danny clenched his jaw muscles. 'Born on the eighteenth of January 1982.'

'That makes me seventeen,' said Danny, confused.

'That's right. We have to put your age back so we can place you in high school.'

'High school.' Danny thought he might vomit. 'I've already finished my final exams.'

'Attending a high school will give you a history, some legitimate records, a reference and school photographs.'

'Who's going to know?'

'It's okay, Danny. It's been specially chosen because of its non-threatening environment – it's a private school.'

'A private school?'

'If you're to assimilate into life outside, you'll need connections to survive. To anybody else you'll be just another new kid.'

'From where?'

'As far as the school is concerned, you're transferring from another high school.'

'Which one?'

'Don't panic, Danny. It's all in the profile, which you'll have plenty of time to read.'

'Who'll know about me?'

'No one, Danny – as few people as possible, but no one at the school.'

Danny eyed him dubiously. How could he believe anything these people said?

'Here's your new Medicare card and social-security number. You'll be entitled to a government allowance for at least two years and you'll be boarding with a local family who run a guest house for university students . . . Less accidental crossover with students from the school.'

What family? Where? If he didn't slow down, Danny was sure he would explode.

'I know it's a lot to take in, but we have to start somewhere. Here's a credit card, and a statement with your banking details.' Danny peered at the growing pile of paper in front of him. He picked up the plastic card embossed with his new name. 'There's a fifteen-hundred-dollar limit. You'll need to practise your signature and sign the back of it.'

Danny's mouth hung open.

'Every cent will need to be accounted for by the likes of me.' He reached into his pocket and pulled out a mobile phone. 'This is yours. You must keep it charged and switched on twenty-four hours a day. You'll be monitored for the rest of your life.'

He scrolled through the numbers already stored in the phone's memory until he came to 'Code Blue'. Danny was starting to feel like a CIA agent being briefed for a special operation. 'What's that?'

'You'll need to change the name to disguise it. It's a special phone-link that will connect you with the nearest police station. Should you ever need to use it, the police will treat your call as an emergency. Don't look so scared – it's just a precaution in case your identity is ever discovered.'

'And what do I tell *them*? Do the police know about me? Do they know who *Geoffrey Wickham* is? Because that's a joke – they hate me.'

'They don't know who you are. Geoffrey Wickham is just one name on a list of at-risk persons who may require police protection at any time. They don't know the reasons.'

'But they know how it works. Somebody will figure it out!'

'They have a list of names. Some are witnesses, some are persons under threat. Not all the people on the list are convicted criminals. The police don't know your details.'

'Who does? Who makes the list? How many people know about me?'

'All of the people involved in this entire process want to give you the best possible chance to make a life for yourself. The handful who know in any detail about your new identity are on your side.'

'How many?'

'Five. I know everything, and the other four know enough to do their jobs.'

Danny didn't speak. He couldn't. He would be walking around calling himself *Geoffrey Roland Wickham* and at least five other people would know exactly who he was. Jonathan Fisher counted them off on his fingers: 'Your new counsellor, who'll know your name, your case history and what you choose to tell her about your new life. A second parole officer . . .'

Danny slumped forward in his chair and rolled his eyes.

'In case something happens to me and I can no longer be assigned to you, a second officer will be kept up to date with what's going on, which gives me someone safe to discuss the matter with.'

Danny listened, his head in his hands. It was all beyond his control anyway. He'd probably be killed as soon as he left the Centre. In a way that might be easier. 'That's three,' he observed baldly.

'And someone in the Police Department will be briefed . . . someone higher up.'

That was that then. He might as well shoot himself on national television.

'And the public servant who originated these documents and put all this together – but they don't know any specifics or who it was for. The biggest threat to your identity is from past contacts, people who could expose you . . . like resuming contact with family, friends or former inmates, who knew you in here during the past seven years. Obviously we've taken all that into consideration in regard to your relocation.' Addressing the disturbed expression on Danny's face he added, 'There isn't any reason to think that the cover story you were given here was exposed, is there, Danny?'

'I don't know. Sometimes I felt like they all knew . . . and there was that kid who I . . . who kept at me, he knew something . . .'

'You mean the boy you choked with a towel? The one who called you a pervert?'

Danny glared at him.

'He didn't know anything, Danny.'

'No? My mother told me what that jerk supervisor said to the papers. The boy could have read that once he left here. If he didn't know who I was then, he probably does now! And what if I run into any of the others on the outside as *Geoffrey Wickham*. Don't you think they might put two and two together?'

'Your release is not without risks, Danny. A lot of people have been working on it. This is your profile, the life story of Geoffrey Wickham.' He slid a file across the desk. 'Take it back to your room, read it, front to back, until you know it off by heart, until it becomes second nature. Okay, Geoffrey?' Danny closed his eyes and nodded slowly. What other choice did he have?

Clues

'A time to weep . . .'

Rachel, 2008

Rachel McKenna positioned the cups in neat rows inside the overhead cabinet. She moved a wad of mail from the counter and dropped it into a tray beside the microwave, where her husband, David, would find it when he came home. That was their agreement. She did not look at the individual envelopes: a letter addressed with her former name could trigger a panic attack. She rolled back the reinforced-glass patio doors that led to the walled courtyard of a substantial garden. 'Time to come in, boys.'

'Okay, Mum,' said Martin, catching a wayward punt from his younger brother. 'Come, on Thomas, *inside*.' He repeated his mother's instruction, hugging the pigskin possessively to his chest.

Thomas dragged his feet, looking up at the afternoon sky, which was tinged with volcanic pink. He didn't get it: there was still plenty of light to play in.

Martin understood: he had been born under the shadow of the event, pulled into the void of his mother's longing for the older half-brother he had never met. He had absorbed her fears and taken it upon himself to protect her from them. Martin was her rock. He knew why he had to be driven to school and picked up every day, why at thirteen he had never had a sleepover at a friend's, why he had to play in the back yard, always in sight of his mother or father. In death Benjamin had remained three years old, but the parts of him that had been conceived in Rachel's mind, all her hopes and dreams for him, had been transposed onto Martin. He straddled the gap between death and life, between a dangerous world and safety, occupying a strange position across the two families, one that had been suffocated by grief and one that watchfully survived. And now by some form of unnatural mathematics he was the elder brother and protector not only of Thomas but also of Benjamin.

Martin had always been aware of her need to preserve Benjamin through him. His earliest memories were marked with traces of the little boy in the photographs above the piano – the one *he* had liked to 'play' – sitting on the red stool, *kerplunk, kerplunk. His laugh was like a crystal bell*. Martin was sure he'd heard it.

Memories of Benjamin became braided into his own. The pain in his mother's expression that accompanied every loving look or protective touch. The downward line of her mouth, even as she laughed at some heroic toddler feat he had achieved on the backyard swings. The 'happy tears' that dropped onto his first drawings, soaking into the paper, distorting and swelling it, the colours bleeding into one another. The panic in his mother's voice when he got ahead of her in the driveway on the way to the car.

Thomas, spared this neurosis, was terrifyingly normal. He'd come along much later and was fearless and uninhibited. Thomas magnified Rachel's anxieties and apprehensions, and increased her swamping need for control. Her all-consuming anxiety ruled their lives.

Thomas reclaimed the discarded football from a patio chair and kicked it through the doorway into the back of the couch. 'What's for tea?'

'We're having an omelette, then Dad will be home to take you to karate.'

Thomas made a face.

'You don't like karate now?'

'The instructor doesn't like me.'

Rachel wasn't convinced.

'He kicked me.' He rolled up his trouser leg, looking for bruises.

'He kicks everybody. That's his job,' said Martin, clipping his brother's backside with his bare foot as he shut and locked the patio doors.

23

'Piss off!'

'Boys!' Rachel's face was tense: one of her headaches was brewing. 'I'm sure the instructor didn't mean to hurt you, Thomas.'

Martin laughed. 'I wouldn't bet on it.'

'Learn to kick him back,' she concluded.

Thomas shrugged his shoulders. 'I'm only nine. But one day I'll kick his arse.'

His mother frowned at the language. Looking at Thomas's ruddy face, she was disturbed by his vitality and wondered how much longer she would be able to contain it.

She had good days and she still had bad days. The good days were days of forgetting, when she lived in the present. In all the intervening years the pain had not abated. *Time does not heal.* People should know that. All the blame and recrimination were still there, lurking under the surface. Her biggest fear was happiness. Happiness led to complacency and she'd been there before. Happiness brought with it guilt that she wasn't mourning Benjamin. Love for her other sons was stalked by the accusation that she was forgetting *him*. Moving on, letting go, abandoning her baby to his fate over and over again.

None of the hate mail, no matter how vile or insane, could ever match her inner voices. She had had to learn how to shut them out, forever blocking the ears of her soul to the nightmare words in court and printed in newspapers. Only she and Mathew, Benjamin's father, really knew who he was before *they* had taken him, before he had become public property – a cypher for every parents' nightmare. The inward death of outliving an infant child – of knowing that their baby had been tormented and discarded – had torn them apart. What love could withstand such an onslaught? The only way they had found to survive was to block the pain, to pull a curtain across each other's faces.

The guilt of abandoning Mathew to his grief had initially been overwhelming – watching him disintegrate, when he had wanted to draw close to her and drown out the horror with another sensation. Hatred had been an elixir. Before long she had been unable to bear the sight of him, to imagine that they could ever be close to each other again, that anyone could be close to her, or even near. They were each alone in their despair, seeing and hearing through a ten-foot wall of cracked glass, drowning behind it. The blackness solidified in her lungs with every attempted breath. The raging disbelief and the endless sobbing. The bewilderment. The first fifteen seconds of every waking day as reality swept in again, demolishing every good and sacred thing in its path.

She had wanted to blame Mathew for being weak, for not being there when it had happened. For stopping her returning to work when the baby was six months old – because if she had been at the building society that day, counting notes into the palm of a stranger's hand, Benjamin would have been safely tucked away at a nursery. She couldn't quite nail it down or make it stick, but she had blamed him anyway. The deeper truth, the one that was hardest to bear, was that she knew he blamed her. He had never said so but she knew.

She was the one who had taken Benjamin shopping, who had let go of his hand for the briefest of moments. *Why had she let go?* Turned her back on him, let him out of her sight. There was a perfectly good mini-market on the next corner. She should have gone there, and their life with Benjamin would still be intact. It was her fault. Hers. Who else's? Somehow she had to believe it was Mathew's.

'How can you touch me?' she had wailed, as he tried to pull her to him. 'I cannot *feel.* Do you understand? I don't want to.'

Why hadn't he gone out to kill those bastards, like any real man would? She had chosen the wrong mate, that was clear, one who couldn't protect his young. She had pushed him further and further away: she hadn't wanted to try to move on with him. Everything that represented moving on, every once-normal event, had been another spadeful of dirt burying all she had ever loved deeper and deeper under the cold, hard soil of a God-forsaken planet.

When she looked in the mirror now she saw a stranger, her pretty features soured by a cancerous grief. Her once flirtatious eyes were dull and empty after years of retreating from public stares. The hardness of her expression was captured by the cameras of stalking journalists, who threw around the F-word – *forgiveness* – in search of a saleable soundbite. As if it were her job to forgive the little ghouls who had done it; as if there was a timetable of normal reactions.

'Do you think you'll ever be able to forgive them?' The obscenity of the question. It wasn't an answer they were after but a reaction they could film or print.

She wanted to turn on them and scream, '*Let me rip your firstborn from your belly and hurl it under a speeding truck and ask you about forgiveness!*'

'Tell us how much you hate them.' The question behind the question. She wouldn't give them what they wanted. Her face became a hollow mask she showed to those who refused to leave her alone to deal with her pain.

Despite the guilt, escaping Mathew's bottomless need for her had brought relief. Leaving him had allowed her to close herself off. They had finally parted 'friends' before they could maim each other further. Only then had either of them begun to mourn properly.

Somehow, even though *she* had pushed *him* away, it was Mathew who needed to be free of her, to immerse himself obsessively in every aspect of the trial and the endless legal proceedings, doing now in Benjamin's memory what he couldn't do then. The further she withdrew from the public, from people, to regain a private sense of what she had lost, the more he externalized his pain and rage. He was like someone she had never met, talking about people she didn't know, holding pictures of a baby that belonged to *her*.

For nearly nine months she had lived 'indoors', guarded fiercely by her family as she rebuilt her memories of life with Benjamin and protected them from the horror of what had come after. The only way she could keep him safe was to separate him from the story he had become. In those first months, she envied the mothers of stillborn babies or those taken in their sleep by cot death. People wrapped their arms around those women and honoured their grief. Not like the faces that turned away from her, with a strangled half-sentence on their lips. No platitude forthcoming.

Any bereaved mother, in her unreachable grief, has some refuge at the bottom of the well of sadness where her heartbreak and memories of her child can wash over her. A place to drown and die, where the loving words of those outside can be heard from a distance. For mothers like Rachel, parents of the murdered and defiled, the pit was full of snakes. The house of mourning was desecrated with vile graffiti, peered into by tourists and anthropologists; one woman's agony another's peep show.

Instinctively Rachel constructed a wall around herself and dealt only with the loss of Benjamin, steadfastly refusing to let the details penetrate her mind. Her baby was gone and he was not coming back. She would never hold his face against her cheek, smell his hair or kiss him again. He would never call her name. He would never hesitate, and look to her for reassurance, before letting go of her hand and sitting down at his desk for his first day at school. He would never score a goal or sing in a school concert. He would never phone her from university just to say hi. She would never see him arrive home with his first car, girlfriend or broken heart. There would be no wedding; she would never hold his child in her arms and marvel at its likeness to Benjamin. All these things that she would never have – they were enough to mourn.

She had refused to attend the victim support groups recommended to her – to sit and trade horror stories, to identify with other broken women, whose mundane lives had intersected with evil. She wasn't like them: there was something wrong with those people. They had some-how taken their hands off the wheel – lived in the wrong area, turned down the wrong road . . . allowed the wrong people access to their children.

Eventually she had met David, a friend of a friend, the first person since time had stopped who hadn't asked how she was 'holding up' or looked at her as if she were terminally ill. He steered her away from her thoughts and walked her slowly back into life – or, at least, to its edges. He had given her Martin, then Thomas. He knew what it cost her to risk children again, and he put himself between her and the world. That he would give his life to protect her and their sons she was certain. No man could offer her more.

'Martin won't let me play on the computer.'

'Let him have some time to himself, Thomas.'

The nine-year-old threw himself onto the couch behind his brother. 'Can't play football, can't go to the park, can't play video games.'

'Switch the television on and shut up, Thomas. Anyone would think you'd got ADD.'

'I wish I did. Then I could take drugs and do whatever I want without getting into trouble.' He pointed the remote at the little red light under the black screen.

Rachel chopped onions on a board and threw them into a pan. She took five eggs from a carton and began breaking them over a bowl. Thomas flicked through the news channels.

'With speculation about their locations mounting, following a suspected leak from inside the Corrective Services Department, the killers of Benjamin Allen may have to be relocated again. The victim's father, Mathew Allen, said in a statement tonight that he was sickened.

'Once again Australian taxpayers are footing the bill to protect the perpetrators. Meanwhile the public should be asking, "Who will protect us from them?"'

The newsreader's voice was abruptly cut off as Martin pulled the cable from the wall. A bowl toppled in the kitchen, sending the remaining whole eggs onto the tiles, where they shattered, sending out gelatinous tentacles.

Habits

'By their fruits you will know them.'

Liam, 2008

As his colleagues from the Creighton and Davis real-estate agency talked around him, Liam took another drag on his cigarette, then drew the second-hand smoke back into his nostrils as it left his mouth. It ate up a considerable amount of money to smoke, and cigarettes were filthy, let's face it. Smoking was a crap habit. He knew it. He could feel it choking his lungs, dulling his senses. He welcomed it.

When it came down to it, Liam Douglass needed all the habits he could get. He needed habits like other people need appointment diaries. Habits like getting up in the morning and remembering to shave and wash. Habits like eating, going to work and *keeping* appointments in a diary. Without his habits he might have evaporated into the air around him.

'Bullshit!' shouted Colin, cutting through his private thoughts.

Liam ground his unfinished cigarette into the aluminium ashtray, and tuned them all back in.

'Ask Liam. He was there,' said Paul.

'The Bartos woman, did she toss a coin to decide between two houses?'

'She did,' Liam confirmed. 'And then she said, "To hell with it, I like this one better," and did the best out of three.'

'That woman's a nutcase. I showed her fourteen houses in April and *you* get the commission,' complained Paul.

'Well, I sold it to her.'

'No, you didn't. You just stood there and let her walk round. You made yourself invisible, like you always do, and she bought it.'

'Like they always do,' said Catherine, linking her arm proprietorially through Liam's. He gave her a weak smile.

Across the room, a young barman deftly filled a glass with beer. The granite clack of pool balls at the nearby table drew Liam's eye: a red ball oscillated aimlessly across the balding green felt.

'Well, it just proves what I've always thought,' began Colin, downing the last of his beer. 'If they're gonna buy the fucker they're gonna buy it, if you're lucky they'll buy it off you.'

'It's got nothing to do with luck. Liam is a *quiet* genius. Just because he doesn't walk around gushing or doing the hard sell —'

'We leave the gushing to you, Cath.'

'I don't gush.'

'I give them the same spiel as you do,' said Liam.

'You're not that bloody good. The *genius* of it is that you sell anything at all.'

Colin was getting on Liam's nerves. 'I know what I'm doing.'

'No, you don't,' goaded Colin. 'It's just like with Cath here. She thinks you're unreadable and mysterious, the strong, silent type, and that she's lured you out of your cave, roused the man in you –'

'Here we go!' Catherine rolled her eyes. 'Fuck off, Colin. How many times do you need to be told?'

'– that you've fallen for her when she just happens to have crossed your path and stopped you in your tracks. It's all her own doing, and you've got no more idea of how you ended up with her than you have about how you sold that house today.' Colin tore open a packet of crisps and turned to Paul. 'He's like one of those little toy cars that keeps going in a straight line, banging up against the wall.' Colin mimed banging his head against an imaginary wall. 'If you could move the wall he'd just keep on going.'

'Thanks a lot,' said Liam, reddening slightly. 'I'll remember that next time you ask me for a favour.'

'It's your shout, Liam,' said Colin, closing the subject.

Go and fuck yourself, Colin, you fat prick, thought Liam, smiling (out of habit) as he headed for the bar. He ordered three beers and a Coke for himself. Drink was one habit he was not about to cultivate, no matter how many jibes he had to endure about it from the likes of Colin. He needed habits and routines that were fixed and secure, even if, like cigarettes, they happened to kill you a little at a time. He needed habits he could rely on, habits he could set his clock by. And, yes, he sometimes needed drugs that kept the mind alert, like caffeine and nicotine, and drugs that subdued and sedated. Drugs like Aropax, Valium and the Tryptanol he took to sleep.

Drugs like alcohol, which relaxed inhibitions and loosened the tongue, or drugs that let down the barriers of the mind, that stirred up the silt at the bottom of the pond, he needed like a hole in the head. Did he need a hole in the head? he wondered dispassionately. If all his *harmless* habits were to desert him at once, there were worse things than a hole in the head. His habits were all that stood between him and the unthinkable, all that identified him as one of those who might walk among men.

Apparently it took twenty-eight days to develop a habit and twenty-eight days to break it. Liam had been married to Catherine a whole month and, as yet, there was no absolute single pattern to this thing called marriage that he could readily discern; instead he observed a bundle of concurrent threads, a multitude of separate habits and tiny nuances that he must master or at which he must acquit himself adequately. It didn't matter all that much if he affected the likeness of a good husband or an indifferent one, as long as the likeness was credible.

Liam watched Catherine's impassive face as she slept, her dark hair tangled on the pillow beside him. He was still amazed to see her there when he woke each morning. She pulled the sheet up around her smooth white shoulders, mumbled something and turned over in the bed. He draped an arm across her hip. Catherine shifted her pelvis, pushing her buttocks against his lower abdomen. She moved her thigh to admit his leg between hers, dragging the sheet down to expose a small ripe breast. He ran his hand slowly down her shoulder, across her breasts, and lightly massaged her belly. Her breathing became louder and deeper as she moved under his touch.

Sex, for him, was something new and it bound him to her. The mute physicality of the act gave him a sense of relief that made him feel as real as any other man, and *she* was ardent about him. Every closed door, every ounce of reserve in him, only fuelled her interest.

Without opening her eyes Catherine raised her knees and arched her back against him until he slid easily inside her. He clasped her hips and drew her body towards him, filling her more deeply. Her quiet moans became louder and more urgent, then quieter still as she gave way to sensation.

Afterwards, as they lay folded together, she loved to talk soothingly about her feelings, her past and her unextraordinary hopes for the future.

Alone, closed off from the world, he would enjoy these moments until he found himself unable to respond with the same intimacies. He sensed that Catherine sometimes felt he was holding out on her emotionally, keeping some part of himself to himself. He knew she would never be able to understand the nature of his reserve, or the fears that drove him, and was glad to find she had mistaken it for strength.

Catherine had chosen the terrace house in Avondale Street. He had seen it the week before their wedding, and after Catherine had been through it with another couple she had pulled him aside at work. 'Why didn't you tell me about that flat? It's perfect for us.'

'I wasn't sure.'

'You know how hard it is to get a good flat downtown.'

'No one's rented it yet?'

'No, I told the woman I took through that the wiring was being redone and that it wouldn't be available for two weeks. Luckily for us she needed something today. I'm going to run it past John, and if it's okay with him we're taking it, yes?'

'If you really like it.'

'Well, don't you?'

'Sure. I guess it'll do.'

A month later she had almost finished repainting it. Despite his indifference to his surroundings, even he had to admit that, for a few hundred dollars, she had transformed the place. The once dead, cold and starkly painted rooms were now filled with her warmth and life.

Catherine held a cigarette to the flames of the open fire, then to her lips. Her fingers were covered with wine-coloured paint. She looked up at Liam from her cushion on the floor. 'Here,' she said, handing him the cigarette, then lighting another.

'Is it really cold enough for a fire?' he asked.

'I like looking at it. It's one of the reasons I chose this flat in the first place. What do you think of the colour?' she said, admiring a velvety expanse of purple wall.

'Good. I told you already.'

'Wait till I do the trims.' She stood up and moved over to the tall windows. 'I love this room. I like the way it overlooks the street, and I really like this area. When I first came here, that little park down there was full of children from the pre-school next door, did you notice?'

'No,' he said absently, but he had.

'Anyway, I love it, and I love you.'

'I love you too,' he said automatically, for he thought that he did, and after twenty-eight days it was becoming a habit.

*

In the living room of his cluttered flat, Mathew Allen was surrounded by plastic boxes, full of files; the long table was buried under layers of clippings, letters and email printouts. Through the window he could see the darkness settling in above the red-tiled roofs of the city.

In front of him, beside a half-eaten sandwich, there was a small pile of mail. He ripped open the first envelope: a letter from Dunedin, in New Zealand. After an incoherent preamble – *not usually one to write unsolicited . . . can only imagine your pain . . . outraged by such an appalling miscarriage of justice* – the correspondent went on to say that she was *certain* that that mongrel, Simpson, was a student teacher at her granddaughter's primary school, *something about him . . . could never forget that face . . .*

He took a white-headed pin-tack from a plastic cup and stuck it into a map of Australasia above his desk. The top was labelled with a large A. The map was peppered with coloured pins, some in clusters. A lone white one now marked Dunedin. After all these years the letters and emails still came from strangers all over the world. He'd learnt not to take too much notice of them but he couldn't just discard them either. White pins were for unsupported suspicions or tips, founded on nothing more than a writer's makeshift identification, based on their memory of grainy pictures published fifteen years ago. Green pins were for more detailed information, suspicions grounded on 'something'. Red pins were for tip-offs or supposed inside information, which often turned out to be false or invented. Red pins were often downgraded to white, but none was ever taken down.

Some of the mail was hate-mail, letters about what lousy parents he and Rachel must have been to allow Benjamin out of their sight, gloating over the details of the affair and laughing at their suffering.

'How can you read them?' Rachel had once cried, but he took particular note of them, recording their postcodes and pinning a black pin in the corresponding towns.

He turned to a large, more substantial envelope printed with the logo of the Louisiana State University's Forensic Anthropology and Computer Enhancement Services: FACES. He opened it hastily, tearing the edge of the glossy white sheet inside. When he took it out he saw it was a photograph of an auburn-haired young man. There was something unusual about the image: it was a headshot only, with no background. The round, unsmiling face transmitted no real expression. The picture appeared pixelated in places, computer-generated. He scanned the attached covering letter.

Dear Mr Allen,

The age-progression computer-enhancement of the photographs you forwarded to my colleagues at the National Centre for Missing and Exploited Children has produced the enclosed images, which represent possible adult likenesses of the individuals in question.

The image in his hand was labelled A. He looked inside the envelope and withdrew a second image, B. Another young man stared out at him. This time the face sent a jolt right through him. It was the eyes, the coal-black, unreadable irises. He'd recognize them anywhere.

He laid the images side by side on top of the papers on his desk. A wave of fatigue engulfed him. How long could he keep doing this? Rachel had been right to move on, to remarry and have more children . . . right to live. But someone had to fight on for Benjamin. Someone had to stand up for him.

He knew he wasn't well. Doctors couldn't help – he didn't even consult them now. The last had given him Prozac. He'd taken it long enough to find out that it was dangerous. He learnt that a Prozac state was not unlike a manic state, with flights of impulse, wild enthusiasms and hastily made plans. (He'd nearly driven Rachel mad with his late-night calls. *Slow down . . . What are you talking about, Mathew? I can't do this any more.*) The artificial highs were followed by sudden deep troughs and pessimisms, suicidal fantasies and murderous rages. He'd even bought a gun.

The drug amplified his feelings of regret, but left him unable to cry a single tear. The nightmares were horrendous. And Prozac had done nothing to numb the soul-destroying hatred, hatred so strong that he sometimes thought of himself as the predator. If only they had kept those boys in prison.

The parole hearing had been a joke. As far as he was concerned the board had been taken in by two cunning criminals. He'd been sickened to hear about their 'great remorse', their 'aspirations'. What about his and Rachel's aspirations for Benjamin? Their opinions hadn't mattered. They represented a dead child. Only the living had 'rights'. It had been the last straw for Rachel.

Detective Kendall alone had spoken out on Benjamin's behalf. Outside the hearing he had told the waiting press, 'Simpson and Harris should complete their sentences in an adult prison.' He was retired now and didn't care what the 'official' police position was. He hugged Rachel tightly and said, 'I'm so sorry.' The same words he had uttered after the original trial, as if the insanity of the legal system was his fault.

'Doli incapax,' they had argued – *incapable of malice*.

As the vultures of the press picked over their open entrails once again, Mathew Allen had given them something – something he wanted printed on the front page of every newspaper across the country: *They may think they are safe, they may think they are hidden, but no matter where they are I will find them, even if I have to track them to the ends of the earth.*

The *Herald* had run the entire quote.

I will track them to the ends of the earth! made its way around the world. Within hours every soothsaying civil libertarian with access to a word processor or telephone line was up in arms, screaming their bloody heads off.

These unfortunate boys were a product of the society they were born into, they made a terrible mistake and have served half their lives in custody. We must all now take stock and allow them the chance to make a future for themselves.

Mistake? Future? The public response on hearing of their impending release had been even more rabid: *Let the bastards find out what real jail is all about.* And: *The parents are serving life sentences, why shouldn't they?*

On the first day of the original trial, when he had laid eyes on the two eleven-year-olds in the dock, he had had visions of manually strangling each boy until the life drained from his eyes. What had he become? How had he travelled from a loving father with kindness for all children to this? He hated them and he hated himself. But he would try not to let Benjamin down. It was up to him alone to represent him.

The court process had been endless and baffling, He had no head for the many abstract arguments – the stopping and starting over points of law – but he pledged to be there every day, to hear every word and detail, much of it for the first time. He let the leaden fragments smash against the side of his head in hammer blows that left him nauseated, somehow allowing the words to run through and out of his mind. He did not look at the photographs presented to the jury. While Rachel withdrew further into the sanctuary of her memories and built a shrine to her lost baby, he stood and took all these assaults, as any husband would to protect his wife. A shattered man on the verge of implosion, *he* had nowhere to go.

In the years since, so that he could keep fighting for Benjamin, he had learnt all he could about the legal system. It would have been so easy to throw his hands into the air and give up. Once the victim was buried, the entire process seemed to be about protecting the rights of the bastards who had done it. *He* could not quit or rest while they were at large.

He positioned both of the computer-generated images, face down, on the scanner bed and closed the lid. A burst of light from the machine illuminated his features from below. His face was drawn from lack of sleep. As the images scanned, he cleared away the debris from his meagre evening meal and rearranged the papers on his desk.

The front of his Fair Isle jumper was smudged with white paint and there were splatters in his greying hair. He looked, through watery-blue eyes, at the pictures now slowly loading onto the screen. He logged onto the internet and opened a site from his Favourites list, titled 'Benjamin's Place'. A scrolling banner, which read 'For the Love of Benjamin', repeatedly dissolved and refreshed itself. Below the banner, a little boy smiled out at him, his deep-blue eyes shining with mischief. The site was a memorial to his son, constructed in an attempt to reclaim him. A family album of who Benjamin had been before his face had become an icon for tragedy, before even his very name was irrevocably linked, in the public mind, with those who had killed him.

Mathew Allen smiled sadly at the familiar pictures, photographs of a two-and-a-half-year-old Benjamin: with his young mother planting a kiss on his forehead; Benjamin holding his father's hand in front of a tall ship down by the docks; Benjamin dressed as a monkey and blowing out candles on a birthday cake; Benjamin sleeping like an angel, his black lashes resting on his flushed cheeks. The pictures were accompanied by simple stories, a paragraph or two beneath each, chronicling a small event in his short life.

At the bottom of the page was a list of related sites: 'Victims of Crime', 'Mothers against Murder', 'Sustained Sentences for a Safer Society'.

When the scanned images of A and B had uploaded, Mathew Allen created a new email message with the picture files attached. He selected all the names in his contacts list and pasted them in the address line. Exhausted, he leant back in his chair, moved the cursor over the send button and clicked.

Shame

'Hide not thy face'

Geoffrey, 2008

'Hey, Wickham –WICK-JAM!'

Geoffrey Wickham looked up from his workstation. It sometimes amazed him that, even after seven years, he could still be thrown by the use of his 'new' surname. His baby-faced colleague, Nigel, clutched an outmoded laptop to his chest. 'Another one for you. If it's going to be complicated the owner would rather upgrade. Sounds like a virus.'

'Leave it there,' he said.

'Thanks so much, *Geoffrey*,' said Nigel, amusing himself with one of his funny voices.

And *Geoffrey*, like *Nigel*, was – as far as G. R. Wickham was concerned – the name of a faggot. He deftly inserted a set of tiny screws into a computer back plate and turned them slowly into place. *Fiddly little fuckers.* He'd been working in this shit-hole for nearly five years and knew enough about fixing computers to start a business. Nigel's father had even offered him the store manager's job, but he preferred to avoid people, preferred to stay out the back and keep his hands busy. Let Nigel suck up to them – he was good at that.

He could hear him at it right now, buttering up some dithering old fuck-wit at the counter. 'Not a problem. Leave it with us overnight, and if Geoffrey can get it fired up, he'll install the new modem for you.'

'See you tomorrow,' called Nigel. Geoffrey heard the sound of the door shutting in the front of the store. He rebooted the clunky laptop and waited while it searched for the newly installed modem. He dialled the connection and clicked the history file on the menu. Sure enough, there among the list of innocuous sites were the headings 'Free Porn' and 'Hot and Horny Teens'. It wasn't just the computer that had a virus. The old fart was just like the rest of them: another hypocrite. They were all at it. They made him sick.

He checked the modem settings, then shut the computer down. He took a crumpled suede jacket off the back of his chair and let himself out through the rear of the store.

The night was turning cold as he walked towards the steps at the end of the laneway. Up ahead the green-painted door of the Bali Hut restaurant opened. A slight

Indonesian man swung a heavy bag of garbage up into a nearby skip. He smiled with perfect teeth and nodded in Geoffrey's direction.

Geoffrey remembered his disbelief on leaving the secure unit. At first he'd thought it was the shock of living in a capital city, but pretty soon he realized that the whole world had changed. As if he wasn't alienated enough already, now he couldn't even recognize himself in the faces around him.

At the top of the steps he entered the anonymous comfort of the busy shopping strip and headed past the fast-food outlets towards the city centre. Here, dozens of illuminated plastic trademarks transmitted their hollow code – *'Eat this!'*; *'Wear this!'*; *'Get laid!'*

Every store competed with its neighbour for his attention: a cluttered jeweller's, a crowded coffee bar, the narrow red stairwell of a tattooist, a bare window displaying a chiffon wedding dress on a headless torso, lit only by one cold white globe. 'Lovely girls!' yelled one of the thugs outside the Venus Lounge. 'Real girls, live on stage,' he hissed, almost in Geoffrey's ear.

At the intersection, where the strip met the highway, stood the Orient Hotel. Young people spilled out of its doors and into the street, where they drank in small, animated groups. Some sat on the kerb, smoking and talking. Beautiful young men, clothes chosen for their careless, masculine impact, pretty and plain young girls made glamorous, displayed to devastating effect. Geoffrey watched their easy communication, heard their lubricated laughter. He saw hands lightly touching shoulders, arms reaching around waists, effulgent faces that flickered with the recognition of being known.

He pressed the button at the crossing, then ran between two cars and crossed to the other side. A huge pair of crimson plastic lips was suspended over an entranceway with 'Carmen's' painted below in an energetic script that suggested it had been written in lipstick.

The cave-like interior of Carmen's glowed with hot-pink light. Geoffrey sat at the bar. 'Vodka and lemonade.' A square-jawed brunette dropped a scoop of ice into a glass, covered it with the clear spirit and soft drink from the tap.

He turned on his barstool to face the room. In the far corner a duo played a slow song with a Latin American beat. Two girls danced in front of the small stage, leaning into each other; one wore a tight red dress. Geoffrey sipped his drink and rolled an ice-cube around in his mouth. The girl in red gave him a little wave. He stared back. She waved again; he lifted his hand in response. Her girlfriend whispered something in her ear. The girls hugged each other and laughed.

Fuck them. He bought another drink, moved to a table near the bar and lit a cigarette. The buzz of the vodka moved in a steady line from his head to his feet. He let himself relax.

'Can I have a light?' A well-built man sat down opposite him. Geoffrey held out his cigarette. Instead of taking it from him the man leant over and held the hand steady as he touched his cigarette to Geoffrey's. His grip was firm and Geoffrey could smell the not-unpleasant odour of his body. Once the cigarette was alight he let go of his hand. 'Thanks. I'm Mario.'

'Geoffrey.'

Mario drew hard on his cigarette, then jerked his head to the girls on the dance-floor. 'The bitch in the red?' said Mario. 'She's onto you.'

'Onto me?'

'*Into you.* Whatever . . . Chicks don't do it for me.'

Geoffrey's heart beat a little faster. Mario wasn't the first guy who'd come onto him at Carmen's – half the clientele was gay, for fuck sake. Why should he care? *Each to their own.* He could see the outline of Mario's powerful arms through the thin sweatshirt he was wearing. He didn't seem queer, but now that he looked at him closely there was something feminine about the shape of his mouth.

Mario laid a rough hand over his. Geoffrey pulled away, but not before a pulse of excitement ran through him. 'It's cool,' said Mario, judging his mistake. 'Maybe next time.' He got up.

Geoffrey let a few seconds pass before he fled to the men's room. He washed his hands several times, with soap. As he dried them he heard movement in one of the cubicles, shuffling and banging followed by a muffled moan. *Fucking faggots, they'd do it anywhere.*

Back in the bar he nursed his third double vodka. The girl in the red dress walked towards his table, taking slow, deliberate steps, as if she were in danger of falling. 'Hi.' She sat down beside him. 'My girlfriend said I should ask you to dance.'

'I don't think so,' he said coldly.

'Oh, come on . . .'

Geoffrey turned towards the bar and saw Mario watching him. Mario pursed his lips and winked. The girl grabbed Geoffrey's arm and pulled him up.

He towered a full head above her as they danced. She pressed herself against him. Her fat blonde girlfriend danced nearby, her arms wrapped tightly around a bald man in a loud shirt.

'I gotta go,' said Geoffrey.

'I'll go with you.'

'Come on, then,' he said, aware of Mario's watchful eye.

She waved goodbye to her friend and followed him off the dance-floor and out at the rear of the building, stumbling on her heels in an effort to catch up with him. 'Slow down.' She grabbed his arm.

'Where do you live?' he asked.

'Canley Vale.'

'*Canley Vale?*' He was becoming annoyed. 'Look . . .'

She began fumbling with his shirt.

'What are you doing?'

She kissed him. 'Let's go to your place.'

'No,' he answered flatly.

'Round here,' she said, pulling him into the laneway. She dropped to her knees and began to undo his jeans.

He looked down at the top of her head, and at her desperately groping hands. '*Stop it!*'

She stood up and looked up at him drunkenly. 'What?'

He pushed her forward, face up against the wall, and lifted her skirt from behind. She arched herself up towards him. He tore at her G-string and pushed himself inside her, forcing her against the wall. After several hard thrusts, she gasped and began to moan, writhing beneath him.

'Shut up!' He put his hand over her mouth and quickly finished himself off.

She turned around and leaned against the brick wall, breathing heavily. 'I'm Courtney,' she offered, tugging at the hem of her dress.

He stuffed his shirt into his open trousers and looked at her lumpen face, the kohl-rimmed, lifeless eyes, the stupid lipstick-smeared smile. 'See ya, Courtney.' He fastened the button on his fly and walked away.

Alex Reiser, Globe *newspaper, 2008*

The offices were being refurbished. A crew of workmen were busy, breaking up a row of lavender-cloth-covered dividers. A carpenter used a claw hammer to prise the last of a laminated shelf from beneath a bank of windows that overlooked the city. Despite the nondescript architecture, the building was prime real estate, with million-dollar views.

From his desk, currently crammed into a corner of the undisturbed side of the room, Alex Reiser could see all the way to the harbour. Over piles of jumbled, upturned desks he watched the foamy white trail of a distant ferry. He stretched out his legs, rested his feet on a low filing cabinet and returned to the book he was reading. He shifted restlessly in his chair and scratched his large round head. 'Oh, give me a break!' He groaned, throwing the book onto the floor. What author of any real ability would write, 'When his cold hand cupped her atrophied breast, she knew without knowing that all hope was dead'?

Outside the city was buzzing with activity, cars stream-ing between the soaring buildings. Alex was annoyed that he would have to spend the next few hours writing a review of this rubbish. *Ghosts of a Dead Marriage*. The title was enough.

He left the book where it was and made his way, via a maze of office furniture, to a kitchenette area where the tearoom used to be and filled a chipped green cup with steaming black coffee. Somewhere behind a stack of partitions a female colleague let out an angry squeal. 'Who jammed the fucking Xerox machine?'

'Get a grip, Penny!' called Alex, from inside his furni-ture fortress.

'I bet it was you, Reiser!'

'Prove it,' he replied, holding his coffee aloft as he negotiated his way back to his desk. *Fucking machines were always fucking up*.

One of the new cadets, an extremely tall girl with short bottle-blonde hair, walked between the desks carrying a basket of mail. She was so thin that Alex could count the ribs beneath her pink silk-jersey sweater. She stopped near his desk and dropped some-thing onto his computer monitor. When he saw the large manila envelope, addressed to himself in his own handwriting, he sighed deeply. 'Damn.' He sat back at his desk and stared at it as he drank the last of his cof-fee. When he had finished he reluctantly picked it up and opened it. Attached to a substantial manuscript, was a letter.

Dear Alex,

Thank you for your submission.

While your novel *Timor Lost* is impeccably researched, and beautifully written, I am unable to offer you publication at this time. Unfortunately we already have two forthcoming titles in our list on similar themes. I am also aware of a theatre project of the same title.

As always this is only one opinion and I wish you well in finding a publisher for your manuscript.

Ghosts of a Dead Marriage lay at his feet where he had flung it. He kicked it savagely, almost tearing the back cover from the spine.

On his computer screen the incoming-mail icon flashed. He watched the spiralling blue arrow.

At last he heard a loud ping. A whole string of emails appeared, three from the editor, one from his mate Penny, with several ideas of interest he might like to follow up, an invitation to a book launch at Collins Book-City Superstore and an email with an attachment. He recognized the sender's name immediately.

Two images, pasted side by side, loaded onto the screen – foreheads, eyebrows, eyes, noses, mouths and chins. The first face was labelled A, the second B.

Alex Reiser studied the faces carefully. *Is this what they look like now?* Certainly the second image triggered some sort of recognition in him. He paused briefly before reading Mathew Allen's accompanying note.

Dear friends and supporters,

These pictures were created by a forensic modelling program. Distribute or display them where you can.

Mathew Allen was tempting Fate, thought Alex. No Australian newspaper would be able to print these images, not after the High Court injunction that protected the offenders' new identities. There was certainly no way *his* editor would let the images go to print, but if these pictures were accurate . . . what a story! Alex looked furtively over his shoulder, making sure that no one else was seeing what he was seeing.

He marvelled, for a moment, at Mathew Allen's stamina. He felt for the man, he really did, but after fifteen years surely it would be healthier to give it up, let it go and get on. Maybe he had finally gone off his rocker. Then again, how would he behave if something happened to one of his daughters?

During the trial he'd had nothing but admiration for the quietly spoken man, his upright dignity, as he sat, day after day, through the harrowing details. Details that many seasoned police officers found hard to recount without emotion. As he saved the pictures on the screen, he remembered the frightened children seated in the dock, feet barely touching the floor. Even knowing the charges against them, no matter how intently he studied their reactions all he had ever been able to see were two eleven-year-old boys. 'Just a pair of average scruffs like the rest of us,' as one commentator had aptly put it.

What did Mathew Allen hope to gain? Even if the pictures did look like them, they could be anywhere. Maybe after all these years they should just be left in peace.

Peace? He knew what Allen would think of that. Where was *his* peace? All he had ever wanted was for them to stay in prison.

When their release was announced, Alex had been conflicted. He'd done a series of passionate follow-up articles about the Allens called 'A Life Sentence for Some'. In it he had calculated the cost of the boys' new identities and chronicled the psychiatric and social support provided for their rehabilitation and compared it to the scant assistance offered to the Allens. The series had won him a prestigious Walkley Award, for excellence in journalism.

Despite his advocacy for the rights of the victim's family Alex knew that the truth was never quite so one-sided. His experience as a ward of the state from the age of fourteen had given him an acute affinity with the neglected and abused. He had seen the inside of enough foster homes to know that 'childhood' was not a luxury afforded to all children.

He considered himself one of the lucky ones. With a mother who had fallen into and out of mental illness, he at least had had one parent to be returned to and elderly grandparents to visit twice a year. When she was lucid, his mother was the brightest, liveliest person in any room. For seven years he had also had the love of a father, not some deadbeat who had walked out on his responsibilities but torn in half in a banana field in Vietnam, after stepping on an M26 'jumping jack', a device perfectly designed to cut a man's legs out from underneath him. The detonation was felt almost seven thousand miles away by an idealistic young mother and a seven-year-old boy.

The news had been delivered on the same day that the Yanks had put a man on the moon. A television had been rolled into the assembly hall at Alex's school and he had witnessed the ghosting black-and-white broadcast of the historic moment, linking the two events for ever in his mind.

In care the worst cases were always the long-term placements who no longer hoped for rescue by their real families. Eventually the light went out in their eyes and they armed themselves with hatred and cynicism. The greatest agent of moral corrosion he knew of was to believe oneself not unloved but unlovable.

He chewed the end of his pen, remembering how badly he wanted to get interviews with Simpson and Harris, now that they were adults and could speak for themselves, not through the mealy mouths of lawyers. *It was the stuff of novels really* . . . He dropped his pen onto the cluttered desk and sat back in his chair.

Doubts

'As small as a mustard seed'

Liam, 2008

He shuffled sections of the greasy broadsheet, opened one and folded it to fit his half of the undersized café table. His fingertips were black with newsprint. Apart from the real-estate section, Liam didn't read the papers any more, if he ever had. Newspapers hadn't been allowed to circulate in the Meadowbank Correctional Centre. He didn't know exactly what had been written about him all those years ago. Even now when people occasionally talked about *it*, he knew, from what they said, that their knowledge of events far outstripped his.

Of course there was plenty of stuff on the internet but he had worked far too hard to distance himself from his past to go within a hundred miles of it. Besides, he knew his nerves would never take it. He was a different person now: he deserved a chance. That was the mantra they had given him. 'You deserve a chance, Liam. Never forget that.'

'If you've finished with the paper, Liam, I'll take it,' said Catherine.

'Sure. More coffee?'

'We're late,' she said, looking at her watch.

'I'm not going back to the office. I've got an inspection at three.'

She looked annoyed.

'I'll see you at home.' He kissed her cheek.

'No, you won't. We're all going for a drink, remember?'

'I don't think I'll come.'

'Why not? Come on, Liam, you did this last time.'

'I went last time.'

'That was weeks ago, and I had to talk you into it.'

'So? It's not compulsory, is it? I see those people every day at work.'

'Those people are our friends. You see me every day at work.'

'Don't make a big deal, Cath. I just feel like staying home.'

'Well, I don't.'

'Go, then. I'll cook something and we'll have dinner when you get back.'

'Liam, you're becoming a fucking hermit, you know that?'

Driving to his appointment, Liam's mind wandered, as always, to other things, circling malevolently around the unalterable reality of his past. He barely registered the streets along the route through town, automatically shifting gears, changing lanes and crossing a busy intersection.

A red Daihatsu sat outside number twenty-eight Park Road, a young couple and their son waiting beside it. Liam greeted them warmly, then led them up a pleasantly overgrown path, under a huge poinciana tree, to a solid but featureless house. 'Once you're inside, it's so private you wouldn't even know you were on the main road,' he said, as the little family headed up the polished hall. 'Have a look through, take your time. Great light in here. Good views from the kitchen and the rear deck. You'd never be built out . . . Master bedroom has its own bathroom.'

The couple peeled off to investigate the facilities, leaving their four-year-old son in the lounge. Liam walked back into the kitchen to give them some space. The little boy followed close behind. Liam gave him an awkward smile.

'Is this your house?' the child asked.

'No,' said Liam. His throat was dry.

'What's in here?' The little boy opened a door.

'Just the pantry.'

'This is my room,' the child announced, stepping inside. 'I sleep in here,' he said, shutting the doors on himself.

'Better come out now,' said Liam, after a few seconds had passed.

The little boy answered with a knock.

Liam felt suddenly anxious, his armpits were damp with sweat.

There was a distinctive knock-knock, from inside the cupboard. 'Who's there?' asked Liam, reluctantly.

'Me!' The little boy pushed open the doors, laughing. Liam managed a lopsided grin.

'Toby!' called his mother, from the front of the house.

Liam began to walk to her. Without warning, Toby reached up and took his hand. It was all Liam could do not to scream.

'Is this a reverse-cycle air-conditioner?' asked the boy's father.

'N-no . . . no, it's not. It's just a cooler, but the roof is insulated and those gas fireplaces are pretty efficient,' he said, recovering.

The couple looked the house over for another ten minutes; fortunately their son followed them into the yard, where he amused himself with a broken laundry trolley. Liam made a few incidental calls on his mobile to keep himself busy. He thought they might never leave.

Back at the flat he swallowed a Serepax and took a shower, leaning against the wet tiles and letting the hot water run off his back for a long time. He dressed himself in fresh clothes and bundled his sweat-stained shirt into the washing-machine. It smelt of fear.

He took a Coke from the fridge and sat down at his computer. He finished some paperwork and emailed it to the office. The computer gave a musical ping as a little envelope icon dropped into his mailbox. He clicked the in-box: more paperwork. He'd had enough for today.

It was the first Tuesday of the month. He hesitated, then clicked on his Favourites and selected Hotmail, typed in his details, and a series of asterisks appeared on the screen as he entered his password. He scrolled through the usual junk, which he subscribed to in order to keep the seldom-used address active, until he saw 'xxShe@hotmail.com Subject: None.' His heart rate increased as he clicked the message open.

Dear G, sorry I missed the last mail date. Things happening here you don't need to worry about. JH having some trouble. OK now. CH is well. Haven't heard from PO. Thinking of you. Miss you. Very happy you have someone. Still hoping meeting might be possible. Won't get my hopes up. Love you. XxShe

It wasn't much but it was enough. A few minutes later, when he had composed himself, he deleted the message, then deleted it from his trash folder.

Dear M, A rough day today. Your message made me feel better. Work OK. Some days harder than others. I will never be able to

tell C everything. Meeting could be possible for July. Can't
promise. Need to talk to PO and others. XyHe

He reread the message twice and clicked send.

'Hi! Give me a hand, will you?' Catherine had opened the front door and was pushing her way into the flat with several heavy bags of groceries. Liam closed the email page and rushed to help her. He took the bags off her and dumped them on the kitchen bench.

'But wait, there's more!' she said, holding up a finger.

'I'll go.'

'No. You unpack, it's just small stuff.'

Liam put the items on the counter in ordered groups – fridge stuff, tinned stuff, bagged stuff, bathroom stuff. There was enough for a couple of weeks.

'There you go,' she said, plonking down one last bag of groceries and a bottle of red wine.

'What happened to drinks at the pub?'

'I went off the idea.'

'What's this for, then?' He indicated the wine.

'Oh, we'll see.'

She was in a funny mood, he thought, as he stuffed several bags of pasta into one of the pantry drawers.

Catherine sat at the kitchen table, sipping a glass of water while she watched him work. Liam took two yellow sponges and placed them on the pile of 'kitchen stuff'. He pulled out a colourful package from the last

66

remaining bag, a glossy box he didn't recognize. It was printed with pink text and a picture of a dove – probably one of her expensive face creams or hair products, he thought, then studied it more closely. Crystal Clear Midstream Pregnancy Test. He looked at Catherine, who was watching him intently. She smiled. 'Are you pregnant?' he gasped.

'That's what I'm about to find out. You look like you're going to faint, Liam.'

'You never said anything . . . I thought you were on the pill?'

'I went off it.'

'Why?'

She pulled a dumb face. 'I went on it so that I wouldn't get pregnant and I went off it so I could.'

'Yes, but you said . . . We talked about it . . .'

'Liam, calm down,' she said, putting her arms around his shoulders. 'It was me who didn't want to have kids . . . Just let me use the test and find out. If I am . . . you'll get used to the idea.' She kissed him playfully and left the room.

Used to the idea? How could she possibly know what she was saying?

Oh, God! Please don't let her be pregnant . . . *Why the hell should God listen to him?* Please, God, for the child's sake – for hers! He knew that for him ever to hold a child, to know the love of a child, would tear his heart out of his chest. Please, God, don't let it be true.

67

She'd been in the bathroom for ever. What was she doing in there? He wanted to break the door down. He wanted to nail it shut and lock her in.

When she emerged she had a strange teasing smile on her face, as if she had done something really clever, as if the whole thing had been a great big joke. She held up a strip with two pink lines across it.

'What does that mean?'

'I'm pregnant. I did it twice to make sure.' She held her arms out to him. 'You're not angry with me, are you?'

'No, not angry.' Shock reverberated through his body, his mind grappling to process the implications of her news.

Catherine saw his panic and laid a hand on his cheek. 'Don't worry, Liam,' she whispered. 'I know you'll make a wonderful father.'

Detective Kendall, 2008

The retired inspector looked down at the coloured tablets he held in the palm of his hand. For several seconds Phillip Kendall considered throwing them over the railing into the grevillea bushes. A willie wagtail dropped onto the rail, then jumped to the deck. The bold little bird ran in short, erratic bursts, fanning its tail to signal each change of direction, then flew off again.

The nausea, a result of his recent chemotherapy session, made him suddenly change his mind. He swallowed the tablets and washed them down with cold tea from a tray on the nearby table. An uneaten plate of skinless white chicken and mashed greens lay untouched beside it.

A young woman appeared at the patio doors and looked out at him with concern. He picked up a fork and made a feeble show of poking at the broccoli as she walked quietly towards him.

'Dad,' sighed Lauren Kendall, 'you've eaten practically nothing.'

'I'm just getting stuck into it now, love.' He pushed some of the vegetable into his mouth and swallowed. It tasted of cardboard. He tore a small strip of flesh off the chicken breast and nibbled it. 'I might feel more like it later.' He put down the fork.

She moved the tray aside. 'These are for you,' she said, laying down two computerized mug shots. 'If they're who I think they are, I probably should have thrown them into the bin. I know Mum would've.' She handed him his glasses.

Phillip Kendall's face took on a professional cast. He studied the pictures carefully. 'Where did you get them?'

'They came in an email from Mathew Allen. I printed them out for you.' She rested a hand on his shoulder.

'Good girl.' He patted the hand.

Lauren picked up the tray. 'More tea?'

'That'd be great.' His eyes remained fixed on the pictures in front of him. Mathew Allen was skirting around the law by circulating images like these, but he didn't blame him. Thirty years as a policeman had shown him that everybody deals with grief in their own way, and some cope better than others. Nobody asks to become a victim, and nobody is ever prepared for what follows. He had done his best to support the Allens over the years, to keep in touch. His relationship with them had altered his life, and in all probability the trauma of the investigation, and the controversy surrounding the early release of their son's killers, had triggered the decline in his health that had ended in a diagnosis of cancer.

'Operable,' the doctor had said. If the tumour in his bowel could be reduced by chemotherapy he had a 'fair' chance of successful surgery and survival. His mistrust of doctors, though, ran very deep. A naturally lean man who didn't smoke or drink, he usually discarded whatever pills he was prescribed and he was loath to surrender what remained of his life to a regimen of toxic drug treatments. He had agreed to this first round of chemotherapy only after Lauren's urgings. With his system reeling from the effects of the poison, now pumping through his veins and irrigating even the healthy cells of his body, he didn't rate his chances of living out the year.

Apart from the unwelcome interference of doctors, *he* was strangely at ease with his diagnosis and with the prospect of death. Despite his inability to comprehend the suffering he had witnessed first-hand in the world, he was a religious man who regularly made peace with his God.

He looked again at the printed faces. His detective instinct still intact, he considered all the ways in which these pictures might be employed or distributed to identify the offenders. He pondered the challenge of locating two young men, of a certain age, in a country of twenty million people. He thought about the moral implications of being party to their exposure. Even he didn't believe they should remain in jail for ever, but he struggled with the idea of them living and working among people who were oblivious to their deeds. The thought of them having access to children while hiding behind new identities made his blood run cold.

A bank of clouds obscured the sun and cast a shadow across the deck. After a few seconds his legs began to ache. He went inside the house to the front room. Still holding the images, he lowered himself into the soft cushions of the comfortable new couch that Lauren had made him buy. He reached for the black Teledex that sat on a side-table near the phone.

'There you are.' Lauren put down a cup of milky tea. 'I hope you're not getting yourself worked up over those pictures.'

'Not much I can do now, love,' he said. She threw a mohair blanket over his legs and left him to rest. If all this fussing was going to help Lauren cope with the reality of losing him, he didn't mind. He'd been exactly the same when June was ill. His wife would have made him fight too, probably in different ways – vitamins, fasting, meditation. For a moment he couldn't help wishing she was there, but the fact that she wasn't made it so much easier – after all, he'd only have to part with her all over again.

He took his glasses from his cardigan pocket and opened the Teledex. He might be out of commission himself but he still had friends in the force; friends who thought like him.

History

'Better is he who never existed'

Liam, 2008

He pulled the razor across his cheek in quick light strokes, leaving tracks in his shaving-foam mask. He found it hard to look at himself in the mirror. Catherine said he was handsome, but she didn't really know him – what did it matter anyway?

With every day of Catherine's pregnancy Liam's anxiety grew. Dread lay, like a stone, in his stomach. No matter how he looked at it, he could not think his way out. He should never have imagined he could have a relationship in the first place, should never have dragged Catherine into the black hole of his life. He should have been grateful simply to exist. He washed off the foam residue and buried his head in a towel.

'Eggs?' called Catherine, from the kitchen.

'Yes, please.'

It wasn't enough to carry the stone around, to be crippled by the fear. He had to convince her with his every word and gesture that he was *pleased* – and, despite the 'shock' of her sudden announcement, overwhelmed with joy. How could he explain anything less?

Catherine set his breakfast on the table in front of him. He plunged a toast finger into the yolk of a perfectly cooked five-minute egg. Catherine put a green napkin beside his plate and poured his tea. Liam noticed that she had become increasingly interested in the details of domestic life.

Finally she sat down opposite him.

'Aren't you having any?' he asked.

'No.' She wrinkled her nose. 'I feel a bit off.'

'Oh, right,' he said awkwardly, attacking the remainder of his egg with a spoon.

'Are you getting used to the idea?'

'Yes,' he lied. What he *was* getting used to was that Catherine would do, say and get exactly what she wanted, no matter what they had agreed, that life with her wasn't safe, that, like everyone else, she couldn't be trusted. His initial fears about responding to her advances had been replaced by a new sense of safety. Catherine and coupledom had been a safe place to hide, until now.

'Do you know that he's already the size of a lemon?'

Liam fought the visualization forming in his head. 'He?'

'He, she . . . although I feel sure it's a boy.'

He lowered his spoon. 'You can't know that.'

'It's a just a feeling. Mothers know sometimes. I can close my eyes and picture his little face . . .'

He laid the spoon on the plate in front of him. His appetite had vanished. He wanted to run out of the room screaming, to get away from her and the thing she carried inside her, but he knew he had to stay and be *interested*. What normal husband wouldn't be? Oh, God! He had made another terrible mistake. There was nothing for it but to surrender to his role. 'How long will the nausea last?'

'Probably a few weeks.'

'Are you sure you shouldn't take some time off?'

'I'd like to work as long as I can.'

'My mother always resented my father because she had to work right up until I was born,' he volunteered.

Catherine looked at him in amazement. 'That's the first time I've *ever* heard you talk about your mother.'

Liam's mind was in turmoil – he wasn't even sure exactly what he had just said. 'I mean, she had n-no choice. She had to w-work . . . I've told you about my mother before?'

'You've given me the family history.'

'Well, she worked. That's all.' He got up abruptly from the table.

'Did you love her?'

'Of course I did.' He rinsed his plate vigorously at the sink.

'It's all right, Liam . . . You just talk so little about your family, and never about your feelings.'

Liam felt he was being tested in some way.

'Wouldn't you like to get in touch with your father?'

'I've told you, he's an alcoholic.'

'I know that, but now that you're going to have children of your own, wouldn't you like to get in touch?'

'What the hell for? He made our lives a misery.'

She was staring at him. 'I just want our child to have a family.'

'Look, you've got enough to worry about with . . .' he struggled to say the words '. . . being pregnant.'

Catherine was looking at him incredulously.

She just didn't get it. How could she? Suddenly it struck him – a revelation: he would have to tell her everything. Then she would understand that she had to have a termination. Even Catherine would see that she couldn't bring his baby into the world.

'I'm going outside for a cigarette.'

From somewhere in the living room the phone rang. Liam went towards it, lifting the red scatter cushions on the couch until he found it. 'Hello.'

'Liam?'

'Margaret. How are you?'

'In an uproar as usual – the dishwasher's just fallen out of the wall again. I suppose you pair are very busy?'

'No. Not at all, just having a quiet Saturday morning . . . It doesn't happen very often, not for me anyway.'

'Can I have a word with my Catarina, then?'

'Yeah, sure, I'll just –'

'And, by the way, Liam, I couldn't be more pleased for you both. Congratulations! Gavin was just so thrilled.'

'Oh . . . yeah, thanks . . . It was a huge surprise.' Liam held out the phone to his wife. 'It's your mother.' Catherine took it from him and sat on the couch.

Liam went outside, lit a cigarette and began to pace up and down on the patio, watching her through the glass as she talked and laughed. Was she ever going to consult him about anything again? Or had he already served his purpose as a sperm donor, a disposable commodity in a process that was only ever about her? He stubbed out his cigarette and flicked it over the rail.

'When did you tell them?' he asked, when she had hung up.

'A few days ago, why?'

'Oh, nothing. What's it got to do with me anyway? Who else have you told?

'What's wrong with telling people?'

77

'Everyone at work knows already, do they?' Liam pulled on his jacket.

'No. Why? Where are you going?'

'Out! Out of this house, away from you.'

Catherine was staring at him in astonishment.

Outside in the driveway he reached into his pocket for his keys and remembered that Catherine's car was being serviced. He was supposed to pick it up for her later that morning. If he took the car she wouldn't have any transport. Fuck that! He needed the car: he needed to drive, to get far away. He wondered if Catherine had ever gone without anything she wanted in her entire life. In the absence of other choices he was beginning to hate her.

He drove through the central business district, past the busy Ice-Creamery and the Saturday-morning market crowds. Parents dragging children, children dragging parents, and the sort of children who hang around the energy of other people's families, skirting through the market on bikes or milling about in pairs waiting for something to happen, anything that would connect them to the greater whole.

His mobile phone rang in his pocket. He pulled it out, saw Catherine's name, turned it off and threw it onto the passenger seat. He stopped at the intersection near the Creighton and Davis offices, where Colin was leaning on his silver Jaguar, arms crossed over his ever-expanding belly. Liam watched his mouth moving soundlessly as he lectured his colleague, Paul, on some area of his expertise. Liam sickened at the thought of the crude innuendo he would have to put up with from Colin when he found out about Catherine's pregnancy. He accelerated rapidly through the intersection. They were probably talking about it right now for all he knew.

He could forget any notion he had of telling her the truth. Tell her what? 'You're carrying the child of a monster. Kill it before it's too late'?

Liam crossed the railway bridge and drove blindly through the industrial estate, soon leaving the car yards and warehouses of the township behind. He drove through the open countryside, past the speedway and its empty, makeshift stands. His eyes took in only the road ahead and the broken white line that measured out the endless kilometres before him. He wondered how far he could drive without running out of fuel. How far he could distance himself from the nightmare reality of his life. How far he could drive 'away' from himself and how long he could stay there.

Slowly he began to look at, and really see, the physical details of the world around him. Yellowing paddocks, a distant green shadowed hill, a stand of camphor laurel trees, a bare farmhouse, a dairy, the endless still sky. He wound down the window and let the air rush past him.

How could he change what was already done? He still existed – blood still flowed through his veins – but for him the world had stopped a long time ago.

Up ahead at a small junction there was a general store. The fuel gauge was nearly on empty. He resisted the urge to turn off into the nearby patchwork of farms, accelerated towards the carefully restored stone building and pulled in alongside the single petrol bowser. A group of Jersey cows were feeding on the ridgeline opposite as he filled the car.

Inside the Berridale Emporium a round man in workshorts and a singlet carefully stacked apples on open tiered shelves. He looked towards Liam and ambled over to the counter.

'Twenty bucks worth of fuel,' said the man, looking at the readout on the terminal. 'Anything else?'

Liam hesitated and took two packets of crisps from a tray on the counter. 'Just these.'

'Twenty-four ninety.'

Liam fished the exact amount from his pocket and placed it in the man's hand; he noticed crescents of black earth beneath the shopkeeper's fingernails.

'Makes a nice change from plastic,' said the man, clamping the twenty-dollar note in the till. 'Most people don't know what real money looks like nowadays . . .' He smiled in such a friendly way that Liam felt almost bereft at the thought of leaving the store so soon.

'Do you have a farm here?'

'The whole ridge, a bit of dairy, orchards.' The man pointed in various directions with his thumb to indicate the vicinity of each enterprise. 'Root crops. Dairy. That's our milk there.' He pointed to a glass-fronted fridge. 'Best milk you'll get, not homogenized. Pasteurized but not homogenized. Got some unpasteurized too. Have to label it "Pet food only". Drink it meself. Been drinkin' it since I was born. Pasteurization just allows farmers to get sloppy. A clean dairy farm don't need no pasteurization.' He walked over to the fridge and opened the door. 'Here, have one on me.' He handed Liam a two-litre container of milk. 'You'll taste the difference.'

'Thanks.'

'Of course, if you want the big supermarket chains to buy up your milk for a pittance you gotta do what they tell you. Me? I like to keep things small.'

The rhythm of the man's steadily building argument was having a soothing effect on Liam's frayed nerves.

'You looking for a farm?' asked the man.

'No, just taking a drive. As a matter of fact I'm a real-estate agent,' added Liam, awkwardly, 'but it's my day off.'

The farmer eyed Liam curiously, his youthful clean-shaven face, his tailored pants and well-cut shirt. 'Aha!' He shook his finger. 'That's another story! No end of you people coming round here talking up land prices. I wouldn't even look at selling this place under one million.'

'Well, from what I've seen you'd probably get it.'

'Then where would I go? People round here start getting that sort of selling price they'll need the same kinda money to buy back in.' He pointed to his head several times. 'Loony tunes – only people who benefit is you lot!'

Liam nodded: he could hardly deny it.

'It's all arse-up. My granddaughter won't be able to buy into a shoebox in the outer limits, let alone anywhere else. Whole generations are going to be held hostage by the wealthy. People should hang on to their land and hand it on to their kids. You got kids?' He lifted a box of butternut squashes from behind the counter and deposited it in a nearby trolley.

'Thinking about it.'

'Don't think about it. Best investment you'll ever make. What's all this for,' he waved his hand over his head, indicating the entirety of his business, 'if you don't have someone to hand it on to? Apart from you and your greedy lot!' He laughed.

'So you're definitely not interested in selling, then?'

'No, but plenty are,' said the man, turning back to his work.

'Thanks again for the milk.'

'My pleasure. I know you'll be back for more when you taste that . . .'

In the car, Liam propped the milk between the front seats, and started the engine. The farmer's dog emerged from the rear of the adjoining shed and rounded the building. The black-and-white collie barked excitedly and ran towards Liam's departing vehicle.

As the Berridale Emporium receded into the distance Liam's momentarily raised spirits began to sink. The farmer's rapture for ordinary life, his relentless enthusiasm and cheerful wisdom had lifted him out of himself for a short while. He had been fascinated to meet someone so rooted in his life, so vitalized and defined by what he did. *You are what you do.* An integration of body and soul not possible for Liam, whose very survival depended upon separating himself from what he had done. *He* would never be whole again.

The road crossed a small creek and cut sharply into the hills. At the top of the ridge, where the paddocks unfolded, Liam left the car at the edge of the pasture and began walking. He waded through the tall oat-grass, carrying the farmer's milk. He followed the ridgeline for a time, then made his way across a cultivated field of turnips, towards a copse that straddled a narrow gully. Here behind the trees several outbuildings took him by surprise; further along behind a windbreak of monastery bamboo, he found a small, well-kept weatherboard farmhouse, freshly painted in tones of pale green and cream. He could clearly see the dormer windows of the north-facing attic.

Not wishing to trespass, Liam walked the full boundary, following the line of the bamboo until he arrived at the front of the property. Access was via a narrow but sealed road that led down the opposite side of the ridge and reconnected somewhere with the main road he had driven along.

He followed the rough gravel drive to the front gate where, to his amazement, a vivid new yellow and red Creighton and Davis sign had been posted. To Liam's professional eye the house appeared unoccupied. On the faded grey timber veranda he pressed his face to a window and peered inside; across the darkened room he could make out a fireplace surrounded by lacquered woodwork and, deeper in, through an open doorway, the black-and-white tiles of a country kitchen. The unfurnished rooms confirmed his first impression. He leant on the timber handrail and looked across the fields at the 'pleasant rural views', imagining a life here for himself, Catherine and the child.

Liam continued his walk, travelling upwards over open paddocks until the ground finally began to descend. There, he looked out across the open vista to an expanse of farms and forest. He opened the plastic container he had been carrying and gulped the now tepid milk. He sat on the ground and ran his hands over the wild grass, massaging his palms against the coarse texture. He couldn't remember the last time he had been alone and at one with the elements.

He lay back and looked at the sky above, clear, blue, blemished with a few hazy streaks of cloud. He breathed in the clean air and felt the endless space around him. Happiness was a possibility, but he was not allowed moments like these and his eyes filled with tears. If only he could go back to a time before he had forfeited the right to be happy, to a time before *it* had happened.

He tried to remember when he had last felt safe, sifting through memories of his early childhood for remnants of joy, unconditional love, or even security. He found nothing he could hold on to, and quickly realized that what he really longed for was a return to the womb, to be completely unborn.

He let the hot tears roll down the side of his face and cried for the life he had lost and the life that had been taken. He closed his eyes and drifted into oblivion.

Catherine, 2008

'The mobile number you have called is switched off or unavailable . . .' Catherine dropped the phone onto the bed, and sat down beside it. Liam never turned off his mobile, *never*. Her face was disfigured and red from crying. She couldn't quite believe what was happening. Liam had been gone for nearly eight hours. Why didn't he call? She was so angry she wanted to pack her things and leave. She wanted to call her mother and get her father to pick her up – Liam hadn't even left her the car, for God's sake. What on earth had got into him? She wished she wasn't carrying his child. What could he have been doing all this time? She had no desire to bring up a baby on her own. If only he would call!

She wiped traces of makeup from her eyes with a tissue and lay down on the bed with her knees pulled up to her chest. For the first time in her life she felt utterly powerless, humiliated, which made her angry all over again. Who was he to treat her like this? *Where the hell was he?*

She leapt up off the bed and went to the bathroom. She turned the tap on and watched as the column of steaming water thundered into the bath. Throwing in a handful of lavender salts and watching them sink to the bottom, she recalled Liam's outburst and faced the unpalatable truth that he really didn't want the baby. She should have talked to him about her own feelings now that they were married instead of blindsiding him. He had every right to be angry and hurt, to feel as powerless as she did now.

She dropped her robe and stepped into the warm water. Her small breasts were already swollen and the nipples had darkened. She sat down slowly, letting the water close around her abdomen as she ran her hands over the tiny mound of her barely pregnant belly. *Is this what happened when you gave your body over to a new life? You lost control of your own?* As the heat of the perfumed water pervaded her body, the anger and despair leached out. She had to talk to Liam and take his reservations into account; she should have talked to him before.

Catherine wrapped a towel round her damp hair and began to massage some cream into her shoulders. As she tied her robe around her, the phone rang shrilly. She ran to the bedroom and picked it up. 'Liam? Where are you?'

'I'm at a road-house down near Lindisfarne. I've booked into a motel across the road.'

'A motel? What are you doing there?'

'I'll be home tomorrow. I'm just too tired to drive any further. I've been driving all day.'

'Are you all right?'

'Yeah . . . Look, I'm sorry I stormed off. It's not your fault.'

Catherine began to cry. 'You don't want the baby, do you?'

'We'll talk about it tomorrow, Cath. I don't know what I want, but we'll work it out together.'

'Okay, Liam . . . *I love you.*'

'Bye.'

She held the receiver for several seconds, stunned. She felt that the power in her relationship with Liam had shifted completely and without warning. Hunched naked on the edge of the bed she was swamped by a deep sense of unease: *something was off.* Imaginings of the future now contained a sense of foreboding.

In the morning Catherine lay alone in bed unable to shake off the apprehension she felt. Even after Liam called again to reassure her that he would be home that afternoon, she had to force herself to get up and face the day. She made tea and sat in the kitchen, thinking about something her mother had said when she had told her that she and Liam were getting married. 'He seems a very likeable young man, but what do you really know about him after six months?'

At the time Catherine had laughed. They were in love: what else did she need to know?

The only personal records Liam possessed were kept in a shoebox in the linen cupboard. Catherine took it down from the shelf and carried it back to the kitchen with her. The box held a few papers; a résumé, a multimedia diploma, a school report from Meredith Smith-Baxter College and a short reference.

During his time with us I have found Liam to be a cooperative and courteous student, who quietly completes work set to the best of his abilities. He has shown a particular interest in media and computer studies, which is reflected in his results. It is my belief that Liam will be a solid contributor wherever life may take him.

She unfolded a stained and creased birth certificate: 'Liam Jon Douglass. Born: 1 June 1982. Father: John Scott Douglass, surveyor 5/8/1947. Mother: Brenda Halliwell, domestic, 16/3/1959.'

Wedged into the bottom of the box were two identical photographs of Liam's formal graduation dinner. Catherine had seen the picture before and had offered to frame it for him but he had seemed as uninterested in it as he was in any reference to the past.

Initially she had enjoyed the idea that Liam had no prior attachments, that he was all hers to monopolize, but now it seemed sad that the father of her child had no history to bestow, and no family to speak of. She examined the photograph. It told her little. A wide arch, of silver and pink balloons and white streamers, was suspended over a stage. The black drapes, behind the assembled students, were peppered with silver stars. A sequined banner read, 'Live Love Life'.

Although Liam stood at the centre of the group under the arch, he appeared somehow set apart, separated from the rows of smiling youths on either side of him. His eyes looked past the camera and his mouth was a thin, closed smile. It seemed to Catherine to have been an odd affair, none of the usual pink taffeta ballgowns. Many of the girls wore unusual outfits, and her eye was drawn to the raven-haired girl with dark eyes, whom Liam had said he'd been friends with. Catherine felt an involuntary stab of jealousy, as if the girl in the red bolero knew things about Liam's past that she never would. She collected the documents together and held them. It wasn't much to show for a life. No pictures of his childhood. Not a letter or even a photograph of his mother. She knew the reasons from what little of the family history Liam had told her.

After years of his father's drinking, his mother had packed their things and returned to Scotland. Liam was to fly out from Australia and join her in a few months' time when she was settled and had found him a school. His father had given up: he travelled around so much with his work that he hadn't fought to keep his son.

Liam had counted the days as he waited for word from his mother. Eventually his father had received a call informing him that Liam's mother had suffered a cerebral haemorrhage and died. His father would not, or could not, provide the money for him to travel to Glasgow for her funeral. His Scottish grandmother died six months later. The following year Liam had left his father and, using the small amount of money left to him by his grandmother, applied to attend the college in Wentworthville. He hadn't attempted to make contact with his father since and had told Catherine that as far as he was concerned his father was already dead.

It was a sad story, and when she thought of Liam waiting for a call from his mother that would never come, her eyes filled with tears.

She could see that Liam's father had failed him badly, but after all this time, surely, in the absence of so much history, even an alcoholic father would be better than none. If only she could get Liam to contact him, his father could at least provide her with a sense of his past or him with a few mementos of his mother. After almost ten years maybe he had mellowed. And if that wasn't possible, what about his mother's side of the family? By all accounts she had loved and fought for him, his grandmother too. Surely someone from that branch of the family tree would welcome news of a nephew or cousin.

She propped the portrait of Liam's graduation dinner on a corner shelf in the kitchen, took the documents to the printer in the bedroom and made copies of several pages. She slid them inside a Manila envelope and folded down the flap.

Mathew, 2008

The back lounge of the Flag Hotel was windowless, cramped and overheated – the perfect haven for the hard-core early-morning drinkers who owned the stools at the bar. Mathew Allen sat under a tarnished mirror, printed with the figure of a cricketer parrying his bat. He knew why men came here. He used to come here to drink until he was legless. It was a hidden place where no one judged and people left you alone to guard your sorrows. Today, as he waited for his friend Father Robert, he drank ginger ale through a straw and watched the blue light of the soundless television play on the faces at the bar. Even at lunchtime the place made him feel as though it was already dark outside. After the conclusion of the trial this bar had become his second home.

He wondered how many nights Robert had sat there and drunk whisky with him until the rage had swelled inside him, and he had smashed his fist on the table and wept like a baby. More often they sat in prolonged silence, the priest offering nothing but his presence, aware that the gospel was not always delivered in words.

And when he had frequently demanded, 'Why?' Robert was never fool enough to insult him with a ready answer.

Mathew and Robert, 1994

'I have no explanations, Mathew. All I know is that you're still here and somehow you must go on. Sometimes there is nothing left but to lean into God.'

'There is no *God*, Robert.'

The priest nodded. 'Sometimes it's almost worse to believe in a God who appears to oversee the evil in the world and do nothing about it. It might shock you, but there are times when I find it hard to convince myself that God exists.'

'A priest?'

'I sometimes think I became a priest to escape everything I see in the world – all of this.' He looked across at the weary barmaid and sozzled punters. A couple exchanging heated words across a table. 'And the rest of it . . . love, responsibility. Sure I convinced myself I had a calling. We can convince ourselves of anything. I may be a priest, Mathew, but it doesn't mean I haven't struggled or doubted.' He sipped his whisky thoughtfully. 'What you're going through, I can't pretend to know. But I do feel the pain of what you share with me. I can sit with it. That's my real calling.'

'What do you believe in?'

Robert pinched the bridge of his nose and closed his eyes for a moment. 'On a good day? When I feel effective, when I've lifted a weight off someone for a few moments, I do feel the power of God – but after all the things I've heard, the things I've witnessed people go through, it's people themselves I believe in, their ability to overcome almost anything and go on living.'

Mathew slugged his whisky and eyed the priest sceptically.

'If God represents a place big enough to offload what we can't carry,' continued the priest, 'then I'll always be his man.'

'I want to kill them,' said Mathew.

'I'd be surprised if you didn't.'

'I think about it in detail, how I'm gonna do it. The terror in their eyes. I want them to know that no one is coming. I want to tell them, "This is for Benjamin." They have to suffer.' He sat back against the wall and swirled the Scotch in his glass before swilling the last of it. 'When I do it in my mind it feels good. Two twelve-year-olds up against a grown man . . . I make myself sick.'

'About the same odds they gave Benjamin.'

Mathew checked the older man's face for signs of judgement and found none. Robert offered him a refill from the whisky bottle. 'No, I've had enough.' He covered his glass. 'I'm not sure about you, Robert. Aren't you supposed to tell me that that would only make me the same as them?'

'They're normal reactions. We all have darkness and light inside us. It's what we decide to do that matters.'

'I really do want to kill them. I think about it a lot.'

'You're walking through Hell right now, Mathew, but you will get to the other side. How are things with Rachel?'

He shook his head. 'It's a lost cause. I can't talk to her. Most nights, when I'm not with you, I don't go home. I go to Ewan's. Jen always keeps a plate for me. They don't care what time I come in or how drunk I am. Apart from you, Ewan is the only person I *can* talk to. He saw what they did. I feel so guilty he had to go through that. I can see in his eyes when we talk about it – he's got pictures in his head. It's fucked him up. I'm supposed to be the older brother.' Mathew's eyes were wet with tears.

'I'm sure you'd be there for him in a crisis.'

'He's always been smarter than me, more able to find the right words. It used to really piss me off sometimes.' He wiped his face and almost smiled. 'If I go to Mum's she starts hovering around me like I'm a sick child – like I'm the victim. She adored Benjamin, but to spare me, I suppose, she never falls apart in front of me. I can see she's been crying. Dad just sits there like he's been shot – like this is just one parenting scenario beyond his map of the world, completely outside his comprehension. "I don't know what to say, son." I doubt he'll still be here at Christmas. He had a tumour removed from his neck last year, and I just keep wishing he'd passed away a happy old man before this happened. I avoid them all, I can't help it – I can't stand to look at their faces. Especially Rachel . . . I can't see us ever being the same again.'

'Maybe if Rachel understood how isolated you feel, perhaps you could talk to someone together.'

'She can't stand me to touch her – I get it, I totally get it, but who's there to get me? She'll always be the heart-broken mother of my dead child and I'll always be the husband who couldn't protect them.'

'There's a group. It's not just about bereavement, it's for people who've lost family to violent crime.' Robert fumbled through his wallet and pulled out a small card.

Mathew waved it away. 'I told you, she won't go.'

'They also have a group just for men . . . The way men and women cope with trauma is often very different.'

'Honestly, Robert, what's the point of any of it?'

'Well, that's the hardest question . . .'

'The only reason I can talk to you is because you don't pretend to have the answers.'

The priest filled Mathew's glass with water, and pushed an open bag of cashews in his general direction.

'Underneath it all, I'm just so fucking lonely. Part of me knows Benjamin is dead and the life I lived with Rachel is over. If I could go out tomorrow and find a normal girl, a happy girl with a kind heart, if I could paper over the past and have more kids with *her*, I would. The other part of me can't let Benjamin go. I don't know what to do with myself . . . I used to be somebody's father. Now I don't know what I am.' He looked into Robert's face and was embarrassed by the empathy he saw. 'Didn't you ever want children?'

'I was married once.'

Mathew was surprised.

'We thought she was infertile. I would've done the IVF if it had come to that – but we found out it was me. My ego couldn't take it. For some reason adoption I could rationalize, but she wanted to go ahead with a sperm donor so the baby would be half "ours".' He laughed.

'I couldn't do it. It's the most pathetic choice I ever made. I can't regret it . . . Now I have many children in my life by many different fathers – but I'll never know what it is to have a child of my own.'

'She left you, then?'

'No. She stood by me. I had an epiphany and skulked off to the priesthood.'

'Jesus.'

'Mmm.'

Mathew fell silent, staring down at the tabletop for a while. 'Sometimes when I'm smashed I walk over to the cemetery and lie down on the grass next to him,' he confided quietly. 'I talk to him, like you'd talk to any three-year-old. I dumb it down and tell him that the boys are being punished, that we miss him. It gives me comfort because that's where his little body is. After all the searching and having him taken away, knowing he's there gives me some relief. We always said we believed in cremation for ourselves but after what happened, the thought of inflicting any more damage, of burning his body, just seemed obscene.'

'You wanted him laid to rest.'

'Yeah. I remember Mum used to say after Ewan and I had moved out – we'd come home for Christmas and be out till all hours – what we did when we were away she didn't have to worry about but when we were back under the same roof she couldn't go to bed until we were both in ours . . . It doesn't last long, but that's the feeling.'

Robert fingered the card on the table. 'Some of the people at this group had children who were murdered – and worse.'

'What good will that do me?'

'People wounded in that way are the only people who can really know what you're going through. They may have passed through stages you have. Your experiences may even help them.'

'I don't know if I'm ready for that.'

'I'd be happy to go with you.'

They had attended a single meeting together. Mathew was already half cut when Robert picked him up. He knew that Robert understood, that he would want to be drunk himself if he was in Mathew's shoes.

Mathew sat through the meeting in total silence, witness to different versions of the same story. Though the background and the details differed the endings were inevitable. It was his story. It helped a little to know that he was not alone in his fantasies of revenge, that other men wished suffering and death on those who had murdered their loved ones. Some who had come through it insisted it would pass, that hatred would be replaced one day with forgiveness. For the moment hatred was all Mathew had. He had never been able to make himself go to a second meeting.

Mathew, 2008

A chorus of 'Hey, Father!' broke out as some of the old-timers greeted Robert at the bar. He shook a few hands, then came to Mathew's table. The two men embraced warmly. The priest unbuttoned the studs on his fur-lined bomber jacket but made no attempt to take it off. He held a black helmet under one arm.

'Can I get you a drink?'

Robert glanced at the amber dregs in Mathew's glass.

Mathew caught the look. He had stopped drinking some years back, but had been tempted occasionally to start again. 'Ginger ale, don't worry.'

'It's not that. Would you mind if we got out of here and just walked for a bit? I've been on the scooter all morning.'

'Sure.'

The pavement outside the dour hotel was wet from a fleeting shower; a row of ugly red and yellow wheelie bins marred the view across the flagstone square to the river-front reserve. 'Shall we cut through the park?'

Mathew nodded. It was all the same to him. They took the signposted cycle track that wound between the giant camphor laurels.

'God, they're beautiful,' said Robert.

Shafts of yellow light pierced the pattern of overlapping leaves. Mathew followed his friend's gaze and saw the enormous spread of the overhanging canopy, the shivering leaves. He smelt the camphor in the air. 'Aren't they supposed to be a noxious weed?'

'It depends who's looking at them.'

'I'm sorry about the other night. I didn't realize how late it was when I called,' said Mathew.

'Don't worry about it. I wasn't asleep anyway . . . I have some news, actually. I've been offered a position as chaplain in a country school – it's a permanent posting, semi-retirement, really. It comes with a small house.'

'That sounds good.'

'It's a long way up north, past Atherton.'

Mathew was shocked, but tried not to show it. 'I'm really pleased for you,' he said, but his voice was flat.

'I'm looking forward to it, and the job, of course, is a sinecure, but I'll be working with young people, which will be quite rewarding, I think. As I get older, the thought of having a place of my own to potter about in is very appealing.'

'Yeah, right. You deserve a bit of sunshine, Robert.'

'Maybe you can visit me up there sometime.'

Mathew looked at him doubtfully.

'I mean it. I hope you will.'

'I've got a lot on my plate at the moment.'

'And you can call me anytime . . . There's a new guy down at St Andrews. He's young but good.'

'*Please* . . . Robert, you don't have to worry about me. And don't feel guilty about living your life. When do you go?'

'In a few weeks. I made the decision today. You were one of the first people I wanted to tell.'

A bell tinkled. A young cyclist swerved around them and onto the path ahead.

'Don't worry about me, Robert. I'll be all right.'

Chemistry

'An eye for an eye, a tooth for a tooth . . .'

Geoffrey, 2008

Through the carriage window Geoffrey could make out the sign for Thornleigh. Two more stops and he'd be in Headlands. He put his feet up on the opposite seat and stared out at the shale-edged slopes that banked the railway line, the creosoted stones, and the rear yards of the faceless houses, as they shunted past.

At Headlands a bus took him through unfamiliar streets, along a battered promenade lined with Norfolk Island pines, their needles browned and burnt by spray from a polluted sea.

When the bus stopped at the clifftop lookout he got off and passed through the gateway of the cemetery, climbing a path through the grounds, beside sparse rows of slumped and broken early-settlement headstones. Among the lines a small fluted one caught his eye. He stopped to read the inscription. The engraved lettering was worn smooth by years of sandblasting from the buffeting winds. He ran his finger across the depressions that spelt out the few remaining words. 'Sarah . . . beloved . . . of . . . 1883–1890. Drowned.'

Moving towards the more ostentatious monuments on the brow of the headland, he came to the sombre polished-granite and terrazzo stones at the heart of the cemetery. The graves in this section were littered with modern funerary dross – plastic posies, laminated photographs, stuffed toys and foil balloons. Beside a gleaming black obelisk, dedicated to a 'Beloved Mother and Grandmother', he found what he was looking for: a simple white stone bearing the short inscription 'Adam Paul Simpson. In God's care. 1979–2000.' At the base of the stone lay the remains of a dried-flower arrangement. Next to it, weighed down with a heavy stone, was a stuffed red love heart, embroidered with the words 'In my heart always, Olivia'. A token from the half-sister Geoffrey had never met. Where was she now? Another casualty.

He sat down and leant back against the cold stone. Below the slope of the cemetery an implacable ocean rose and fell against the rocks. He had wanted to come here to see for himself the reality of his brother's annihilation. Here, beneath the ground, lay one relative he could safely visit in a strange confirmation of his survival. Further proof that it was all wrong, that there was no justice. It wasn't fair.

Was it *fair*, he thought bitterly, that while he was 'rehabilitated' in protective custody, treated by specialists for dyslexia and educated, Adam had had the shit beaten out of him because of who his brother was? Was it fair that he, who had taken a life, had been released after seven years in a secure unit, while Adam, a heroin addict, had got five years for a series of break-and-enters – not a counsellor in sight – had been beaten and fucked up the arse in jail, and had killed himself before he could die of AIDS while *he* still lived and breathed?

He looked at the clumsy chain-stitch on the heart that spelt out his sister's name: *Olivia*. Addicted to smack herself since she was fifteen. None of it was fair. It never had been.

Danny, 1992

The boy shrank into the chair as the buzzing clippers made another pass above his left ear. The crooked teeth bit roughly into the skin at the base of his skull. 'Ow!'

'Sit still.' His mother wouldn't pay for a haircut, said they were worse than a waste of money. 'Do you want me to do it or not?' she asked. Danny straightened up. The instrument vibrated violently across his scalp.

'That'll have to do.' She shut off the clippers, reeled in the cord and began to sweep up auburn hair from the cement landing.

Danny ran his hand across the soft stubble on his head and looked at his brothers, Damien and Adam, shorn only minutes ago themselves. He held up a cracked hand-mirror and mournfully observed the uneven quarter-inch 'shave', marred, here and there, by several ugly, hairless patches. The whole Simpson family had been branded with the one brutal haircut; even Danny's softer features could not lessen the impact.

At school Danny's teachers saw only another bullet-headed Simpson. They noticed that he was quieter and less outwardly aggressive than the two older brothers who had preceded him, but they thought him sly and manipulative, capable of setting up another kid to take a fall. This was the unfair legacy of being a Simpson. And in a way it was true: he was sly. He had to be. Danny Simpson had been ducking punches all his life, even in his mother's womb.

He had been born a month premature, and his mother had barely been able to look at him – the new male animal in her life – without turning away. For a few days the nurses had brought him to her to feed, but with two broken ribs from her husband's farewell punch, and her ambivalence to the infant, their efforts had been to no avail. An experienced foster-mother had been found, and it was she who had called him Danny.

When he had finally been returned to his mother, so deep was Debbie Simpson's depression, so numbed was she by alcohol and anti-depressants, that she didn't even hear him crying as he lay in a bassinet at her feet. Soon the crying had become a defeated sob and then a whimper. Finally it had stopped altogether.

By the time she had begun to pick him up more often, it had been too late: Danny was an 'unresponsive' baby. Debbie had always suspected it was the six weeks without her that had done the damage.

Danny brushed his teeth, picked up a damp towel from the bathroom floor and tried to wipe a stain off the front of his school shirt. He walked up the short stairwell of the cramped flat and stood at the bedroom door. He pushed it open. A naked man lay face down on the bed beside his sleeping mother. He began to back out of the room. The sleeping man stirred. Debbie Simpson opened her eyes. 'Danny?'

The man lifted his head. 'Don't you know how to knock?'

It was his father. His face was swollen and red. Danny recognized the signs and could smell the alcoholic vapour.

'I'm going to school.'

The two figures on the bed remained inert.

'I haven't got any lunch-money.'

'Jesus, Danny. Tell them I'll pay later.' She shielded her face with a pillow.

Danny slowly closed the door.

His mother's handbag hung on a coat hook in the hall. He slid his fingers inside, pulled out her purse and helped himself to a ten-dollar note, then looked at the remaining twenty dollars. He considered taking that too – she wouldn't know the difference, wouldn't know how much she'd blown at the pub last night or how much his father had taken. After all, that was the only reason he ever came here.

He decided against it and instead emptied the copper coins from the bottom of the bag. Why not? It was his tenth birthday. He should have known that his mother would never keep her promise to pick him up early from school and take him to Birkenhead Towers to buy a set of Viking figures, the ones you could paint yourself. He should never have believed her in the first place. He stuffed the coins into his pockets and hoisted his backpack over his shoulder, taking care to close the front door quietly behind him before he headed off to school.

The front of Adam Simpson's black T-shirt was covered with fine white powder. He popped another tablet from a pharmaceutical foil onto the pile of pills accumulating on the table-top, scooped them up and dumped them in the bowl of the coffee-grinder. On the screen of the portable TV suspended from a bracket in one corner of the kitchen, Oprah Winfrey held up a book: 'Some things are almost too hard to talk about. It takes real bravery to open up and publicly admit that you were wrong.' The sound of the grinder drowned out the talk-show host and sent angry lines of static across the screen. 'If you don't recognize my next guest from that description then I don't know what else to tell you!' He tipped the powder into a measuring jug.

A string of bells on the front-door handle jangled noisily as Danny came in and threw his backpack to the floor. Adam leaned instinctively forward across the table, obscuring his processing operations from view. 'How come you're home?' he said, before pulsing the machine a few more times. Danny watched him silently. Adam now crushed the resistant core of a tablet between two spoons. 'I said what are you doin' here?'

'No, you didn't.'

'What?'

'That's not what you said.'

Adam looked confused, as if his brain had missed a few steps in a complicated equation.

'I forgot my sports kit.'

He poured the powder into a large envelope, then used a funnel to deliver the codeine and paracetamol into a two-litre soft-drink bottle.

'What's that?'

'None of your fucken business.' He filled the bottle with water, screwed on the lid and shook it vigorously.

'What have you gotta do that for?'

'It gets rid of the shit.'

'Where's Mum?'

'Where d'ya reckon?' He swung his head upwards in the direction of the stairs. 'Leave her alone. I don't want her down here.'

Danny dug through the dirty washing, searching for some shorts and his regulation sports shirt. The school was a ten-minute walk away and if he got back by the end of lunchtime he'd be able to go on the bus to play soccer at the sports centre. He hated sport because he was no good at it. The kids who seemed to be built for games and came alive in the presence of a ball, shouting and hooting to one another across the field, made him feel fat and stupid, but the sports centre, with its foyer full of video games, held other attractions. He stuffed the unwashed items into his backpack and shrugged it on.

'Hey, Danny,' called Adam, wrapping the cord around the grinder. 'Don't tell Mum about any of this stuff, okay?

Danny nodded. Adam was volatile, and although he would never want to cross him, it was out of loyalty that he kept his brother's secrets. Unlike his oldest brother, Damien, Adam had never hurt him.

*

A fist thumping the other side of the bedroom wall roused Danny from his Saturday-morning lie-in.

'Damien!'

Danny opened his eyes and looked across at his brother's bed, unmade and empty. A crooked venetian blind above it masked the bright morning light. The underside of the bed was crammed with CDs, boxed Game Boys, items of tagged clothing and skateboard magazines. Damien rarely slept at home now but the pile of booty under the bed kept growing. Their mother never commented on it and was under strict instructions not to touch Damien's *things*.

Danny eyed the items covetously but knew better than to set Damien off on any score. He still had the bruises on his back from when he had walked in on him straddling a naked girl across the bed. He hated sharing a room with Damien. His brother was a pervert and a sadistic bully. He was relieved the bed was empty and hoped that Damien never came home again. In fact, he wished that Damien would die – violently, at the hands of someone as vicious as himself. Yes: Danny would like to be there to see that.

Damien's temporary absence from the flat created a power vacuum and an uneasy peace that could be reversed at any time.

'Damien!'

'He's not here.'

'Danny!'

'What?'

When Danny got to her room his mother was in her knickers, kneeling on all fours, running her fingers through the nylon shag-pile, like a blind woman. 'I dropped a Valium in the carpet and I can't find the other packet.' Danny stood at the door, indifferent to her dilemma.

'Danny, I think Damien's taken my box of medication.' She stood up exposing her long blue-veined breasts, pulled back her thin, bleached hair with both hands and stared at him wildly.

'What do want me to do about it?' He turned away from the spectacle.

'I can't find my pills, Danny.'

'Which ones?'

'The ones the doctor gave me . . . All of them! What do you mean "which ones"? The whole box, Danny. It was under the bed.'

'The ones you take with vodka?'

She opened a wardrobe. 'No, Danny.'

'You got about fifteen boxes. You put them in the cupboard behind the fridge.'

She looked at him warily for several seconds, then pushed past him. In the kitchen she began shouldering the refrigerator sideways across the linoleum to access a small utility cupboard. She pulled out a large Tupperware box and opened it. The box was full of prescriptions, each written in a different hand, and stuffed with tablets, diazepam, codeine and Xanax. She pulled out several empty sleeves marked 'Vicodin'.

'Where's the Vicodin? Fuck. Fuck!'

'What's it for?'

'Pain, Danny. Pain . . . Does Damien know where I keep this box?'

'I don't know.'

'Did you see him or Adam with any of this stuff?'

Danny picked up a foil of pills from the box marked 'Aropax'. 'What are these ones for?'

'Jesus, Danny, stop asking stupid fucking questions, will you?'

She sat down at the table and popped two generic Valium out of a half-empty foil. Danny opened the stranded fridge. 'We got no milk.'

'We got no milk,' she repeated. 'What do you expect me to do about it in my condition? Just eat something at school – tell them you forgot your lunch.'

'It's Saturday.'

'Oh, God, Danny. I'm going back to bed. If you turn the telly on, keep it quiet, okay?' A satin robe hung on the back of a kitchen chair. She pulled it on and closed it around her breasts. 'Make me a hot-water bottle and bring it in, will you?'

Danny filled a pink rubber bladder with boiling water from the kettle. He put it inside a fleecy bag and carried it up to his mother.

After the Valium she seemed less agitated. 'I'm sorry I bit your head off, Danny, but you don't know what's it's like for me.' She cradled the hot-water bottle and covered herself with the duvet.

'What's wrong with you?'

'Nothing, Danny. Just let me sleep for a while.'

'There's nothing to eat.'

She sat up angrily and began rummaging through her bedside drawer. 'Here, get some takeaway somewhere.' She handed him a ten-dollar note, hesitated, then handed him another. 'Take yourself to the arcade.'

Danny quickly pocketed the cash.

'There might be someone coming over later, a friend of mine, so take your time.'

Danny rolled his eyes. She'd had a lot of 'friends' over since his father had stopped coming around. 'How come we never do anything on the weekends?'

'Like what?'

'I dunno . . . Go to the beach or up to Toy Kingdom.'

'Danny, that shit costs money.'

'So? Why don't you get a job?'

She appeared injured. 'It's not like I've never had a job, Danny. I was halfway through my hairdressing apprenticeship when your father got me pregnant . . .' She gave him an indignant look. 'If I had a job, who'd be lookin' after you now, huh?'

Danny looked around the dingy room, then down at his feet. 'Dad said he'd take me to the greyhounds one weekend.'

His mother laughed bitterly. 'Is that right? You might be waiting a long time, kiddo.' She scratched a match across the side of a box of Redheads and lit a cigarette. 'He hasn't got the guts to tell you, Danny, but he's going inside for a couple of years.' She sucked some more life out of the cigarette, all the while watching his face for a reaction.

Danny's face reddened. His ears felt like they were on fire.

'I'm sorry, Danny. Things don't always work out the way you want them to.'

'Shut up! I don't care.'

The following Saturday night, after five happy-hour cocktails at the Lions Gate Hotel, Danny's mother met Steven Parry in the public bar.

When Danny took his mother a cup of tea on Sunday morning, it was Steve's hand that reached out and took it.

'Good service round here, eh, Deb?'

It wasn't the first time he'd found a stranger in his mother's bed and, as far as he knew, it wouldn't be the last. He tried not to think about it. At least she was home and in a good mood.

But Steve was still there a week later, sitting on the couch in his boxer shorts, and passing on orders. 'Fix your mum a sandwich, will ya?' Helping himself to her handbag, groping around for money or cigarettes. 'You got no fags left, Deb.'

'Go and get me a packet of Winfield, will you, Danny?'

'Go on, you heard her.' Steve's right arm was covered with a sleeve of tattoos, a spiral of thorny vines that travelled from the wrist to his unnaturally white shoulder. Inside the vines a red heart was gripped by the eight legs of a fearsome black spider.

Danny found it hard to take his eyes off the artwork. He noticed Steve had a habit of swinging his elbow out and craning his head to examine it closely, as if he had never taken a proper look at it before or was checking that it hadn't somehow altered itself overnight.

Pretty soon Steve was making demands: 'Turn that bloody noise off! I'm watching the news here, if you don't fucken mind.' After a month it was as if he had always been there, a poisonous black cloud, just like their father.

Rachel, 2008

A series of gentle waves lapped quietly against a distant jetty. Rachel turned away from the light and buried her face in the quilt, awake but still dreaming, dozing, drifting off again. The piercing cry of a lone seagull brought her back to consciousness and the unfamiliar room. She sat up, resting on her elbows. Her eyes turned immediately to the bunks at the far-side of the L-shaped cabana. Crumpled white sheets were thrown back and the beds were empty. Across the room in the kitchen nook David wiped a glass at the sink.

'Where are the boys?' She got to her feet and threw a robe over her shoulders.

'On the beach. I can see them through the window.'

'Where?'

He put his arm around her and steered her to the doorway. There they were, less than fifty metres away, kneeling on either side of a shallow trench, digging in the wet sand. Thomas scooped up the slurry from the bottom of the channel and drizzled it over a growing sandcastle. Martin supervised the operation, occasionally buttressing the sides with pieces of driftwood.

David held out a mug of tea. 'Just relax.'

The deck in front of the cottage jutted over the sand, like the prow of a ship. On one side the view stretched all the way to the rock wall, a series of large basalt lumps that fell away into the sea and curved protectively around the bay. A ribbon of shell-covered beach unfolded in the other direction, leading to the rotting pier. The nearest shack was a white matchbox that barely broke the line of a shrubby horizon.

The boys chased the retreating waves of the outgoing tide, dragging antlers of stranded kelp behind them. Thomas swung a piece high in the air over his head, letting it fly with a spray of sand in his brother's direction, then charging into the water when Martin turned to chase him, dunking his head in a wave.

Their mother watched them move up the beach away from her, wet bodies glistening, running now, bounding towards the boulders. Laughing breathlessly as they pursued each other, quickly becoming tiny shapes that moved across the silhouette of the rocks, dropping in and out of sight.

'Perhaps we should take our towels and sit in the shade of the rocks.'

'They're fine, Rache.' He dropped a warm pastry into her lap. 'Have a croissant and shut up.'

'No butter?'

'You packed the Eski . . . I can go to the Co-op later, if you want.'

On the beach three other children filed down the sandy trail that wound through the knee-high spinifex. Rachel saw them first and dropped her half-eaten croissant onto her lap. David turned to look. Thomas was clearly visible on the rock shelf poking in one of the pools with a long stick. Martin had pulled himself up onto a ledge. A boy in an orange T-shirt ran ahead of the other strangers. Martin jumped down onto the sand in front of him.

'It's just some kids,' said David.

All of the children now squatted, hands on knees, around the pool, captivated by something that Thomas was probing with his stick.

'Martin!' shouted Rachel, above the wind.

'Don't spoil their fun.' He sighed. You were going to try – remember?'

Martin looked up.

David answered him with a wave. 'Just let them be.'

'I'm only letting them know we're here'

'No, you're not. You're doing what you always do,' he snapped.

She looked shocked.

'They're not babies. Martin's thirteen going on thirty-five, thanks to us.'

'You mean me?'

'Let the rope out a little bit, for God's sake.'

'Thomas is only nine,' she protested unconvincingly.

David rolled his eyes heavenwards. 'I'm not worried about Thomas. You have to stop doing this to Martin.'

'Doing what?'

'Making him responsible for your fears.'

'Martin understands.'

'Do you think that's fair? It's selfish!'

Rachel was stunned into silence. It was true: Martin was not a little boy any more. He was growing up and away from her, yet she still expected him to regulate his existence according to her fears. The control her anxieties imposed upon the entire family had become a network of superstitions. It was addictive. No amount of compliance satisfied her need for safety.

David was at the end of his tether. He had navigated this minefield with her for years and now, in one conversation, she could feel the walls of protection being smashed down. She knew he was right: she had to relax her grip and face her fears.

David saw the panic in her face. 'I'm not trying to be cruel, but they're my sons too.'

Rachel nodded, trying hard to hold back tears.

'You lost one, no one will ever forget that, but it has to be about them now.' He closed his arms around her.

'Hey! Guess what we saw!' shouted Thomas, racing towards them with Martin hot on his heels.

'A blue-ringed octopus.'

'What?'

'He poked it with a stick and it turned blue.' Martin looked at his mother's tear-stained face. 'What's wrong?'

'Nothing, mate. It's just the wind in my eyes.'

'Jesus, boys, those things can kill you,' said their father.

'We know that, Dad, we're not stupid.'

He moved restlessly in his seat as he watched the other faces in the waiting room, anxious, closed, self-absorbed and bored. Convinced, like him, that no one carried a burden as heavy as theirs. Liam felt strangely removed from himself; he had already done his worst. Perhaps these people were still trying to hang on, to forestall theirs.

Inside the doctor's office, Liam's usual anxiety had disappeared, replaced by a sense of great relief as if he had carried his stone to a place where he could finally put it down.

Dr Rani Patma smiled warmly at him. 'I'm glad to see you, Liam. Marriage is such a huge transition that I'm surprised you missed your last appointment.'

'We were moving into a new flat and it wasn't easy to get away.'

'Catherine still doesn't know about your counselling?'

Liam looked bewildered, unprepared for the doctor's questions.

'We did discuss alternative explanations.' Dr Patma pulled her long, black hair back, and tied it into a loose knot as she spoke.

'She knows I'm on medication for depression and anxiety, but the counselling hasn't come up yet.'

'It would be good to clear the way for your regular visits. Your therapy isn't optional.'

'I know that. I've only missed one visit and I called to reschedule.'

'Okay. Tell me about married life,'

'Catherine's pregnant.'

Rani Patma fingered the ornate Coptic cross that hung at her throat. 'How did that happen?'

'She just did it. We'd agreed not to have kids – she didn't want kids . . . She just went off the pill.'

'She didn't discuss it with you?'

'No, she just thought if she changed her mind I'd change mine.'

'How did you react?'

'I couldn't believe she would do that to me. I felt safe with her, but how could she possibly know what it means?'

'What did you tell her?'

'I told her what she wanted to hear. I've tried to have the right reactions. How can I possibly be a father? I would never have married her . . .'

The doctor studied his troubled face. 'Basically, Liam, this is one of those things we talked about. A huge challenge thrown in your path, one you can't move or change. You can only confront it or go around it. I take it that Catherine wants to have the baby?' Liam nodded. 'And you can give her no reason not to have her baby. You have a number of choices.'

Liam looked terrified.

122

'You can step up and embrace becoming a father, run away from the situation – or you can tell Catherine about your past and let her decide what she wants to do.' She waited for a moment for Liam's response. He stared back at her. 'If you stay with her and become a father, you will have to confront your demons. Confronting the suffering you caused will be very painful. If you tell Catherine, you will risk her rejection and perhaps exposure. She may not want you anywhere near her or the baby. You may need to be relocated all over again.'

He cradled his face in his hands and looked desperately at the doctor for an answer.

'You have to ask yourself which is easier, which is safer, which is right, which is sustainable. Which is helpful to your recovery and which is fair to Catherine.'

He shook his head. It was all too much.

Dr Patma kept talking. 'For instance, what will leaving her and the baby, without explanation, do to her?'

Liam remained silent.

'How will she feel about carrying your baby when she learns about your past?

The doctor got up from her armchair, opposite Liam's, and walked across the room. 'If you say nothing and face up to being a father, what are the possible outcomes?' She folded her arms and sat on the edge of the desk. 'Will you be an adequate father? Is the child at risk?'

Liam looked up at her in horror.

Rani Patma raised a supple hand. 'I'm not suggesting he or she will be. These are simply the issues. What do you think Catherine needs right now?'

'Me to be there for her.' Liam's voice seemed to be trapped deep inside his throat. 'Me to be the child's father.'

She nodded. 'And what option appears easiest?'

'To run away.'

'Relocation, new job, new people. Is it really the easiest option, do you think?'

'Initially, yes.'

'What seems the safest option?'

'For who?'

'You.'

'To run away.' He rubbed at his face with his open hand. 'To stay, to do nothing.'

'Which is more frightening to you?'

'Telling her . . . Having a child.'

'Which is "right"?'

'Getting out of her life. Staying. Telling . . .'

The doctor looked at him with compassionate eyes. 'Which is sustainable?'

'I can't keep running away.'

'Which choice is best for your recovery?'

'I don't know. I really don't know.' He was sinking deeper into the mire.

'Go through the choices. Leaving?'

'Leaving doesn't achieve anything.' He thought for a moment. 'Staying, being a father, could send me over the edge – could be dangerous.'

'But if you do stay, if you do get through it, could it help you to grow? Could nurturing a child restore something to your life?'

'I don't deserve a child.'

'Maybe you don't.' She considered. 'But what about the child? What does he or she deserve? What do they need?'

'Not me.'

'What about telling?'

Liam looked away. 'It's too late for telling. I made a choice to marry and to have a life. I knew Catherine wouldn't take me on if she knew the truth – who in their right mind would?' He bowed his head. 'There never was any question of telling her. It was a choice between letting her go or grabbing a life. I was *never* going to tell her. It's not her burden.'

'So would telling her help in terms of your recovery?'

'I already know. It won't.'

Rani Patma interlocked her fingertips, making a little temple of her two hands, and pressed the point to her lips. 'Do you remember after the trial, when you first received therapy, you were obsessed with "growing" a new baby and giving it back to the mother? You even asked your own mother to have a baby for her . . .'

Liam began to weep. He remembered the dreadful longing and how he had dreamt of the child night after night, of growing a new baby inside his belly, of undoing the deed. He remembered his torment on waking to find that his dream was futile, that things remained as they were and always would.

He had tearfully begged his mother to have another baby and give it to the mother who had lost hers. He thought back to the endless months spent racked with anxiety, rocking his body back and forth on the little bed in his room in the secure unit. Eleven years old, utterly alone with his grief. For six months he had been too ill even to mix with the other children.

Finally they had convinced him that it was not possible to magic up a baby to replace one already dead. When at last he let go of his obsession and faced the permanence of death the real unravelling had begun.

Rani Patma waited politely for Liam to recover, then handed him a tissue. 'It seems to me your mind was constructing a way to undo your actions and to restore life. Of course, the solution it offered was a magical one – obviously the past cannot really be undone by magical thinking – but what if you were to look at this baby as an opportunity for restoration, for the renewal of life?'

Liam wiped his face and listened.

'Just as in your remorse you longed to grow and nurture a new baby to atone for your crime, what if you help

Catherine grow and nurture this baby? Don't you think that might help rectify what has been done?'

He sighed. 'Nothing will ever change what happened.'

'No, it won't. The past is past, unalterable. Your choices can influence only the future. Perhaps you can sublimate all that pain and use it as an opportunity to give, maybe one of the few you will ever have. Maybe the real choice here is between existing and meaningfully existing.'

'You mean dedicate myself to the child?'

'You took a child's life. Now it seems you have the opportunity to give life to one.'

Liam cried out, 'But what if something terrible happens to him?'

'Liam, do you really believe you are a danger to this child?' Rani Patma looked genuinely shocked.

'No! Not me.' He looked up at her, injured by the question. 'What if somebody takes him?' He doubled over and brought his hands to his chest.

'Is that your greatest fear?'

'*Yes!*' He knew what could happen, how short the time a mother's back had to be turned.

'Liam, *loss* is the risk that every parent takes when they bring a child into the world . . . Every father or mother's greatest fear is that something terrible will happen to their child.'

Liam held his hands out in supplication. '*I know.*'

An imposing walnut corridor divided the operational core of the newspaper from the editorial and corporate offices, permanently blocking any view of the harbour from Reiser's new workstation.

Pinned like a fly to the wall, facing out on what now seemed like the interior of a luxury barge, he was obliged to look all the way to the stern, where the new managing editor and his assistants presided over the room from a row of glass-fronted cubicles. The drawers on his new fitted filing cabinet opened with a quiet whisper and came to a stop without the familiar clunk. He was in the process of hurriedly emptying half the contents of one into a faded briefcase, hoping to get in and out quickly, when he was waylaid by one of the new editorial drones.

A *Globe* fixture, he'd been around long enough to have earned the leeway to finish most of his work out of the office, just so long as he stuck his head through the door for meetings and turned in the goods without rubbing his freedom in their faces. He stuffed one last file into the case and attempted to buckle the strap across the fat leather belly.

'Hey, man.'

'Hey,' said Reiser, clamping the latch on the bag, and doing his best to look like he was in a hurry.

'Man, that was a good piece on the Villawood detainees. You really nailed it.'

'Thanks, Cal.' Short for Caleb. Cal had proudly told him on first introductions that his mother had lifted the name from a character in a John Steinbeck novel.

Wow, man. He hadn't bothered to point out that, unlike Cal, Steinbeck was pretty familiar with his Bible.

Just one more egg to suck.

'Shame you couldn't have run it all, especially the stuff about the connection with privatized prison interests.'

'I think that came across. The pictures said it all.'

Cal was the kind of foppish pseudo-intellectual ferret who mooched round the floor at random intervals and sat on his subordinates' desks, bovver-booted foot lifted over one knee, nodding sagely as he patronized seasoned journalists twice his age; people who could actually spell 'succinctly' without resorting to a mechanical aid.

'I was thinking we could follow with a friendlier piece about the success stories of migrants from earlier waves of immigration.'

'Excuse me.' Reiser leant across him, pulled a USB stick out of his desktop drive and slipped it into his satchel. 'Sounds a bit predictable.'

'It's all about the balance.'

Balance. Who gave a toss about balance? What did balance have to do with anything, apart from selling blocks of advertising space?

Late-twentysomething, Cal was representative of the cocksure, self-absorbed kind of graduate journalist who was being actively recruited to infiltrate every aspect of the paper, products of an era in which self-published, self-edited and self-promoting internet copy was churned out at five cents a mile. Technology-savvy young Turks with callow interests, they saw guys like him, who sat with a serious subject for months on end until they could reveal something more than the obvious, as top-heavy dinosaurs. Everything had to be fast, current and attention-grabbing, multiplatform cross-pollinated advertising content posing as journalism. Cal's own stock-in-trade was punchy puff pieces about designer gadgets and rad toys for adult lads. *Ho-hum*. The kind of energetic fluff that snuck its way out of the advertorial section and crawled on its belly over to Arts and Lifestyle.

The days of the extended feature that crossed to the back pages were a thing of the past. Reiser had the sneaking suspicion that he was retained only as the paper's token Jiminy Cricket with a loud-hailer, providing hobbled opinion pieces, cramped essays that provoked a few moments of uncomfortable thinking before they were reduced to an orphaned slug line, without context or consequence.

Increasingly, he craved the freedom of fiction, where he could construct his house from the ground up and move the furniture around, take the reader by surprise, turn out the lights, let them bump into the chairs, feel along the walls and find their own way out. Fiction was the answer.

Research and sound, logical argument were generally a waste of energy unless they could be brought to life by a story that forced the reader's hand.

'I'm working on something at the moment.' Reiser tugged on the waistband of his flagging chinos and lifted them high on his arse. 'A piece about societies changing attitudes to children.'

Cal looked entirely nonplussed.

'Quite a long piece actually. Think Robert Bly and *The Sibling Society*.'

'Right.' Cal gripped both his elbows across his chest and did some ambiguous nodding. 'I look forward to reading it.'

Reiser punched his arms into the sleeves of his quilted anorak and picked up his bags. 'Off to the library,' he said, giving the younger man a wink.

Danny and Graham, 1993

Sunnybank Primary School was surrounded by asphalt yards and playing areas; a group of children gathered on the marked basketball court. An obese boy on the baseline held up a volley ball and the children in the middle spread out. He held the ball to his chest and suddenly threw it towards the legs of a shrieking girl. It missed its target, skidded across the court and out the other side.

Danny Simpson stood apart from the game, watching as the ball rolled past his feet. He bent down to pick it up. He looked at the children on the court and made to throw the ball in one direction. Then, without warning, he tossed it at head height straight at the closest player. It connected with a smack. The boy held his stinging face as the game continued around him. Danny turned to walk away and found himself face to face with a female teacher.

'What was that, Simpson?'

'Bad throw, miss.'

The woman watched him with distaste as he dawdled along the pathway to the nearest building.

Sneaky, sly and cruel he might have been, but Danny Simpson's behaviour was nothing compared to that of the new boy.

'Good morning, class.'

'Good morning, Mrs Barnes.'

'I'd like you all to meet your new classmate Graham Harris.' The teacher placed a hand on the shoulder of the mortified boy, who stood fidgeting beside her.

Graham was tall and slender. He had a slightly fragile, out-of-proportion look about him, a large forehead and an undershot jaw, unreadable dark irises, and the kind of hunted expression that invited the attention of bullies. Danny was immediately fascinated.

'Please say good morning to Graham, class.'

'Good morning, Graham,' the students responded, in a low chant. Some of the boys at the back laughed. Graham turned bright red.

'Please sit down with the blue group.' The teacher indicated a set of tables pushed together at the side of the room. Graham looked back at her, paralysed.

'All our groups are represented by different colours,' she explained.

Graham walked robotically towards the blue group.

'All our readers are marked with coloured stickers to match the group's abilities. This week is blue week, when we call on people in the blue group to present their work to the class.'

Graham stood behind an empty chair at one of the 'blue' tables.

'You can sit down now, Graham.'

He pulled his chair out, bumping it into a desk in the 'orange' group behind. Danny sat staring directly at him.

The teacher distributed small coloured baskets among the groups – orange, yellow, red, blue and green. Each basket contained lists of elementary equations for the students to work through. The more industrious raced through them, taking one list after another from the basket. The quieter, more reflective students plodded carefully through the equations until they finished each list. Danny took his time, completing a single strip throughout the entire exercise. He sniggered to himself as he noticed Graham scribble out and correct his answers on one list. Mrs Barnes wasn't going to like that. Suddenly Graham began to scribble across the whole list. Then he took another from the basket and began to draw crude stick-men in all the answer boxes. Some were urinating in high arcs all over the questions. One figure defecated large missiles that fell from the top of the page. Danny laughed. Graham looked at him and smiled. A serious girl with long dark plaits eyed his efforts.

'Danny Simpson, concentrate on your work and stop distracting Emily. Everybody, finish the list you're working on and put them all back into the baskets. Make sure your names are on the top. We'll mark them after lunch. Blue and orange groups go to the shelves and select a reader, if you haven't already got one.'

Danny shuffled sullenly to the shelves and picked out a book. Graham pulled out *Eerie Tales* at random and returned to his desk. One by one the groups selected their books and settled down to read them.

Mrs Barnes circulated around the room, picking up the coloured baskets as she went. She stopped behind Graham and watched as he very slowly ran a finger along the text. Danny yawned loudly. Mrs Barnes looked coldly in his direction. His book was marked with an orange sticker and still he was having trouble making sense of it. He shielded his eyes with his hand and hunkered down in a show of concentration.

After fifteen minutes of silent torture the teacher instructed the blue group to read a page aloud from their books. Graham became immediately restless.

A girl stood up: 'The old woman cried out for help, but no one heard her. It was cold and wet and . . .'

Graham fiddled with the tub of coloured pencils at his table. He pressed the palm of his hand down on the sharpened points.

'When she was about to give up she heard the sound of –'

The pencils toppled over and cascaded to the floor. Graham knelt in front of his chair to pick them up.

'Just leave them there for now, please,' Mrs Barnes instructed.

Graham stood up. 'I need to go to the toilet.'

'You'll have to wait until Jackie has finished reading.'

Graham sat down, then immediately stood up again. The teacher studied him curiously. 'Go on then, but hurry back. Do you know where it is?'

Graham nodded and left the room. Danny watched him appear outside the window and slowly wander toward the toilet block. He looked back at Mrs Barnes.

As the remaining children in the blue group read aloud, she took the blue basket onto her lap and began flicking silently through the equations. She stopped, a disturbed expression on her haggard face. She drew out the offending sheet of paper and crumpled it into a small ball.

When Graham returned she asked him to read.

'This is a story about a ghost who got killed and now he's dead. It's boring because ghosts are boring. They're not real and they can't talk.'

Several children began giggling.

'Could you please read what's actually on the page?'

Graham held up the book and started again. 'This is a boring book about *stupid* people who believe in *stupid* ghosts –'

'Sit down, please.'

After lunch Graham was moved to the yellow group, where he fell off his chair three times and threw an entire box of SRA reading cards onto the floor.

When Danny laughed loudly at Graham's antics he was sent outside.

The headmaster stood on a raised platform and tapped the microphone in front of him; a couple of hundred restless children filled the internal quadrangle, standing in uneven rows. 'Return to lessons with your class teachers, and be sure not to leave anything behind. Mr Prentiss is waiting on the oval for the athletics representatives. The bus leaves in ten minutes.'

The children began to shuffle forward behind their teachers. Graham marched impatiently on the spot in his line as the queue slowly concertinaed along. The boy behind him became impatient and shoved a stiff arm into his back, causing him to fall down hard, onto the unforgiving asphalt. The remaining students filed past. Graham scrambled to his feet, his face twisted with rage.

In the hallway outside the classroom he ran from the rear of the queue and rammed headlong into his attacker, kneeling over him as he pushed him to the ground. He put both his hands over the boy's face and pressed down with manic strength. Mrs Barnes rushed towards them. She tore Graham off the other boy and pulled him up roughly by one arm.

'He asked for it.' Graham's face was slicked with snot and tears.

The bully was sent to the school nurse with a bloody nose. Graham spent the afternoon in the corridor outside the classroom copying out an apology line by line. Before long Danny Simpson was sent to join him.

Danny sat on a bench while Graham climbed onto one of the steel lockers, stood on tiptoe and looked through the high windows into the classroom below. Mrs Barnes scraped a stick of chalk across the dusty green board, trailing out a row of disconnected letters.

'You're a psycho,' said Danny, looking up at him.

Graham stepped down from his lookout and tried the handle on one of the lockers. 'This school's crap,' he replied.

'What did you come here for?'

'What d'ya mean?'

'Where'd you move from?'

'Didn't move from anywhere. I used to go to Alcott Street, had to change schools.'

'Why?'

'Threw a rock at a kid who kicked me.'

'Got expelled?'

Graham shook his head. 'Suspended, then I came here.' He sat down on the bench and swung his legs repeatedly back and forth. Danny watched him sceptically, not sure whether to believe anything he said.

'Stand up! You're not out here to enjoy yourselves.' Mrs Barnes glowered at them from the doorway of the classroom.

Sent out together on a daily basis, drawn to each other by some sort of toxic chemistry, the two boys formed a strange alliance. Danny developed the habit of meeting Graham on the corner near his house each morning, from where they would double back, past the brown-green lawns of Spinnaker Avenue, to Graham's house and let themselves in. Inside the Harrises' recently built brick-and-tile house, Danny always felt a strange mixture of contempt, envy and excitement. Compared to him Graham seemed to have it cushy, living in a real house, filled with real furniture and real parents who, even if they weren't around much, had actual jobs.

Sometimes they stayed the whole day and watched the dirty videos Graham was always bragging about, the ones his father kept hidden in a beer carton at the back of the garage, behind the hot-water cylinder. They were nothing compared to the stuff that Danny's brothers had shown him at home.

Graham slid the unmarked cartridge into the VCR and pressed the play button. The naked bodies on the television screen ground mechanically against each other. Danny pointed the remote and rewound the film to the start. It wasn't very good porno, just one woman and one man screwing. Danny fast-forwarded any bits that showed the woman's face or where the soundtrack recorded her hollow moans; soon he was fast-forwarding most of it.

If they didn't go down to the river to smoke the cigarettes Danny had stolen from his mother, or go into town to prowl the shops, they were sometimes still at the Harris house when Graham's parents came home, still hanging around in their school uniforms. One night Danny even stayed over.

Christine Harris didn't warm to Danny. She hadn't liked him from the moment she opened her front door to find him sprawled on her living-room carpet, playing Nintendo with Graham.

'Hello.'

Danny sat up and looked at her. Graham kept playing.

'You must be Danny?'

Danny's mouth smiled.

'Well, Graham, maybe your friend would like to stay for tea.'

During a grim dinner of microwaved pasta and over-cooked vegetables, Danny noticed how Christine Harris watched her son's every move, as he pushed his food around the plate and slowly ate small mouthfuls. 'Eat some of the peas, please.'

Graham speared the peas singly, scraping the plate noisily with his fork. His mother grew visibly irritated.

'Come on, Graham, eat up.' said his father, in a placatory tone.

Mrs Harris glared at her husband.

Graham's sister Claire stared at Danny as he shovelled food into his mouth. She wore thick glasses, and over her left eye a flesh-coloured patch. Her good eye wandered and the lid twitched violently every few seconds. She occasionally dropped food down the front of her school uniform as she ate. Her older brother Joel motioned to his mother and she wiped the food away without comment.

No one had to tell Danny to clear his plate. He had already finished a second helping by the time Mrs Harris angrily took Graham's meal away before he could spear the remaining thirty-odd peas.

'What the hell is wrong with your sister?' asked Danny, once they were in Graham's bedroom.

'I told you, she's retarded.'

'What's wrong with her eyes?'

'She's got a spasmatism.' Graham began rebounding a plastic basketball off the bedroom wall.

'A what? Will she ever be normal?'

Graham shrugged.

'Your brother seems weird.'

Graham headed the ball several times and fell onto the bed laughing. 'He's all right.'

'I thought you didn't like him.'

'He goes to a special school for smart kids,' said Graham, in a funny voice.

Danny didn't know what to make of that. 'What are we gonna do now?' He felt suddenly stifled by the orderly bedroom, the pastel-blue and white colour scheme and matching quilt. Graham kicked the ball hard up into the ceiling.

'Stop kicking that ball!' shouted his mother.

'It's Tuesday. She'll go out soon,' said Graham.

An hour later, after his wife had left the house to attend the computer course she was taking at the local adult education centre, Denis Harris settled on the couch to watch a video. Claire was already in bed and Joel was busy doing his homework.

When Graham heard the familiar soundtrack he and Danny shot into the living room and sat on the floor. On the screen a small child of five or six, the Changeling, stared intently at a group of older children playing in a cornfield. A close-up of her ice-blue eyes showed flames beginning to ignite around black pupils. The camera plunged the viewer into a black tunnel of fire. One of the children in the cornfield suddenly took hold of the youngest boy's throat and began to strangle him.

'You know you're not supposed to watch this,' said Graham's father, without taking his eyes off the screen.

'I've seen it before,' said Graham. The children onscreen stood stock still, mesmerized, as the strangled boy gasped for air.

'Shouldn't you be in bed?'

'It's only seven thirty.'

'Well, don't go blabbing to your mum.'

The boy in the film stopped struggling as the last of his breath was squeezed from him. The faces of the children who circled around him were lit by strange half-smiles. Light from the screen was reflected in Graham's eyes. The pupils flickered.

The sky above the cornfield erupted in lightning, and black clouds boiled furiously. Heavy torrents of rain poured down. The spell now broken, the children came to their senses and began to scream in terror at the broken body that lay before them. The Changeling, now a frightened child, ran through the rain to the nearest house to raise the alarm.

Over the next ninety-five minutes the Changeling killed, or orchestrated the deaths of, fifteen victims, slashing, burning, mutilating and dismembering as she travelled through the landscape of a fictitious American rural town.

Danny and Graham were riveted, their attention only wavering during the brief stretches of dialogue or plot development.

'Awesome,' declared Danny, as the Changeling charred the features of victim number thirteen's face with a blowtorch. Victim number fifteen was impaled on a spiked fence. When Graham's father went to the kitchen to get himself another beer and use the bathroom, Danny took the opportunity to replay the impaling several times.

Finally the Changeling, exposed by the town's doctor, is surrounded by an angry mob of townspeople. Trapped at the top of a silage tower and spectacularly beheaded with a ceremonial sword, her haemorrhaging body is tossed to the ground while all the children cheer. The eyelids of the severed head quiver and blink open, a foretaste of the inevitable *Return of the Changeling III*.

Mathew, 2008

Vibrating jackhammers drowned the noise of the traffic. Another swarm of passengers radiated out from the steps of the subway. Mathew Allen tore a piece off his falafel roll and put it into his mouth. Then he swallowed some coffee and put the paper cup down on the stone wall beside him. Across the street, at 401 Chalmers Road, hemmed in among a row of sandstone townhouses, were the legal chambers of Cross and Beardsley. He kept his eyes fixed on the building as he ate. Several times the red-painted door opened. A woman in a black-and-white-striped suit emerged, slipped on a plush cream coat and briskly walked off. Clerks whose faces he recognized went in and out of the building clutching folios.

The flap-flap-flap of a traffic helicopter sounded above him, momentarily silencing even the din of the persistent jackhammers. He could just make out the struts of the machine's landing-skids as it lifted, crab-like, tilting across the outline of the tallest buildings. When he returned his attention to the offices, a round-shouldered, twenty-something man was walking towards the red door. Allen grabbed at the compact camera, hanging from his neck inside his open coat, and leapt up. Hot coffee splashed down the side of his khakis and the falafel roll landed in front of him. He trod on it as he crossed to the side of the open bus shelter and began to shoot continuous frames of the ingoing figure.

He moved quickly along the street and walked up the steps of a public building. As he sat and waited he could see the upstairs windows of the lawyers' rooms. His mind mapped the various vantage-points around the block. He knew there was a rear exit that turned back onto the same street a few doors up – he had a clear view across to it.

Forty minutes ticked by. Time meant nothing to him. He could wait all day if he had to. Finally the door opened and the man emerged. Mathew took a closer look at him through the viewfinder. He was in the right age range, but nothing stood out about him. He took a couple more shots anyway, descending the steps two at a time as he pressed the shutter.

As he did so Tony Cross emerged from the building and saw him. Mathew began to move away.

'Hey!' shouted the barrister across the busy road. 'Give it up, Mathew.' He threaded his way through the traffic and caught up with him. 'Stay away from here and leave my clients alone. What are you hoping to achieve?'

'I know you still work on their behalf. It's because of you that they're out on parole.'

Tony Cross stared at him, and the anger in his face drained away. 'I'm not the enemy, Mathew. They have the right to representation, you have the right to representation. That's how it works. Do you really think I'd meet with them here? You're wasting your time. I'm warning you, just stay away.'

Graham and Danny, 1993

'Get up, Graham! You're already late.'

Danny awoke from a sleepover at Graham's to Christine Harris's shrill demands. He rolled over in his sleeping-bag and looked up at the radio clock: it was barely seven. He pulled the hood over his face. Graham hadn't moved.

'I said up!' Christine flew into the room and tore the quilt from the bed. The boy in the bed curled into a ball and hugged his knees. 'Shower *now*! You're not the only cab on the rank – get up.'

Accustomed as he was to the violent outbursts within his family, Danny had been surprised to find that Graham was subject to a different, almost constant, form of tyranny. It set his nerves on edge. While his mother was rarely out of bed before lunch time, leaving him and his brothers to get themselves off to school, or not, Graham's mother badgered him at every turn.

'Put your sandwiches in your lunchbox.' Graham fumbled through his bag for it.

'Where's your lunchbox?'

'At school.'

'You've lost it?' Christine Harris looked like she might explode. 'For God's sake, Graham. Get a Tupperware!'

Graham fumbled through the open dishwasher tray and pulled out a melamine bowl.

'Not that!' She slapped it from his hand. The bowl skittered across the tiles. Graham laughed in defiance. 'A Tupperware!' she shouted, wrenching a drawer open and slamming a plastic box onto the counter. Graham put the sandwiches into the container, looked at Danny and sniggered. His mother observed them coldly. 'Hurry up.'

'You come straight home after school today. I don't want you hanging around in town,' she called, reversing the red Falcon out of the driveway and heading off to deliver Joel and Claire to their respective schools.

When Danny and Graham reached the school turn-off they stashed their backpacks between the brittle branches of a thick hedge and walked in the opposite direction. They were heading for the Regency Arcade Shopping Centre, where they could steal candy from the bulk food dispensers at the supermarket and eat it brazenly as they moved about the store.

To cover his increasing truanting, Danny's brother Adam had forged him several notes citing migraine, a throat infection and 'sprained feet'. Inevitably, after several weeks, a letter had arrived from the school.

'What the hell is this?' shouted Debbie Simpson, slapping him around the ears with an envelope that bore the school's preposterous motto, 'Success with Honour'. 'What have you been doing every day when you're not at school? Five unexplained absences! They say you've been forging notes. Well? Where do you go? You certainly don't hang around here. *Truanting*, Danny,' she concluded, as if no child of hers had ever stooped so low.

He felt like laughing.

'What do you do with yourself?'

'Nothin'. I just go to the river and read.'

'Read? Go to bloody school and read, would you? That's what school's for.'

Danny thought he might as well quit while he was ahead. He looked blankly at the floor and said nothing.

'Is somebody giving you a hard time? Picking on you?' asked his mother, shifting gear. Danny shrugged to create the impression that he didn't want to talk about it. 'Gotta stand up for yourself. You get to school tomorrow, no excuses.' She fixed him with a look and took hold of his chin. 'If anyone gives you shit, Danny, you tell Damien. He'll sort them out.'

Danny could stand the pantomime no longer. 'Shut up, Mum. Don't be so bloody stupid. If anyone needs sorting out it's him.'

Fortunately for Graham, it was his father who opened a letter about his unexplained absences – he arrived home an hour before his wife did every night. 'Jesus, Graham, what's your mother going to say?'

'I told you, Dad, if you're late they mark you absent.'

'It says here that you were absent three days last week.'

'I wasn't! I came home early one day 'cause I was being picked on. I was there all the rest. I was,' he pleaded.

His father signed the acknowledgement slip at the bottom of the letter, then scrawled, 'virus' and 'temperature'. He handed the form to Graham. 'Your

149

mother has enough to worry about. Just get your name marked off!'

On the last day of term the boys walked to school together in silence. Graham was actually looking forward to collecting the fired clay pot he had decorated the previous Friday, but Danny was in a black mood. Things at home were getting worse: his mother had struck him across the face after he had sworn at Steve. He didn't feel like being pushed around all day by teachers at the school.

'I'm not going,' he announced, as they crossed the road towards the cyclone-meshed playing fields of Sunnybank Public School. He turned left and began walking away, along the nearby bike-track.

Graham reluctantly followed. 'Let's go till after lunch.'

'Do what you like.'

Graham lagged behind, dragging his bag.

Danny glanced back at him. 'Well, fuck off, then.' He walked faster, passing a group of older boys, two on bikes. One of the boys looked disdainfully at Graham as he did a quick shuffle to catch up with Danny.

'Where are we going?'

'Somewhere,' said Danny.

Truth was, Danny didn't know. He just knew he wanted to go somewhere away from people and maybe smash something up.

They walked in the direction of town but clung to the river. On the pier alongside the pulp and paper mill depot they hurled large rocks into the air and watched as the stones plopped heavily into the water, narrowly missing the targeted, filmy-white jellyfish. They peered through a crack between the corrugated steel doors of the depot at the stacks of milled paper inside. Graham suggested they set them alight, but when Danny's disposable lighter refused to ignite long enough to light even their cigarettes, they gave up on the idea.

On their way to the wasteland, near the Battery Road overpass, they passed the rear of a wrecking yard. A skinny tortoiseshell cat walked across the ground of the neighbouring industrial complex and slunk between two sheds. Danny saw it re-emerge and claw its way through a gap under the wire fence. He stopped and stood very still. 'Hear that?'

'What?'

They walked over to the fence and listened. From an outbuilding inside the enclosure came a faint miaow. Looking through the mesh, they saw that the cat was padding furtively across the cement holding a kitten in her mouth.

'She's moving her kittens.' Danny started to climb the fence.

'What are you doing?' Graham looked nervously up and down the full length of the yard. Danny jumped down and walked to the area the cat had come from. There, in a storage bay, behind lengths of galvanized guttering, a small dappled shape moved. Danny went towards it. He reached his hand down, little by little. The kitten hissed in fear. He picked it up by the scruff of its neck and cupped it in his other hand. Danny could feel its rapid heartbeat. He guessed it to be about four weeks old. The kitten fitted neatly into his jacket pocket.

Graham watched eagerly as Danny returned to the fence. When he had one leg halfway over the kitten began to wriggle itself free from his pocket. He reached for it and handed it over the fence to Graham, before dropping down beside him. Graham held the kitten tightly in his hand, patting it heavily. Danny motioned to take the kitten back. Not willing to surrender it, Graham turned away.

'Give it here!'

'In a minute.'

Danny grabbed at Graham, turning him around and prising his arms away from his chest in an effort to reclaim the animal. Graham closed his hands even more tightly around it. 'Fuck off.'

They struggled until Graham pulled himself away from Danny. The kitten let out a squall of pain. Danny ran at Graham, who held it out with two hands, as if to throw it away from him. Avoiding Danny, he turned and fell, landing heavily.

The freed kitten attempted to walk away, but its head listed oddly to the right. The impact had somehow disabled it. After a few steps it began to stagger.

'He's got brain damage,' said Danny, appalled.

'You shouldna took him.'

'You fucken did it!'

'No, I never. You pushed me.'

The kitten began to incline its head repeatedly, in some sort of spasm, towards its shoulder. Something was badly broken.

'Better finish it off, it's fucked now.' Danny stood over Graham, who looked up doubtfully.

'Go on.'

They could hear the bereft caterwauling of the mother cat, now searching for her missing offspring, inside the yard. Graham took hold of a nearby rock and smashed it down on the kitten's head.

Danny picked it up and carried it with him to the overpass. He waited until the road below was clear of traffic before hurling the small body over the barrier.

The two boys ran to the side of the culvert to get a broader view of the road. They could make out the outline of a tiny bundle near the left-hand shoulder of the motorway and were disappointed to see the wheels of the subsequent cars pass by without disturbing it.

Rachel, 1993

Benjamin Allen's clear blue eyes grew wide as saucers, tracking the progress of the blazing sparkler that hissed and burnt on top of the cake his grandmother carried into the room. From his vantage-point on his father's hip, he watched his cousins, as they hovered around the wonder at the centre of the table. He put one hand over his ear and pointed with the other at the dying firework, jiggling his bottom up and down. 'Boom.'

'It's not going to explode, mate, it's just a pretty one,' said his father.

The toddler dropped his hands away from his face but held them out in mid-air.

He watched his aunt Jennifer as she removed the scorched metal stick and lit the five pink candles on top of the cake one by one. The room was full of singing. '. . . happy birthday to you, happy birthday, dear Hazel . . .'

'Everybody ready!' Ewan Allen stood on a chair, trying to fit all the faces into the Polaroid viewfinder.

Rachel leant in beside her husband and put her cheek to Benjamin's, smiling broadly. Hazel held herself tall and took a deep breath, exhaling in a long stream as she turned her head from side to side. The orange flames guttered violently before snuffing out, covering the table with a haze of paraffin smoke. The camera clicked and whirred.

'Happy birthday,' called Benjamin, bobbing forward, straining against his father's grip.

'Yay! Hazel's five today,' said his mother, lifting him onto her lap and handing him a piece of cake.

He licked the buttery frosting and pushed the crumbled chocolate into his mouth. 'I'm three tomorrow,' he mumbled, through his mouthful, holding two sticky fingers in front of his face.

'Not tomorrow,' she said, opening another of his fingers to make the right number. 'But soon.'

When all the cake was gone, the older children surged noisily through the house, climbing on the furniture, jumping up to reach the strings of the coloured balloons that clung to the ceiling.

Mathew Allen plucked one down and put the silver ribbon in his son's hand.

Benjamin felt the gentle upward pull against his fingers as he took off squealing, almost jumping out of his skin, chasing his cousins around the table legs. They pretended to be afraid but easily eluded him.

Outside on the patio a gutted piñata hung from the clothes-line. Benjamin collected foil stars from the paving beneath it, playing close to his father's feet. Pink and white balloons trailed above them as some of the boys leapt down onto the lawn. One of the helium-filled spheres separated itself from the pack and rose into the air, drifting higher and higher. Mathew scooped Benjamin up and lifted him onto his shoulders. Hanging on tight, he craned his neck, captivated by the tiny speck as it disappeared into the ether. Soon all the balloons were in the sky, sailing away in different directions.

'Hey, Benji!' Rachel called from the stairs, pointing the camera in their direction. As Benjamin and Mathew turned, she pressed the shutter and waited while the photo paper was delivered. She fluttered the square in her hand and caught a whiff of the rubbery alkaline developer. The detail of the image steadily emerged, revealing a smiling Mathew holding onto his son's ankles as Benjamin gazed over his father's head, directly at the camera, framed by an unbroken powder-blue afternoon sky.

Ghosts

'Without flesh or bones'

Liam, 2008

Catherine placed her hand on Liam's and directed it over the curve of her belly. 'There.'

Liam craned his head towards her, concentrating intently. 'I can't feel anything,' he whispered.

'There!' she cried again, as the child fluttered inside her.

Liam smiled. 'I still can't feel anything.'

Catherine leant back on her pillows and gave up. 'Well, I can feel him swimming around in there.'

'I'll make you some breakfast,' said Liam, getting out of bed and carefully rearranging the quilt around her. Light from the shuttered window fell in narrow bands across the bed.

'Here.' He took a pile of furniture catalogues from the dresser and dropped them on the quilt beside her. 'Have a look at them. They should send you back to sleep.' Catherine reached down and picked one up. Liam pulled a sweatshirt on and went downstairs.

After several sessions with Dr Patma his terror of the baby had diminished and he had experienced brief moments of hope and anticipation. Reconciling himself to Catherine's pregnancy had brought them closer together; he had even confided something of his therapy to her, telling her only that issues surrounding his childhood had left him ambivalent about becoming a parent. Relieved that it was not her he was rejecting, and understanding the shock she had given him, Catherine had rallied to support him, now including him wherever possible in the process of the pregnancy.

Liam's trust in himself and the relationship was slowly returning. In an attempt to follow the doctor's advice to see the baby as his salvation, he frequently reminded himself of her words that too many had suffered already. But when he sat beside Catherine as the radiologist passed the head of the ultrasound probe across her lubricated stomach, sliding it backwards and forwards, the sight of the unborn child, squirming on the screen, filled him with dread. According to the obstetrician, everything was normal – mother and baby were doing fine. Given that the child had half his genetic material, Liam wondered what unseen deformity it might carry in its DNA. Propelled by the terror of exposure and resigned to the right of the child to its own future, he vowed never to burden it or Catherine with the truth. He created instead new compartments within himself to accommodate the impending reality of fatherhood, splitting himself off from past events until they were buried even deeper.

Liam set a tray with tea and toast on the bedside table. 'Hot black tea, just the way Madam likes it.' Catherine pretended to ignore him as he slid back under the ivory quilt and snuggled close to her. He took her hand and ran his fingers thoughtfully between hers.

'Look at these.' She indicated the elaborate nursery suites in the catalogue, then pointed to a majestic woven-cane cot, wardrobe and changing table.

'I don't want him to sleep in a separate room. Why can't we just put a cot alongside our bed, in here?'

Catherine looked up at him; it seemed he had an opinion on everything these days. 'Because we might want to get a good night's sleep ourselves.'

Liam sat up against the bedhead. 'I don't think you should have to work when the baby's born.'

'I beg your pardon?'

'Not if you don't want to. What's the point of having kids if both parents are too busy for them?'

'I don't want to work for at least six months, but after that . . .'

'Even then, why pay strangers to look after our child?'

She eyed him warily and put the catalogue down.

'I'm serious, Cath. I'll stay at home and look after him if you don't want to.'

'You?' She laughed. 'You make more money than I do for a start.'

The offices of Creighton and Davis were cramped, full of tiny wood-panelled booths. For a thriving agency in a real-estate boom, they spent little on appearances. Although they were equipped with the latest computer technology they relied mainly on the hunger of their sales team to directly market their properties and bring people through the door.

Liam had come to the office five years earlier via a work placement, arranged through the private computer college he had attended after school. He had created the agency's first website and was asked to join the team as a property manager. After two years he had completed a real-estate course and become an agent.

Lately he had been fired with new enthusiasm, keen to sell as many properties as possible and improve his monthly commission. He had almost beaten Colin, Creighton and Davis's star performer, in last month's sales figures. Sitting at his desk in his orderly booth, he calculated and recalculated his current figures. If all his contracts went through this month he might be in a position to put down a deposit on a house. He and Catherine already had a sum put away and her parents had agreed to match them dollar for dollar on any deposit they could raise.

He still carried a torch for the property he had stumbled on that day in the country. At $350,000 it was a fantasy, but the farmlet, one of Colin's listings, had already sold. He still had a copy of the sales flyer pinned to his noticeboard just to remind him of what was possible.

A red light flickered on his desk phone, indicating a call.

'Hello?'

The woman at the other end wanted to look at a townhouse in a new development. Liam had sold her home for her three weeks before, and she was still wavering between a house on half an acre and a townhouse in the city, between investment and lifestyle properties, between staying with her browbeaten husband or setting up alone with her kids. Liam had already heard most of her life story and had the patience required to show her as many properties as her whims dictated until she made up her tangled mind, usually based on some arbitrary absurdity, like the proximity of a down-market takeaway on a nearby cross-street. He had already helped her buy and sell seven properties in the past three years.

As a salesman he understood that, for some people, certain houses represented an idyllic future where everything would fall magically into place. A solution to all of life's difficulties, a place where stale marriages would rekindle and hyperactive or jaded children would bake cupcakes and gossip with their friends around a slow-combustion fire. Liam knew better than to dissuade such fantasies, how to stay in the background and never to stand between the dreamer and the dream, but empty houses didn't always deliver, and Liam was there, quietly waiting, to sell them the next one.

'I'm not sure they'll drop five grand. They knocked back three twenty, and the market wasn't as strong then. Let me talk to them after you've had another look through. One o'clock is fine.'

Catherine appeared in the cubicle doorway. 'I got this for you.' She slid a brown-paper bag across the desk. Liam put the phone down. 'I'll keep moving,' she said, holding up a swag of labelled keys.

Liam opened the bag to find a glossy book on pregnancy and childbirth. He laid it on the desk and flicked through a few pages. There was an irritable rapping on the partition and Colin stuck his head round the corner. 'Have you got the keys to Sheffield Drive?'

'What?'

'The fake-brick shit-box behind the joinery? Virtually no kitchen, you know the one . . . I've got the perfect prospects, met them in the pub last night. He's a meat worker at Austco and she's a throw-back. What's this?' He picked up the book.

'Sheffield Drive is zoned commercial. I think it's one of Paul's. Look on the board.'

'I already did.' Colin turned a page of the book at random. 'Jesus! How perverted is that?' He held it open at 'Sexual Positions for Advanced Pregnancy'. Liam was mortified by the explicit drawings. Trust Colin. He held out his hand for the book.

Colin continued flicking through the chapter. 'Whatever gets you off. Rather you than me, though.'

Liam lunged for the book.

'Here . . . Don't have a cow.' Colin tossed it onto the desk. 'Still coveting that hobby-farm, I see,' he said, looking at the advertising flyer. 'Looks like the buyer is dropping out. Contract was subject to finance and turns out they've been feeding me a line for weeks. Supposed to get back to me today, but I'm not holding my breath. It could well be back on the market at a very good price.' Suddenly he was all business again. 'Surely you and Cath could raise the money.' His nerve was breathtaking. 'Great place to bring up kids.' Liam stared at him. Colin hated kids as much as he despised Liam. 'You must've pulled in close to twenty grand over the past two months. I notice John is kissing your arse. Well, he can kiss mine tomorrow. That farmer you put me onto, the one with the Emporium at Berridale?'

'I never put you onto him.'

'I've signed him up. Starting price of a million . . . Been wearing him down for weeks. His wife's just had a stroke and he needs to be nearer the hospital.' Liam's mouth fell open. How he hated and feared the likes of Colin, soulless bastards, ever ready to prey upon any human weakness.

Colin looked at his watch. 'Tell Paul to leave the keys for Sheffield Drive on my desk.'

'Tell him yourself,' said Liam, selecting property sheets from a file drawer and placing them in a folder for his one o'clock client.

'I can't. I'm meeting a rugby mate for lunch – up from Wentworthville for the day.'

Liam looked up.

'That's right,' said Colin. 'Wentworthville's not far from your old stomping ground, is it? What school did you go to again?'

'Meredith Smith-Baxter College.'

Colin sneered. 'Don't suppose they played rugby there.'

'I don't know. I only came in year twelve. I did correspondence before that.' Dark patches of perspiration appeared at the underarms of Liam's brown shirt.

'Religious weirdoes, were they?'

'Who?' snapped Liam.

'Your parents.'

Liam transcribed several numbers from his desk blotter into his appointments diary. 'My dad was a surveyor with a mining company. We moved around a lot.'

'A drunken surveyor?'

Liam's eyes flashed with anger. Catherine must have told him that. Why did she always feel obliged to make excuses for the fact that he didn't drink? He stood up and tapped the folder of documents against the desk. Colin was still leaning on the partition barring the doorway.

'Colin, would you mind just fucking off?' Liam looked him directly in the eye. 'I've got work to do.'

'Wooh-hoo-hoo! Well, fuck me!' Colin drummed his fingers heavily on the partition and pointed theatrically at Liam. 'Don't get too competitive – we're all on the same team here. Remember that.'

Liam made a show of calmly collecting his mobile phone and his keys from his desk. Internally, his pulse raced as he recovered from the physical effects of standing up to Colin. 'I need those keys by two o'clock,' said Colin, as he retreated from the cubicle.

Liam, 2001

Meredith Smith-Baxter College had been unknown and frightening territory, a progressive school, based on the Montessori method, a senior college for years eleven and twelve only – Liam had been thankful for that. Low-rise modern buildings arranged in a square that opened onto a central courtyard, surrounded by nine and a half acres of landscaped gardens and recreation areas. There was even an organic 'mini-farm' and a saltwater swimming-pool.

At first Liam had felt a measure of contempt for the other students, with their privileged backgrounds and charmed lives. As he observed their self-confidence, freely expressing an opinion and counter-opinion on everything, he began to see for the first time the deficits in his upbringing. In the presence of offspring who were wanted and cherished, he felt more alienated and miserable than ever.

He missed the predictability of the secure unit, where his situation was known to a core group of sympathetic professionals. His exclusion from this new world of happy young people was more than self-imposed and he felt as though he were on the wrong side of an invisible screen.

Despite the armoury of medication he was taking, depression soon took hold. His parole officer, whom he saw weekly at the boarding house where he was accommodated, hinted that it might eventually be possible to arrange a meeting with his mother. The suggestion, meant to lift his spirits and give him something to hope for, stimulated an even deeper anxiety.

One morning the headmistress pulled Liam aside and asked him into her office for a 'chat'. As they sat opposite each other, Liam wondered what he might have done.

The headmistress smiled warmly. 'Things get very busy in a school like this and I have to apologize for not touching base sooner. It's quite an adjustment to change schools, isn't it?'

'Yeah.'

'And in your situation, your history makes it so much harder to relax and be yourself.' Liam rubbed his eye nervously. What did she mean by his history? And his situation? Was she talking about the history the school had been provided with or something else?

'It's okay, I know all about your circumstances.'

Liam's pupils dilated and his head felt light.

The headmistress smiled again. 'It's all right. I'll let you in on a little secret. Many years ago, when he was around your age, my younger brother was also involved in a car theft.'

Liam breathed a sigh of relief. 'A car theft?' he heard himself say out loud.

'It wasn't his idea, but he was involved. He was headstrong but not a *bad* kid. Anyway, he got the right support and turned himself around. I know how easily things can go pear-shaped in a young person's life and how important it is to have people you can trust, people who believe in you, to get back on track.'

Liam nodded blankly.

'It might help to remember that worse things have happened . . . I'm not saying that property crime is okay, of course, but at least no one got hurt.'

By the time Liam rejoined his communications class in the library, Ethan and Shona, his project partners, were busy drawing up a story board.

'Check this out,' said Ethan, unpacking a compact camcorder from its padded bag.

Shona used a protractor to draw dialogue boxes in the frames of the ruled grid. 'So, what do we want to do? Any ideas, Liam?'

'It's a pretty broad concept,' said Ethan. 'Anything that fits into the theme of "a day in the life".'

'Whose life?' Liam was having trouble catching up with the conversation.

Shona rolled her eyes. 'That's what we're trying to work out.'

'Does it have to be a real day? Like what really happened?'

Shona shrugged, 'Nuh, could be entirely fictitious.'

'Yeah, let's do that – make something up,' concluded Ethan, pushing a greasy dreadlock away from his face.

Liam picked up the camera and took off the lens cap. Shona looked up impatiently from her notes. 'So, who's our character, then?'

'I don't know but let's give him something really dramatic. Maybe he's done something really bad, committed a crime.'

'We'll have to film around here,' said Shona, looking out of the full-length windows onto the central lawn.

'What about a ticking clock, a countdown to something?' added Ethan.

Shona looked at Liam 'You're not saying much.'

'What's he done?'

'Who?'

'The character, what's he supposed to have done?'

'Something really bad. Maybe he's in jail already and got the death penalty.'

'What for?' asked Liam, hoarsely.

'I dunno. Murdered somebody during a robbery?'

'Did he mean to?'

'Maybe.'

Ethan's brain was processing the idea. 'What if he's already on Death Row and the clock is ticking down to his execution? My dad has this book about all these prisoners on Death Row, profiles on every person executed in Texas for the past ten years. Height, weight, age, level of education, a description of the last meal they ordered. We could use one of them.'

'What did they eat?' asked Liam.

'Anything they wanted, usually crap, but as much as they liked.'

'All You Can Eat, that's what we'll call it.'

'Yeah. I'll bring the book in tomorrow.'

True to his word, Ethan brought *Farewell to Texas* to school the following day. Liam was transfixed. Headshot after headshot of male malefactors. Arrested, charged, depressed and frightened, a clipboard on their chests, they looked born to kill and born to have their lives extinguished by a heartless state. Nobody smiled for the camera.

Profile number twenty-six. One Chester Lake, who appeared to be about fourteen years old, was just eighteen when he abducted his niece and strangled her because she had threatened to tell her parents he had molested her. 'A double cheeseburger, French fries, apple pie and a Dr Pepper': his last request. 'I'm sorry': his final words after more than twelve years on Death Row. Liam closed the book.

'You all right, Liam?' asked Shona. He tried to smile. 'Maybe you can choose the subject and write up the basic facts of his story.' He looked doubtful.

'You can take the book home with you and bring it back on Wednesday,' offered Ethan.

Liam found his accommodation at the boarding house an impersonal relief from the forced interaction at school. He felt reassured by the fixed mealtimes and looked forward to the privacy of his room. Tonight he was eating at his desk while he studied. He picked at his macaroni cheese and began to read some more profiles in Ethan's book. After a while he imagined that he could see in their faces who was innocent and who was guilty. Over a small sample his intuition proved right, but the more profiles he perused the more his strike rate dropped. He read their stories, whom they had killed, their sordid motives, denials or admissions of guilt, their clumsy remorse and belated Christianity. The more he knew about each individual the less certain he became.

Birth dates, race and height, how long they had stayed in school. Some of the faces were painfully young. He identified with them all. Their final statements, spoken to those who gathered to witness their executions, were printed below their crimes. Quite a few apologized to the families of those they had killed and said that they hoped seeing them die would help them to find some sort of peace.

Liam felt a terrible keening sadness as he read the detailed descriptions of the last meal each had ordered. Many of the meals seemed very ordinary, as though the condemned man was trying to relive one normal or fondly remembered experience before his life was taken away. He noticed that those who appeared guilty and unrepentant ordered a long list of dishes, trying to extract some small bonus from a withholding world before they were eternally expelled from it. Most of those who proclaimed their innocence to the last wanted nothing except the symbolic meal of 'peace, hope and justice' ordered by one inmate.

Liam thought about his last meal. What would he order? Certainly not cold macaroni. If he were about to be put to death for his crimes, would he be able to raise the enthusiasm to conjure up a favourite meal? He wondered how many prisoners actually ate what was delivered to them. What happened to the contents of your stomach when you were electrocuted or given a lethal injection? When he had had his tonsils taken out in the secure unit he hadn't been allowed to eat for a day beforehand because he might choke on his own vomit.

What interest could food hold in the hours before death? Maybe it was purely a distraction. He decided that his last meal would be a glass of water.

Liam chose profile number twenty-three, Eugene Williams, as the subject for the video production assignment story line. Eugene was twenty when he had entered a Stop and Go garage in Houston, Texas, armed with a .38-calibre pistol and demanded the contents of the till. He was convicted of capital murder after shooting James

Leopold in the chest when the terrorized store attendant, also twenty, reached for something beneath the
counter. Williams was arrested a few streets away, running from the scene. His last meal on earth was nachos
and a red-pepper salad.

In his final statement he asked to be forgiven and for
the death penalty to be fought. He also read a short poem
by Mary Elizabeth Frye for his mother who attended the
execution.

> Do not stand at my grave and weep.
> I am not there, I do not sleep.
> I am a thousand winds that blow,
> I am the diamond glints on snow.
> I am the sunlight on ripened grain.
> I am the gentle autumn rain.
> When you awaken in the morning's hush
> I am the swift uplifting rush
> Of quiet birds in circled flight.
> I am the soft stars that shine at night.
> Do not stand at my grave and cry;
> I am not there: I did not die.

Liam was deeply moved by the poem. He ran his
finger over the image on the page. Eugene Williams was
a young white man, with a boyish face, who had taken a
wrong turn. He was not a monster: he had killed a man,

but he had not set out to do it and he had paid the ultimate penalty for his crime.

Ethan had been unable to convince Liam to play Eugene in the film. Although he participated fully in drafting the story of prisoner 4132, and helped film the kitchen scenes, neither Ethan nor Shona could persuade him to appear in front of the camera. Liam was immovable on the subject.

'All you have to do is sit there, Liam.'

'I can't be in it.'

'Can't? You mean won't.'

Liam felt desperate. If Ethan insisted on him being filmed he would have no choice but to cry 'sick' and not turn up. Ethan caught the pleading look in his eye and relented. 'You really don't want to do it?'

'No.'

Ethan shook his head. 'OK, but you're going to have to get familiar with the camera.'

At the class screening, the students were even more animated than usual. Between each of the five seven-minute films, Mr Bradshaw allowed time for discussion. The first film was a montage of sequences of action, shot over the course of a day at the school, set to music. Time-lapse footage showed students arriving and rapidly filling the quadrangle. It was so good that it could easily have served as a promotional clip for the school.

Liam felt slightly depressed by the film, the sense of time passing so quickly and the rapid, seemingly meaningless movements of students around the school grounds. Catching a glimpse of himself among the crowd, in the CCTV-like footage, sent a stab of adrenalin through him.

The third film, *All You Can Eat*, was shot in black and white and opened with a frame on Ethan's eyes staring blankly ahead. In the following scene he ran away from a service station while a police siren sounded. Once apprehended, Ethan looked hopelessly out through a car window as it pulled away. There followed an apparently unrelated sequence, shot in colour, of stove jets hissing and exploding into flame, ingredients being sliced and chopped and thrown into a sizzling pan. Scenes of food preparation were intercut with shots of a wall clock counting down from two thirty to three o'clock.

Finally the meal was assembled on a plate and placed on a tray.

At four o'clock the tray was placed heavily on a metal surface in Ethan's 'cell'.

The film ended abruptly with a mug shot of 'Eugene', a.k.a. Ethan, an outline of his personal details and crimes printed below with a description of his last meal.

The rest of the year at Meredith Smith-Baxter flew by. With his exams completed Liam was preparing to be relocated, once school was over, to a new area where he was to begin his adult life. The hot topic of conversation among the students was the school graduation dinner. At Shona's suggestion Liam went to the Salvation Army store and found a near-new electric-blue suit that he matched with a black shirt and a lurid geometric-patterned tie. He had grown so tall in the previous six months that a series of raw-pink stretch marks had appeared, at odd intervals, on his back along the line of his spine.

His face, too, had changed, his features now somehow more in proportion to his lanky body. Admiring his suit in the wardrobe mirror, adjusting the lapels, buttoning and unbuttoning his jacket, he saw, as though from a great distance, that he could possibly be called hand-some. Even his unruly dark hair, uncut for several weeks, had decided to behave itself.

At the venue Liam found himself seated at the end of a long table opposite Shona and her mother. Shona wore an extravagant black flamenco dress with a tiny red bolero. He could smell the soft-pink rose she wore behind her left ear. He looked away as she caught him staring at her, occupying himself by devouring several unidentifiable canapés from a nearby tray.

Shona's mother ordered a whisky from the drinks waiter and looked repeatedly in his direction, talking loudly to the woman on her left in a raspy voice that frequently broke down into husky laughter. 'God, I'd kill for a cigarette,' she said, turning to her daughter.

'You can't.'

'I didn't say I was going to . . . Do you smoke?' she asked Liam.

He shook his head and swallowed another pastry.

'Nobody does.' She sighed. 'And it's a good thing. Stay smart and don't touch them.'

'Oh, Mum, leave him alone.'

'I used to.'

Mrs Wilcox and Shona looked at him with renewed interest.

'When I was a kid.'

'I had my first cigarette when I was sixteen,' confessed Mrs Wilcox. 'My mother recommended them for keeping the weight down. She wanted me to be a dancer. Can you imagine? Stupid woman. She'd been smoking most of her life and it never kept her weight down, not until she got cancer and died.'

Liam looked across at Shona for some sort of cue. She laughed.

Before dinner each class of graduating students was called to the stage at the front of the room to be presented with their reports and references. When all sixty-four students were assembled onstage a professional photographer ushered them into rows of standing and seated to take a series of shots. Because of his height Liam was asked to stand in the centre of the back row, where he towered over the young men on either side.

'Say "cheese".'

. '*Cheese!*' The photographer's flash illuminated the smiling faces. Liam blinked, the white imprint of the photographic lamp hovering behind his closed eyelids.

'Where is your family tonight?' probed Mrs Wilcox, as plates of turkey breast and spinach ricotta pie arrived at the table.

Shona glared at her mother.

'My dad moves around a lot.'

'Oh, really? So does Shona's.'

'OK, Mum, stop it,' said Shona, firmly. Mrs Wilcox smiled, cut a tomato wedge in half and put it into her mouth.

When her mother joined a handful of parents on the small dance-floor Shona took the opportunity to pour the remaining whisky into Liam's empty glass. He looked at her dumbly. 'Well, you don't want her to drink it, do you?'

He obediently skulled the neat spirit and pulled a face. 'Won't she know?'

Shona snorted. 'She's already had four doubles . . . Have you changed your mind about coming to the after-party?'

'No.' Liam felt the heat of the alcohol settling in his stomach.

'You're joking, right?'

'No, I can't. I'm moving tomorrow.'

'Yeah, I know, but . . .'

'She's a good dancer,' said Liam, watching Mrs Wilcox grind and bump with somebody's father.

'She should be. She danced at the Moulin Rouge in Paris when she was young.'

Liam had no idea what the Moulin Rouge was.

'That was where she met my father.'

'Where is your father?'

'He left us for one of his students.'

'Didn't you want him to come tonight?'

'He sent me a card . . .'

In the foyer Liam lined up with his classmates to view the photographs, already printed and on display for sale. Shiny faces smiled out from the glossy squares of coloured paper. Liam selected an 8 x 10 enlargement and bought three copies. He held one of the prints carefully and studied it. Without warning, a surge of bodies pressed against him from behind, causing him to bump the photographer's table. '*Shit!*'

Behind him Ethan wrestled playfully with another youth in a white suit. 'Sorry, Liam. Cole won't tell me where the after-party is.' He let go of his victim.

'If I tell you, I'd have to kill you . . . Everyone gets on the bus first.'

Ethan slapped Liam's shoulder. 'You coming or what?'

As if alerted by some secret signal the young men and women of Meredith-Baxter's graduating class were emptying from the reception hall, spilling down the ugly orange and purple carpeted steps of the foyer and out into the street. Two white minibuses stood waiting in the drive.

Caught in the tide, Liam found himself walking beside Ethan and Cole. Shona's head bobbed above the crowd as she pushed her way towards him.

The students began climbing onto the buses. Shona lifted the ruffled hem of her dress away from her red sandals and stepped up. 'Come on,' she called, taking Liam's hand and pulling him on board. A trail of students followed up the rear. 'I knew you'd come.' She squeezed herself onto a seat next to him. Liam looked up the aisle, then at Shona's smiling face. 'You can't chicken out now.'

The buses pulled slowly away into the night, leaving behind a small crowd of waving parents.

When they finally reached the designated community hall and picnic grounds, Liam had resigned himself to having a good time. Climbing down from the bus, he saw that a semi-circle of seating 'logs' had been set up around the lighted hall, and several forty-gallon drums blazed with fire. Music sounded from the hall. Galvanized tubs, full of ice and soft drinks, stood on the grass alongside the steps to the building. Bottles of liquor and six-packs of beer appeared as students dug into their backpacks to liberate their stash.

A crowd gathered around the flaming drums, drinking their contraband. Shona pulled Liam down onto the log next to her and handed him a peach wine-cooler. He sipped the sweet drink and winced. 'That's a chick's drink,' called Cody. 'Here.'

Liam held out one hand and caught the icy wet can that Cody tossed to him. 'Thanks.'

'Don't thank me. I didn't buy them.'

'You fucker, Cody!' called another boy from out of the darkness.

Liam drank the beer. A pleasant buzz crept over him and his private thoughts began to meld with the joyous, crazy, tipsy laughter and talk of those around him. He watched the showers of amber sparks that randomly shot up from a nearby drum into the infinite black night. Somebody offered him a cigarette. He experienced a brief sensation of his head spinning as the nicotine-rich blood percolated to his brain. At some point Shona slipped her hand into his. When the beer ran out one of the boys gave him the remains of a half-bottle of Southern Comfort. He drank it neat. It tasted good.

A loud chorus from Chumbawamba's 'Tubthumping (I get knocked down)' rang out from the hall.

'Come on!' called Ethan from beside the fire.

Liam got to his feet and went with Shona and the other couples to the hall. Inside, the students had already formed a circle by linking arms over shoulders as they shouted the lyric of their unofficial anthem.

The newcomers barged playfully into the ring, breaking and re-forming the circle in unison. The unwieldy chain of drink-loosened bodies repeatedly broke down, as the revellers fell and got up again, adding to the hilarity of this spontaneous eruption of solidarity, a rowdy salute to their impending futures. Liam had never had a reason to laugh so hard. All around him ecstatic faces mirrored his euphoria. At that moment they felt that anything was possible.

When he left the hall and stepped out into the cool night, his head was spinning. Shona fell against him, laughing, and they stumbled back to the fire where they sat huddled together. She leant forward and kissed Liam on the lips. He kissed her back.

A can exploded near the hall, showering a group of girls with beer. 'You fucking dickhead, Heinzy!' Everyone moved towards the commotion, leaving Liam and Shona alone on the log.

Liam's perceptions were slowed by the alcohol. He could see people collecting near the steps of the community hall but he couldn't focus long enough to make any sense of what was happening.

'You don't say much, do you, Liam?' said Shona, holding onto his shoulders.

'Not much to say,' he replied drunkenly.

'I bet you have lots of secrets.' She poked him in the chest. Liam laughed and grabbed her finger, imprisoning it in his fist. She pulled it away. 'What *are* you hiding?' she teased.

Liam was feeling more and more light-headed, as if he was in danger of lifting outside himself and floating away. He looked at Shona's face, her sweet Cupid's-bow lips and soft brown eyes. It occurred to him that she was someone you could tell things to, someone who would try hard to understand. He was struck by an overwhelming desire to unburden himself to her.

'Hey, *Shona*?' A skinny blonde girl was fishing drinks out of the watery slush at the bottom of one of the galvanized tubs. 'This yours?' The blonde girl wiped her face blearily with a wet hand, smearing blue mascara across her cheek. She dropped a bottle of wine-cooler at Shona's feet.

Liam opened it and began to drink. 'I do have secrets.'

'Oh, yeah?' Shona stood up and brushed herself off. 'I need something to eat.'

He grabbed hold of her clumsily and tried to kiss her again. As he pressed against her, Shona became aware of his growing erection. 'I think I know your secret,' she said, holding him off.

Liam shook his head. There was something he wanted to tell her but his thoughts were tangled. Suddenly he felt nauseous, bile rose in the back of his throat. His head hurt, as though a steel band was being tightened around it. He lunged forward, over the back of the log, vomiting violently.

'Oh, God!' Shona stifled a laugh 'Are you all right?'

Liam couldn't reply. He kept vomiting, even after his stomach was empty. It was as if he was unable to hold his very innards down. Shona made him drink some water but it came up again. He kept trying and eventually succeeded. She splashed some on his face. His head felt a little better.

'Sorry.' Liam wiped his mouth. Aware of the spectacle he was making, his awkwardness and embarrassment returned. He began to sweat heavily, his heart palpitating. He was overcome with the need to get out of there, to lie down somewhere and sleep it off. *Thank God* he was leaving tomorrow and would never have to see any of these people again.

Waiting outside the transit centre the following morning, clutching his ticket, head thumping, he remembered, with horror, how close he had come to telling Shona the night before. How in his inebriated state the desire to reveal himself to her had become almost irresistible. As the hydraulic doors of the interstate bus hissed open, he vowed silently that he would *never* drink again.

Mathew, 2008

The Rodeo pickup had been parked outside the Military Road Workers Club for nearly ten minutes. A black-and-white cattle dog waited patiently on the truck-bed in the shade cast by the front cabin, tongue lolling from its mouth. Mathew Allen had tailed the vehicle from a white stucco villa in Ravensbrook Gardens, across the bridge, to a building site on the docks, then to this tradesmen's waterhole.

At three in the afternoon, apart from two other vans covered with signage, the car park was virtually empty. Sunlight burnt his arms through the windscreen. He flipped the visor down, sucked some water from a plastic bottle and turned on the radio – some left-wing reformer stridently advocating a better, fairer social-security system that didn't punish or stigmatize the poor.

He punched the tuner button through the static until he found some classical music. He didn't need any more voices in his head.

The Ravensbrook address had been sent anonymously, written across a copy of the forensic photo projection of 'Offender B'. The sender had circled the face with a red marker and drawn an arrow pointing to an additional sentence: 'Evil resides here.' Mathew had seen little reason to give this tip-off any more credence than the other cryptic voodoo messages he was regularly sent. Some people had elaborate imaginations and way too much time on their hands. There were hundreds of twisted nuts out there and he figured he had received mail from most of them. It was impossible to be shocked any more by what they said: the stimulus of a brutal crime and private pain made public was irresistible, luring them out from under their rocks to offer bizarre clues and confessions, taking credit for a crime already solved and providing explicit details.

In the years since his son's death, Mathew Allen had had an ongoing education on just how sick the world really was. He'd had no idea.

The fact that the address was a local one agitated him even more. As part of the conditions of their release, neither Harris nor Simpson was permitted within the greater Henswick area, but over the years people had speculated on whether or not the conditions of their parole had been properly enforced. Internet rumour had it that Danny Simpson had even visited Benjamin's grave.

It galled Mathew to imagine that he could unwittingly run into one of them and never even know.

When the local paper ran a story quoting an associate of one of Simpson's brothers, laughing off the strict terms of their release, claiming that 'Danny' had visited the area 'several' times and 'did as he pleased', Mathew decided to check it out for himself.

On the car radio, Beethoven's Overture to Prometheus was surging towards its manic crescendo. Impatient now, he flicked the switch, cutting short the climax. He pulled the keys from the ignition, left the heat of the car and strolled casually in the direction of the pickup. A panting dog was tethered to a U-bolt on the truck, with no water that he could see. *That wasn't very nice now, was it?* He offered his closed knuckles for the animal to sniff; it wagged its entire body and submissively licked his fingers. He rubbed its head and woolly neck while cataloging the contents of the pickup's tray – the usual fixed toolboxes, several large bags of Skimcoat plaster, a length of poly pipe tied with a red rag. He felt for the dog's collar as he continued to pat him and lifted the bone-shaped identity tag. 'Hey, Barney.'

The dog quivered all over at the mention of his name.

'You want some water, buddy?'

A white Moto Guzzi Eldorado rumbled through the parking lot and out the other side. Barney gave three sharp barks.

'Shoosh.' Mathew Allen left the dog and went back to his Nissan, returning with the water bottle. He drizzled some into his hand and held it out. The dog sucked it up gratefully, making big smacking sounds with its tongue. He unhooked the animal's lead and beckoned him down. 'Come on, Barney, that's a good boy.'

The dog followed him to his car. In the back of the little station-wagon he gulped water from a paint tray as Mathew fired the ignition and drove away. A few blocks later he turned into a Hungry Jacks drive-through, bought a burger, threw away the bun and tossed the patty into the back. The offering was devoured in one mouthful. Barney looked only slightly perturbed when his new chaperone opened the hatch door and beckoned him out onto the grass by the river.

Mathew waited until six p.m. to send a text to the number on the dog's collar: 'Lost dog, Barney, found wandering'. Within seconds his phone was vibrating. 'Mathew here.'

'Hi, I'm Justin, Barney's owner. Where did you find him?' asked the caller.

'He was down near the water, below Ravensbrook Bridge.'

'Man, how did he get all the way up there? I don't even know how he could have got off the truck.'

'I'm just dropping my wife off at her sister's in Faulkner Road,' said Mathew.

'That's not far from me.'

'Right. What's your address, then – Justin, you said?'

'Yeah, Justin Lucas. Number four forty-eight Pembroke, white Spanish arches out front. I mean, I'm not home now, but I can be there in five minutes?'

'Sure. I'll drop him off as soon as I'm done here.'

Mathew was already parked under the cool sprawl of a poinciana opposite the villa when the Ute pulled up. He observed booted feet stepping down from the Ute's cab, and caught a flash of the copper-tanned face under the rim of the labourer's cap as its owner turned to retrieve a bag and made for the front door. Barney immediately woke up, got to his feet and peered out of the window, wagging his tail. Freed from the stranger's car, he pelted into the house, dragging his lead behind him.

At the doorway Mathew held a hand over his eyes to see beyond the glare of the free-standing halogen light that lit the room. Two scaffolds spanned the walls; the room had been gutted.

Barney broke off from licking Justin's face to bark hoarsely at the incoming visitor.

'Bit late now!' admonished Justin. 'You must be Mathew.'

He nodded, still taking in the empty space, the bedding roll and pillows on the stripped hardwood floor. 'You live here?'

'No, mate, it's a job. I crash here. Work late, early start. Saves driving in and out from my parents' place.'

'Looks like it'll be a nice reno when you're done.'

'It's all right, yeah. Thanks for bringing the dog. I was driving around in circles looking for him. Someone must have unclipped his lead.'

'Who owns this place?' said Mathew, looking around the room.

'Some real-estate group – bought up the whole complex, want to turn them around quick.'

'What about before that?'

Justin patted his dog. 'Haven't a clue, mate. From the smell of the back room, I wouldn't be surprised if had been used as a squat. Why?'

'I think I may have known a guy who lived here a little while back.'

'Been empty for months, as far as I know.' He took off his sweat-stained cap and combed his fingers through a frizz of surf-bleached hair.

'How old are you, Justin?'

The young man cocked his head. 'Twenty-three.'

With no reason to disbelieve him, Mathew Allen was immediately relieved. Tall, blond and amiable, Justin Lucas was five years too young to remember a day in 1993 when the whole of Henswick had stopped to take stock of where their children were. The freckled tradesman seemed to be a genuinely nice kid. 'Look after that dog, then.'

'I will.'

Code Blue

'Let your yes be yes and your no be no'

Geoffrey, 2008

The phone rang three times. Geoffrey looked at it from his position near the window. He stared the device down, almost willing it to ring again so he could tear it from the wall and smash it into a thousand pieces. He hadn't been to work for three days now, not since he'd read the article in the Sunday paper. He'd called in sick on the first day and had spoken to no one since.

From under a pile of discarded clothing, the hollow trill of his mobile phone sounded again. Ignoring it, he looked at the street below, observing a young mother half in and half out of her car as she clipped her child into a safety seat. A little leg and sandalled foot kicked impatiently. A hunched old woman in an adjacent yard tugged uselessly at a clump of weeds that grew along the fence line of her barren garden.

The aluminium kettle on the stove gave a lisping hiss. He dumped a spoonful of instant coffee into a mug and poured boiling water over it. He took a carton of milk from the fridge; the milk separated into tiny curds as he poured it into the coffee. 'Fuck.' He lit a cigarette and drank the sour coffee. Sitting down on an armchair in the small alcove that served as his living area, he picked up a folded newspaper from the floor and opened it to page fifteen.

Under the headline 'HIGH COURT RULING FLOUTED' there was a picture of Mathew Allen standing on the steps of the court building. He reread the short article beneath.

> Mathew Allen was acquitted today on contempt of court charges after circulating computer-generated images of Graham Harris and Daniel Simpson on the internet. The forensically modelled images show a probable likeness of the perpetrators, as they would appear today, almost two decades after they were convicted of the brutal murder of Mathew Allen's only son, Benjamin. Lawyers for Mr Allen successfully argued that the modelled projections did not constitute a breach of the special High Court ruling in regard to the publication of 'recent photographs' of the released offenders and that the internet, as a 'territory', was otherwise outside the jurisdiction of the Australian courts . . .
>
> Legal commentator Callum Keating contended that this 'leaves the way open for a major legal loophole

regarding publication of information about their identities'.

The article added, helpfully, that 'While the pictures have been withdrawn from locally based sites they can still be accessed via sites outside the country.'

Geoffrey folded the paper in half and studied the portrait of a weary Mathew Allen smiling at the camera; the look in his eye claimed a victory of sorts in having brought the issue once again into the news. He threw the paper face down onto the floor.

Rage welled inside him. What did Allen want? Why was he hounding him? Why couldn't he just let the whole thing die? In his anger it was easy for him to see himself as the victimized prey, easy to forget why Mathew Allen would suffer any consequence to hunt him down or see him dead.

He stood up and began pacing back and forth between the kitchen and the window, picked up the cigarette packet that lay on the counter, took out the remaining cigarette and tapped it against the bench. He would need to go out soon to get more. He put the cigarette back into the packet and returned to his pacing, stopping briefly in front of a makeshift desk to stare at the screensaver on his computer. He knew what he had to do but for three days he had been unable to do it.

The phone rang again. He put his hands behind his head, pulled his elbows in front of his face and arched his back. 'Fuck!'

In the bedsit's tiny kitchen he knelt down and disengaged the kickboard from the base of the upright stove, then dragged out a multi-patterned satchel from the cavity. He withdrew a small laptop from the bag and held it to his chest, then slammed it down onto the kitchen floor. The machine impacted with a smacking sound but remained intact. He retrieved it and hurled it down again. The screen flew back violently as one of the hinges sheared off and the plastic body split.

He turned a tap on at the sink and smashed the device several times against the edge of the counter. Using a nearby skillet, he delivered a final blow. Plastic shards flew into the air, the hard shell cracking open in several places to expose the workings of the computer drives within.

He dropped it into the sink. Tiny bubbles filtered to the surface as the remaining cavities filled with water.

Sitting down in front of the desktop monitor he logged onto the internet. He typed in a search for Mathew Allen and quickly found the 'Benjamin's Place' website. He didn't wait for the pictures of Benjamin to load before clicking 'Links'. He selected 'Justice Without Borders' from the list and was taken to a site that acted as an exchange for information about convicted felons, crimes and sentencing issues, missing persons, children abducted in custody disputes, and sex offenders. He typed 'Benjamin Allen' into the search field.

Among taglines for articles about the trial and those expressing outrage at the 'soft sentencing' or early release, Geoffrey read, 'Harris and Simpson, is this what they look like now?' He scratched an itch at the back of his neck; his shirt clung to a damp area that had formed between his shoulder-blades. He clicked the link. On the screen two faces quickly uploaded.

Face B on the right mesmerized him. He scoured every feature. He couldn't know if it was an accurate likeness of Graham Harris now, but the hair follicles on his scalp contracted as he looked into the eyes of the Graham Harris he had once known. Eventually he tore away his gaze to examine Face A. He scanned the image anxiously, comparing every feature to his own. The auburn hair, the rounded cheeks, the broad nose and the dimpled chin were all there but combined to create a completely different face from the one he had grown into. He hit the print button and waited impatiently as the printer head droned back and forth and the resulting document was delivered to the tray.

He took the image with him to the bathroom, stood in front of the mirrored cabinet and studied his face, masculine if not handsome, with the stern mouth and cold blue eyes. He held the picture up to his face and saw a clumsy resemblance, as if a bad artist had drawn someone who looked a bit like him – a distant relative, perhaps – but had failed to capture anything that triggered any real visual recognition. He changed his expression and even the technical resemblance disappeared. The forensically modelled projection stared ahead grimly. Geoffrey made a wide grin, exposing his teeth. Apart from the auburn hair, uncannily cut in an approximation of his current style, the two faces, one on paper, the other of flesh, held no apparent connection to each other. He crumpled the page in his hand and flushed it down the toilet.

He'd been half out of his mind for three days. He let out a strangled laugh. It took hold of him, spasming deep in his belly. He laughed until tears rolled down his face, until he began to wheeze. He dropped to the tiled floor and held onto the side of the bath for support. Several minutes passed before he finally regained his composure.

Now that he was free to leave the confines of the flat, he felt far too exhausted to face the outside world, wanting only to eat a good meal and sleep for a very long time. He needed to phone in to work, check in with his parole officer and put the wheels back on his life before things started to unravel.

He made it as far as the bed, lay down and closed his eyes. If he could get an hour's sleep, then he could think about going out for food and cigarettes.

When he opened his eyes again the room was shrouded in darkness. Only a faint glow of evening light bled through the dull-white Terylene curtains. For a moment he wondered if he had slept right through to the next day. He dragged himself up and peered outside. Across the neighbouring rooftops he noted the streaks of faded orange that tinged the darkening sky.

After showering for the first time in three days, he shaved and dressed. He drained the sink in the kitchen and separated the laptop debris into three different garbage bags, which he carried from the flat slung over his shoulder. He deposited them in bins on three separate streets, the last before the steps to the Underground.

Three days in captivity had given him a heightened awareness of the small freedoms his narrow life allowed; for as long as he could remember he had had no remaining ambition, other than to walk free, unmolested and anonymous. An episode like that of the last few days served to remind him that he could be exposed at any time. No matter how many years passed he would always be an uninvited guest at life's table. As he boarded a city-bound train and stood near the automatic doors, silent strangers brushing involuntarily against him, he began to breathe a little easier.

In the city he walked in the direction of Quayside with the intention of getting a meal and a beer at one of the busy eateries. Passing a closed tobacconist's stall he felt instinctively in his pockets for his cigarettes. They were empty: he'd left his last cigarette in the flat. He felt in the side pockets of his leather jacket. The right-hand one held his wallet and keys. In the left his fingers found something cold and hard: the neatly crafted pocket-knife he often carried when fear gripped him. He hadn't thought to take it since the weather was last cold enough to wear the jacket but he felt glad of it tonight. He took it out and opened the blade with the fingers of one hand. He pressed the point against the hardened skin of his thumb, then shut it and slid it back into his jacket. Struck by sudden panic, his hand flew to his shirt pocket. His mobile was there. For one minute he'd thought he'd come out without it.

The smell of stale urine and hops rose from the doorway of a nearby pub. Inside the men's bar, he dropped a series of coins into the slot of the cigarette machine. At the bar he ordered a beer and found a book of matches. Only when his cigarette was finally alight and he had taken his first drag did he look around him. Apart from a one-eyed drunk at the bar, the room was empty. Through the internal glass doors that led to the main entrance, he could see a steady traffic of younger clientele coming and going from the lounge. The smoky sweet scent of barbecued meat reminded him that he was ravenous.

'Where can I get a feed?' he asked the man behind the bar.

'Through there.' He inclined his head. 'In the bistro.'

He pushed his way through a small crowd clustered at the rear, lifting his beer away from his body. As he side-stepped a table of diners he collided head on with a younger man. The wiry blond held a plate of food to his chest in an effort to save it. 'Whoa!'

Geoffrey swore loudly as the contents of his beer glass splashed in a frothy arc across an empty table. 'Sorry, mate.' Inwardly he blamed the other man but he knew enough not to buy extra trouble.

'Forget it. Shame about your beer.'

Geoffrey watched as he carried his food over to a table of young men and sat down to eat. When one of them glanced at him, he quickly looked away. By the time he had collected his meal and found a table he noticed, with some relief, that the blond was gone. He tore into the buttered steak, mentally plotting the route he would take home and the supplies he needed to buy from the 'all-nite' supermarket.

A beer thudded onto the table in front of him. He looked up to meet the eyes of the blond man. 'Thanks.'

'No worries.' The man smiled down at him. One of his front teeth crossed the other and was diagonally chipped, giving his smile an awkward appeal. Geoffrey realized that he couldn't be more than eighteen or nineteen. He gave a guarded smile back and continued to cut his meat.

'The food's pretty good here. The chef's a mate of my brothers.'

Geoffrey nodded and chewed. The youth's friendliness was not lost on him but he knew the dangers of human contact. He allowed himself to crave neither friends nor intimates, who could threaten the integrity of his fortress-like defences. Keeping people out was a small price to pay to preserve his limited freedom.

Other, more basic, urges were not so easy to fight. He fought them anyway, pushing them down into the back of his consciousness or avoiding temptation wherever he could. In any case he would never have allowed himself to admit to the overwhelming attraction he felt towards the tanned young man in the pale blue shirt.

'Well, enjoy your beer,' he said, winking, and moved back into the crowd.

The night air was heavy with moisture as he walked the half-mile of dockside that led back to the commercial centre. A light rain began to fall, adding to his discomfort. It wasn't the shortest or safest route back to the Underground, but it was mostly deserted. He crossed the street and stopped briefly to look out across the oily black water, a heartless expanse that immediately depressed him and threatened to swallow him. He turned away from it, leaning against the Victorian cross-patterned iron rail.

On the opposite side of the street stood a row of cavernous factories, days away from being gutted and refurbished, built from rough-cut convict sandstone. Aeons of invisible suffering mixed with crumbling mortar. Loneliness, abandonment and degradation, all there in the empty rain-slicked street. What a desolate landscape, and yet he felt at home in it. This was how the world really was; places like this didn't lie.

Looking towards the lime-painted doors of a corner warehouse, he saw the outline of a figure emerging from the cross street he had just left. Steady footfalls on the wet bitumen broke the comforting silence. Geoffrey turned abruptly and walked at a pace to maintain his lead on the stranger. Instead of continuing directly towards his destination, he turned impulsively into the next laneway. As he climbed the shallow rise away from the waterfront, he thought he heard footsteps again and looked back to see the figure, in a pale shirt, turn into the laneway after him. The soles of his feet tingled painfully as a feeling of vertigo flooded through him. Was that the young man from the hotel?

Geoffrey walked fast now, turning left towards an open square of parkland. He cut across it, heading in the direction of the yellow light that spilt downwards from the eaves of a distant toilet block. He could make out the silhouettes of two people near a stand of trees at the park's far entrance. As he moved closer to them they melted into the darkness. He rounded the brown-brick building and entered the anteroom of the men's toilet. Not knowing if he was still being followed, he looked back out into the darkness. His light-blinded pupils registered nothing.

Despite the cold he was sweating heavily. Reluctant to leave the illuminated sanctuary, he stopped to splash himself with water. He pulled the hem of his shirt loose from his trousers and wiped at his face. When he uncovered his eyes and looked at himself in the mirror, he saw the blond youth standing in the doorway behind him. Geoffrey spun around to face him. 'Why are you following me?'

The boy gave him a strange look.

'What do you want?' Geoffrey fingered the knife in his pocket.

The boy moved forward slowly 'Isn't it obvious?' He laid a hand on his arm.

Geoffrey pushed it away. 'I'm no faggot.'

'Didn't say you were.' The boy edged closer.

Geoffrey's stomach churned. 'Look, you've got the wrong idea.'

The boy's face was now very close to his. 'Don't you like me just a little bit?' His grey-blue eyes looked right into Geoffrey's.

Geoffrey looked back at him, as if he might kill him, then reached down and felt the boy's crotch. They kissed. Geoffrey pulled him into the nearest cubicle and began to undo the fly of his own jeans. The boy pushed the stall door shut and immediately dropped to his knees. Braced against the rear of the cubicle, looking down at the silvery blond hairs on the back of the tanned neck, Geoffrey was overcome with a wild excitement, every nerve ending in his body screaming as the boy fondled him, then took him into his mouth. Geoffrey groaned, one hand caressing the boy's scalp while the other found its way into the jacket pocket and held the knife.

At that moment something heavy slammed powerfully against the cubicle door, which exploded inwards, smashing his elbow and sending the boy sprawling backwards. Pain coursed through Geoffrey's arm.

'Stay exactly where you are.' The man held up a badge of identification. His partner bent down, secured the boy's arms behind his back and handcuffed him. 'I'm arresting you both for offensive behaviour.'

Geoffrey held his elbow and stared up at the two policemen. His brain was still reeling.

The boy began to cry. 'We didn't do anything wrong.'

One of the policemen grunted in disbelief.

'You do yourself up,' the second officer instructed Geoffrey, as he took in the sordid tableau – the cracked toilet cistern, the graffitied walls, thick with salacious invitations, phone numbers, and pornographic promises. How anyone could raise a hard-on in this filth was beyond him.

The next twenty minutes passed in a blur. Bundled into the back of an unmarked police car, alongside the blond stranger who kept glancing at him in expectation of camaraderie, he could only look out of the window as the neon-lit night streaked by.

From the moment of his arrest he had been trying to work out if he should stay silent and ride out the consequences of this cataclysm or if he should phone in a 'code blue'.

At the police station they had taken his belongings from him. He watched silently as his mobile phone was slipped into a plastic bag and placed in a metal drawer. The number he needed was engraved deep in his memory: when he closed his eyes he could see the digits hovering above him, like a tattoo. Still unable to come to any decision, he declined the duty sergeant's offer of a phone call and was ushered into a bare interview room.

Alone, he counselled himself to stay calm. 'Offensive behaviour' was a misdemeanour charge. *Don't panic, stay calm, stay focused.* Wait and see what happens. Just answer their questions, get bailed and get out of there. He could sort it out with his parole officer later. He stared at the arsenic-green walls, glowing dimly under the sickly fluorescent light. *Come on.* He ran the jagged nail of his thumb along the corner seam of the laminated table edge.

The door opened, and the officer who had arrested him came in, followed by a younger uniformed officer. The detective looked at him from weary eyes as his colleague turned on a video recorder at the back of the room and sat down alongside him.

'Let's get this out of the way and we can all go home.'

Geoffrey looked back at him.

'About twenty-five minutes ago, at nine forty p.m., you were arrested for offensive behaviour in a public toilet in Observatory Park. Do you wish to deny or confirm that you were in the process of receiving fellatio from another male in the public toilets there?'

'Yes, we were . . .' Geoffrey broke eye contact.

The officer nodded. 'Have you ever been to that public toilet before?'

Geoffrey shifted in his seat. 'Maybe . . . a long time ago.'

'When?'

'Maybe once last year . . . I don't know exactly. Why?'

'To be honest with you, mate, we're not really all that interested in the sex life of your average queer but there have been a number of violent assaults on gay men in Observatory Park over the past five months.'

Geoffrey listened attentively. He had started to wonder where this was headed.

'You had a small pocket-knife in your possession?'

'Yeah?'

'What do you carry that around for?'

'It's a multi-tool. I use the scissors at work to trim leads and wires. I don't know anything about any assaults.'

'The young guy you were with, where did you meet him?'

'I saw him in the pub on North Head Road. I've never met him before – he followed me when I left the pub. I noticed him behind me before the park – I stopped in the toilet and he came on to me in there. I don't even know his name.'

'Did he get rough with you?'

Geoffrey shot the policeman a withering look. 'Him? No.'

The officer made a neat pile of the few papers in front of him. 'Well, we won't keep you longer than we need to. Officer Hartley will take you downstairs, where you will be charged and fingerprinted. Then you can get out of here . . . You might want to think about getting a motel room next time,' he added, without smiling.

Geoffrey barely heard the man's words. His face had turned white and he stared at his hands spread on the surface of the table. *Fingerprinted.* He looked up at the video camera mounted on the opposite wall.

The detective rose to his feet. 'All right, let's go.'

He silently complied with the officer's instructions as he was charged, photographed and finally fingerprinted. Like a doomed man presenting his bare neck for the guillotine, he mutely held out his hand to be scanned by the flat glass optical block. As the light flared beneath his palm, he felt entirely disconnected from his body, frozen. He knew the implications of the technology, that his palm and finger- and thumb-prints would immediately be uploaded to a national database to be electronically sorted and matched to any print on record.

He gazed down at his hands. If not for the absence of ink on his fingertips he would have believed he was eleven years old all over again.

'Sign here,' said the officer.

For a moment he didn't recognize the name printed on the statement. He moved the pen slowly, carefully trawling out the letters in his distinctive neat cursive. Geoffrey Roland Wickham. *Who the hell was that?*

'That's it, mate. The duty officer will give you back your property on the way out.'

'Nicholas!' The second arresting officer from the toilet block rounded the corridor corner and held out a document. The detective studied the page and looked at Geoffrey. He exchanged several quiet sentences with his colleague.

'If I could just have a word in here.' He ushered Geoffrey into a nearby room. 'We might have a complication.'

Geoffrey looked up at him dumbly.

'It appears that your sexual partner might be under age. His licence has been altered to make him older.' He put the photocopy on the table.

'See here?' The officer pointed to the year of birth: 1990. 'He's scratched out what looks to have been a two and turned it into nought. The licence gives the birth month as May. According to him, he turned sixteen a month ago. We're running a records check now to verify his age.'

Geoffrey looked uncomprehendingly at the small photocopied square floating on the white page and at the tiny photo-portrait of the boy, showing the same crooked grin. 'I don't understand.'

'If the boy turns out to be under age you'll be looking at a charge of sexual assault,' the detective explained.

'Sexual assault?'

'A minor cannot consent to a sexual act.'

'*Consent?* He came on to me . . . I didn't know how old he was. How old does he look to you?'

'If I was planning on screwing round with him, I'd probably make it my business to find out . . . I'll take that,' he said, withdrawing the page.

Geoffrey watched the photocopied image of his assassin as it slid across the table in the detective's hand.

'Just wait in here until we find out. Maybe you've got nothing to worry about.' The detective checked his watch and left the room.

Sexual assault! Geoffrey screamed internally. If the boy was under age he was fucked. Sex with a minor – he'd go straight back to prison. His heart palpitated wildly. What if they locked him up, remanded him without bail? What if they got hold of his record, *his real record*, what then? *That fucking stupid faggot kid, why did he have to follow me? FUCK.* What was he playing at? He'd done his best to fob the idiot off, to avoid him. Then it occurred to him. *They knew!* They knew everything about him. The whole thing was a set-up. The boy was in on it. He struck his forehead with the base of his palm. *Fuck! Fuck!* Idiot! But how could they know? How could they predict his every move? *Stay calm, stay calm.* He scanned the walls of the interview room, looking for the overhead camera. What if they were filming him right now? Shit. What if they had been watching him the whole time? What if they had seen where he had dumped the dismembered laptop, recovered the images?

Breathe. Surely it was all a coincidence. He inhaled deeply, the way he had been taught in therapy, then exhaled, deflating his entire body.

He stared at the door. What were they doing? How long did it take to check an ID?

He leant on the table and held his face, pressing his fingers and thumbs tightly across his cheekbones. The boy was probably telling the truth. Why wouldn't he? But even if he was over sixteen, they still had Geoffrey's fingerprints. What if they cross-checked his prints with the fingerprint archive? They'd know exactly who he was.

Not this. 'Not this again,' he said aloud.

Danny, 1993

'Do you know about fingerprints, Danny?' asked Detective Phillip Kendall, quietly.

'Yeah.' Danny looked at his feet below the desk, then up at his mum. Debbie Simpson rubbed savagely at a patch of dry skin under her mascara-caked eye, her bony hands dropping repeatedly onto the black vinyl handbag on her lap. She was desperate for a cigarette.

'Do you know how they work?' continued the detective. Danny shrugged. 'Can I go home now?'

'No, Danny, not yet. We still have more questions. We need to know what happened on Friday evening.'

Danny examined the fingers of his open hand – the plump, pink fingers of a child. Black ink still stained the tiny ridges on his skin.

'Everybody has a different pattern on the skin of their fingers. Our skin is oily and when we touch things we leave those patterns behind. Do you understand?'

'Yeah.'

'Now, Danny, you told us that you didn't go near the overpass, that you weren't there with Benjamin, but we don't think you were telling us the truth.' Danny looked past the detective at a faded spot on the interview-room wall.

'How long is this going to take?' interrupted Debbie Simpson, heaving her handbag to her chest.

'As long as it takes Danny to tell us about last Friday,' Detective Kendall answered, in a calm, deliberate voice. *He* had all the time in the world. He lifted out a small exhibits bag from the file-tray in front of him. He smoothed the plastic flat across the contents of the bag and held it up for Danny to see.

Danny crossed his legs and looked away.

'We found this crayon box below the overpass, do you recognize it?'

Danny shook his head.

'You don't remember taking a box of crayons like these from the newsagent in the Regency Arcade earlier that day, when you were there with Graham?'

'Nuh, I never took nothin'. We never went to any newsagent's.'

'Then why do you think that your thumbprint, the special pattern made only by your thumb, was found on this box?'

'I don't know! Graham might've put it there.'

'Graham? Was Graham at the overpass?'

'I don't know.'

'If you weren't there, Danny, when did your fingers come in contact with the crayon box?'

'I dunno, we have crayons like that at school. Somebody might have got them from there.'

'Your palm and fingerprints have been found on the handrail at the overpass.'

'Been there millions of times.'

'To the overpass? I thought you never went that way. Didn't you tell us you hadn't been there for months?'

'I never went there on Friday.'

'But you've been to the overpass many times?'

'I've walked home across the bridge.'

'And to get to the bridge you have to cross the wasteland?'

'Yeah.'

'So you have been to the wasteland.'

'Yeah, I already said so.'

'With Graham?'

'Sometimes . . .'

'Well, we think that you and Graham were there again on Friday afternoon.'

Danny held his hand over his mouth, clutching his chin. He shook his head.

'You see, Danny, we know you were there because that was where we found Benjamin, and we found some things near Benjamin that tell us you were there. Now maybe you were there by yourself . . .'

For the first time in the interview Danny's eyes showed real fear. He shook his head twice. Debbie Simpson had had enough. 'Just say if you were there, Danny. *For God's sake*, did you have anything to do with what happened to this kid or not?' Her upper lip twitched and she blinked several times – the interview seemed to have careened off the map and into alien territory, even for a Simpson. 'I tell you what, Danny . . .'

'Mrs Simpson, in order to clarify his version of events, Danny needs to know that you're there for him. That you won't be angry with him.'

'Angry with him!' she repeated indignantly.

'That you'll support him, whatever happens.'

'Just get it over with, Danny, if you was there. Just tell the truth.' *Apparently there was a first time for everything.*

'Do you think we'll find your fingerprints on the crayon that was at the scene?

'Don't know anything about any crayons. I didn't touch him, I swear.'

A knock at the door was quietly answered by Detective Metcalfe.

'I am beginning to wonder, Danny, looking at the evidence, whether you were at the overpass by yourself on Friday afternoon,' Kendall continued.

'I wasn't at the overpass.'

Kendall peered down at a page handed to him by the second detective. 'Well, according to Graham Harris,' Danny's eyes widened, 'the last time he saw Benjamin, he was with you. He says that he wanted to take him to the nearest police station, but you wouldn't let him.'

'He's a liar,' Danny shot back.

Kendall noticed the muscles on the boy's jaw clenching and releasing as he stared defiantly back. 'He says you suggested leaving Benjamin by the river and that he wanted to call the police but you wouldn't let him.'

His heart sank. There were so many near-truths in this account it was obvious that Graham was spilling his guts in the interview room on the other side of the building.

'Well, is that true?'

Danny was confused. He had been denying even going to the Regency Arcade that Friday afternoon, denying he was with Graham, denying he had ever clapped eyes on Benjamin.

'Is Graham telling us the truth about that day, Danny?'

The stony-faced eleven-year-old jiggled his knee up and down under the table, cornered now, nowhere to turn.

'Because he says that when he last saw Benjamin, you were leading him down Barracks Lane in the direction of the overpass. Is that true, Danny?'

'No.'

'So Graham is telling us lies, is he?'

'Yeah.'

'Why do you think Graham would say that you were both with Benjamin, that you led him by the hand through Battery Cove, away from the downtown area towards the docks, that he wanted to return the child to safety and that you led him away?'

'Because he's lying, trying to *blame me*.'

'For what, Danny?'

'For everything! He's trying to blame it all on me.'

'But you weren't at the Regency Arcade. You've never even seen Benjamin Allen. Isn't that what you've been telling us? But we know that you're lying, Danny, because we have you both on CCTV footage leading the child away from the shopping centre. You're wearing a very distinctive red and white Adidas windcheater, the one we took from your house earlier today, and Graham is wearing his yellow jacket. Graham knows that, Danny. That's why Graham has stopped lying about it and started telling the truth.'

Danny stared straight ahead, his mind searching frantically for a way out of the maze. It found none.

'Danny, was you there?' asked his mother.

'He's a bloody liar,' cried Danny.

'Given how many different stories you've already told us, Danny, I'm not so sure.'

'It was his idea.' He clenched his fists and put them under the table against his thighs.

'What was, Danny?'

'To take a kid.'

Phillip Kendall shot his colleague a knowing look. *Here it comes.*

'It was Graham's idea to take that kid.' Danny appeared on the verge of tears, but none ever came. 'He hates babies. Graham wanted to take a kid . . .' continued Danny, unevenly. Now that he was ready to implicate himself to put the blame on Graham, the words were sticking like gravel in the back of his throat.

Detective Metcalfe passed him a cup of water. Danny drank from it.

'And you were looking for one in the Regency Arcade Shopping Centre?'

'Yeah.'

'And that was where you first saw Benjamin?'

'Yeah.'

'Tell us what happened?'

'He was just standing there . . . outside the shop, playing with the doors, swinging on the handle. Graham was laughing at him and he started giggling.'

'Did Graham speak to him?'

Danny twisted his mouth and shook his head. 'Nuh, he just started walking and when the baby followed us out he held his hand.'

'You all left together?'

'Yeah, but I never touched him. You can see in the picture from the video, Graham's got his hand, not me.' Danny knew exactly what he was doing, and so did the detectives, but for the moment their job was not to confront Danny's self-serving lies and half-truths but to open him up gently to let the story slip out whole onto the interview-room table where it could later be dissected. Get him talking, keep him talking. Capitalize on his motivation to lay the blame on Graham.

Like all good liars, Danny knew when to concede a point, when to admit what was no longer deniable, how to stick to either side of the facts and deftly manipulate or leave out the details that would hang him. If Graham was going to spill his guts, Danny sure as hell wasn't going to stay silent. Let Graham be the fall guy. Graham was lying through his teeth anyway, crying like a baby, trying to blame him when it was all *his* fault.

Graham, 1993

Detective Sergeant Stuart Grisham unloaded a tray of boxed juices and tea in Styrofoam cups. Senior Detective Sergeant Harry Townsend repositioned his chair to face the anxious child on the other side of the table. The boy was flanked by his mother and father and watched closely by an attending solicitor. Christine Harris folded her arms across her chest.

Townsend held his big hands together, thoughtfully fingering the edge of a paisley tie with spatula-like thumbs.

Graham Harris blinked back at him like a frightened gerbil.

'If we can just go back a bit to the part where you and Danny decided to skip school for the day.'

Graham's eyes darted in his mother's direction. She glared back. 'You said that was Danny's idea.'

He nodded warily.

'But you'd skipped school together before?'

'Few times . . . not lately.'

'He knows better than to hang around with Danny. We tried to put a stop to it,' his mother interrupted.

Townsend nodded tolerantly and leant further forward, speaking directly to Graham. 'But mates sometimes don't listen to their parents, do they? And Danny was your friend, right?'

'Yeah . . .'

'Do you always do what Danny tells you to?'

'No.'

'You weren't scared of him?'

'He gets me into trouble . . .' He looked again at his mother, who was measuring his every word.

'That's why I sit away from him in class,' he lied.

'What sort of trouble?'

'Sometimes he makes me do things.'

The detective waited.

'Like nicking and other stuff . . . and smashing things in people's front gardens.'

'Graham.' Denis Harris sighed.

'So he's the boss?' Townsend continued.

'Other kids are afraid of him, but sometimes I tell Danny to do things and he does,' he said, lighting up proudly.

'What do you tell Danny to do?'

'Just stupid things, nothing bad . . . He'll do anything. He's not afraid of teachers.'

'He's a hard man, is he? Tough, like?'

'Sometimes he is. He's tough, but sometimes he's like a girl – he plays with stuffed toys and he's already eleven.' Graham nibbled at the straw of his blackcurrant juice box.

The backwards and forwards of Townsend's casual questioning laid the foundation for probing deeper into the inconsistencies of Graham's story.

'So after you'd decided to wag school together you just wandered around all these different places and then went to the Regency Arcade and nicked some things?'

'Danny wanted to steal some pink sunglasses off a stand outside Soul Patterson's but I ran away,' said Graham, painting himself as an innocent.

'What would a tough guy like Danny want with those?'

Graham shrugged. 'He wrote bad words in crayon on the toilet wall.'

'You saw him do that?' said Townsend, studying him carefully and flagging something in his notes.

'Yeah . . .'

'Did you use the crayons?'

A brief look of panic crossed his face. 'No, I never . . .'

The detective turned to another page in his notebook. 'And later you came across a lost boy?'

'Yeah, we saw that boy with his mum and then later when he was lost we were just helping him.'

Townsend caught the other detective's eye.

'So you saw the same boy before?'

Graham's expression became furtive.

'Were you looking for little boys, then?'

He shook his head. Christine Harris glanced up at the solicitor.

'Why did you lead the boy out of the shopping centre, instead of looking for his mother?'

'I don't know. It was Danny's idea.'

'But you had hold of his hand. Where did you and Danny plan to take him?'

'We didn't know where his mum was. I wanted to take him to the police station but Danny wouldn't let me.'

'Do you remember calling him over about an hour earlier?' He gestured with his finger. 'Like this?'

'No.' He pulled his feet up onto his chair and swivelled towards his mother. He seemed to understand the implications of the question. 'I never, Mum.'

'Just tell them what you told me, about what Danny said to you,' she urged impatiently.

Graham looked at the floor.

The detective allowed a few seconds to pass. 'In his interview, Danny said that you often talked about "getting a baby" and taking him away from his mother.'

'Danny wouldn't say that,' he said, his eyes becoming wide.

Townsend's silence reiterated the accusation.

'He's lying, Mum, he's lying.'

Detective Grisham leant towards Townsend and whispered something to him. Townsend nodded thoughtfully and took a sip of cold tea. Anxious about the hushed words, Graham became tearful. 'You don't believe me.'

'I want to, Graham.' As he looked at the fragile, not unlikeable little boy, it was true. 'But we need your help to clear this up. You need to tell us everything that happened.'

He grabbed fretfully at his mother's arm. 'We never took a kid, Mum.'

'For goodness' sake, Graham, talk to the detective and tell him what happened so it can all be sorted out. You're already in trouble – shoplifting and truanting!'

'We believe that you and Danny took the child to the wasteland by the docks and that you were both involved in his death.'

Graham's parents listened in horrified silence, as the detective continued with his statement, registering for the first time the full extent of the allegations against their son.

Denis Harris gripped the table in front of him with two hands. The lawyer seemed to stir from some faraway meditation, a look of sick astonishment on his swarthy face.

Graham blocked his ears and wailed, 'I never.' He crawled across from his chair onto his mother's lap and clawed at her neck. 'I didn't.'

'Stop it, Graham. Sit up. It's all right.'

'When I left he was with Danny,' he cried, hysterical now.

His mother prised his hands from her shirt. 'Stop it, Graham.' Tears welled in her eyes.

'Then why didn't you tell someone? Why didn't you call the police?' the detective persisted. 'Why would you lead a lost boy all the way to the docks?'

Graham remained mute, his black irises flickering.

'You said earlier that Benjamin had only got a bruise on him before you left him with Danny. Was he bleeding?'

'No.'

The detective reflected for moment. 'So how is it that you have blood on your jacket?'

At the mention of blood Graham became rigid with fear. He looked for a long time at his mother. Several seconds passed. 'We did take him . . . but we let him go at the docks, that's all.'

Christine Harris went limp and the blood drained away from her face. The thread of hope that this was all a tangled misunderstanding finally snapped.

He began to wail loudly. 'I'm gonna get all the blame 'cause they say I've got blood on my jacket. They're gonna put me away, Mum.' He tore himself loose from his mother's protective grip and launched himself at his father. 'Dad, make them let me go home.'

Denis Harris restrained his son's flailing arms and held him close to his body. 'Be quiet, son, don't say anything else.'

The solicitor took the opportunity to call time out to advise his client.

When the charges were read out, Graham was undoing the seal on a carton of chocolate milk, weeping only briefly as his mother slumped over the interview table and cried. Denis Harris left the room clutching his arm and collapsed in the corridor outside.

Danny was charged that same night. He responded by saying, 'That was Graham, not me.'

Both boys' accounts had been full of inconsistencies. Graham's lies were more fantastical and elaborate and therefore more transparent; under pressure he admitted to most of them.

Danny, a veteran of brutality and intimidation, never wavered. 'It's him that's got hold of his hand.' To any questioning of his honesty, he responded, 'I was there, and you weren't.'

Graham's extreme distress during the interviews convinced the investigating team that he was perhaps less culpable and more in need of help. Danny, on the other hand, was a hard, cold figure, with a tight lid on his emotions. Viewed from the outside he remained the unflinching embodiment of the evil seed. A born troublemaker with a criminal pedigree. His failure to act like a frightened child left little room for adult sympathy.

That Graham and Danny were two halves of the same aberration, who on their own would never have brought themselves to commit such brutality, was a far more complex psychological puzzle to contemplate. In a world full of iniquity there are lots of Dannys and lots of Grahams. Sometimes they find each other.

Alex Reiser, 2008

In his retreat at the rear of the reference library, sitting at the head of a far table, with his laptop out and his papers spread in a fan around him, Alex Reiser copied a list of online newspaper articles onto his flash drive. He inserted the stick into one of the library computers, in the private study bay behind him, and sent the files to a central printer.

The pages, retrieved from the service desk, were the yield of a morning's internet trawling. He laid them out across the table: instance after instance of children from across the developed world, killing other children, all telegraphed by graphic headlines. He felt increasingly perplexed.

BROTHERS FILM BRUTAL ASSAULT ON
MOBILE PHONE – Footage shared with
classmates.
INTERNET FEUD LEADS TO FATAL KNIFE
ATTACK BY JAPANESE SCHOOL GIRL
FIVE-YEAR-OLD NORWEGIAN GIRL LEFT
FOR DEAD IN SNOW. Killed by playmates
SIX-YEAR-OLD MICHIGAN BOY SHOOTS
AND KILLS CLASSMATE

As he jotted down the key dates and details of what was
by no means only a contemporary phenomenon, Reiser
felt a rising sense of despair.

And then there were the school shootings:
COPYCAT SHOOTER OPENS FIRE WITHIN
DAYS OF COLUMBINE. He shook his head as he
looked down a printed list of carnage carried out by
gun-toting juveniles across America. It had continued
pretty much unabated since 1860, when a Kentucky
student had shot and killed a classmate who had threatened to shoot him. It was clear that children were capable
of great cruelty. Born innocent perhaps, but also without the ability to reject, contain or suppress their
instinctual reactions, impulses and curiosity. A conscience was developed over time. The mistake was in
believing they were not capable of such things. The
extent of violence children were capable of committing

on each other was shocking, but it was the last headline that struck him most forcefully: 'MURDER OF A CHILD BY BOYS. Two-and-a-half-year-old drowned in running brook by two eight-year-old boys.' It had happened in 1861.

In a set of eerie similarities, more than a century earlier, two eight-year-old boys had led a trusting toddler away from the strip of wasteland where he was playing. Reiser felt the hair follicles on his forearms contract as he continued to read. *'Taking him by the hand, the boys walked him through a patchwork of fields, brooks and reservoirs, along a secluded laneway where'*, according to the coroner of the inquest, held at a local tavern, *'seduced at the instigation of the devil, they did kill and willfully murder'* him. The coroner, in his summing up, had observed that, despite there being no fathomable motive for the *'horrifyingly brutal'* attack, the boys had demonstrated the *'capacity to commit the crime'* and had exhibited *'mischievous discretion'* in luring the child to a secluded place, and in not disclosing events to any adults, despite the search for the missing baby, they had demonstrated proof of their *'consciousness of guilt'*. They were, he concluded, capable of distinguishing between good and evil.

As he scanned the dramatic prose, his attention was caught by the judges' comments at the eight-year-olds' subsequent criminal trial. He had advised the jury that they must 'first satisfy themselves that the prisoners were capable of discerning between right and wrong. If so, "*whether they knew the effect of the act they were committing*"; if not, then the presumption of malice would be rebutted and the crime reduced from murder to manslaughter.'

When the jury wasted no time in returning a verdict of manslaughter, he addressed the children in front of the packed courtroom: '*You have been very wicked, naughty boys . . . I am going to send you to a place where you will have an opportunity of becoming good boys, for there you will have a chance of being brought up in a way you should be, and that in time, when you come to understand the nature of the crime you have committed, you will repent of what you have done.*' The sentence of '*one month's jail followed by five years in the reformatory*' was greeted with unanimous cheers of approval.

Reiser was surprised by the judge's enlightenment, no doubt a product of the growing Victorian zeal for social reform, especially in regard to the betterment of children.

Even the leading newspapers of the day were philosophically restrained, advising the public to 'remember that these boys are only wild in the degree that all our boys would be without religion and education'.

'Conscience admits of degrees, it is weak and has not arrived at its proper growth in children.' One went as far as to declare it 'absurd and monstrous that these two children should have been treated like criminals in the first place'.

It was a progressive view reiterated almost a hundred and fifty years later in the sad case of the five-year-old Norwegian girl, whose sweet, guileless face stared up at him from the printed pages. A cherished daughter, who had gone out to build castles in the freshly fallen snow with two six-year-old local boys and never come home. She had been beaten and left to die by her playmates. Reiser was moved when he read that the devastated community had rallied around all three families, protecting the surviving children. Incredibly even the girl's distraught mother expressed her concern for the school-age killers: 'They need compassion and must be treated as children, shown kindness and concern rather than vengeance.' In a country where the age of criminal responsibility was fifteen, the event was seen as a collective tragedy, not a crime.

That the Norwegian press had maintained a united front in agreeing not to publish the young offenders' names or descriptions further amazed him and, with his part in covering all aspects of the Allen case, gave him pause for thought. Remembering the vitriolic hostility and near-lynching mood that had surrounded the Allen case, Reiser saw that, while childhood violence seemed to cross national and social boundaries, the reaction to it was very much influenced by context and culture. He unstrapped his briefcase, pulled out a clutch of well-fingered notes and dropped them onto the table.

And then there was all this, he thought, spreading the paperwork around the already crowded table. Hyperbolic editorials and sensational coverage from the time of the Allen murder and trial: 'FREAKS OF NATURE', 'Throw away the key', 'EVIL SEEDS' and 'A crime like this, committed by children, is unprecedented in history.'

He gave a little groan. How many times had he seen that gem between quotation marks? It made for sensational copy, but simply wasn't true. Looking at the disturbing collage of child killers and victims spread before him, Reiser considered the unpalatable fact that children had been killing children for just about as long as adults had been killing them. It seemed to him that some communities were inclined to accept that nothing ever happened in a vacuum, that we were all co-authors of the environments into which children were born, while others were driven strenuously to project the 'evil' of the world back onto such children.

As far as he could ascertain, from a long career of looking into societies maladjusted, every crime was a coalescence of events and influences. It was this intersection between Fate and circumstance, genetic and environmental heritage that had fascinated him all his life. In a society that denied its own hand in the suffering of nameless millions, children were a symbol of innocence and purity, therefore children could never do what we as a species were entirely capable of doing: kill. Killing in the home, close up and personal, killing on the street, over trifles, killing in foreign fields, anonymously, killing in prisons and slaughterhouses, killing other people's children in the name of democracy, killing for God. If not killing ourselves, then turning a blind eye to it through complacency, indifference and greed.

Meanwhile, held up as emblems of innocence, many children were simultaneously pursued on all sides by the forces of darkness. Starvation, neglect, psychological cruelty, Munchausen's by proxy, genital mutilation, Ritalin, slavery, paedophilia, religious indoctrination, female infanticide: somewhere parents were doing it to their children. Statistics offered a dispassionate glimpse of the reality for many, and it was hard not to be numbed by them. Every ten seconds a child somewhere died of hunger or neglect, twenty-two thousand every day. Statistically their mothers were more likely to be killed by male partners than a stranger and they themselves had most to fear from the men closest to them to whom they were not biologically related. Apparently there was nothing more potentially deadly than a violent *de facto* parent.

Killing was primal. Not killing was a product of an amygdala-friendly environment and a complex web of social conditioning.

He lifted his glasses and rubbed his eyes. The subject matter was onerous and left him with a sense of responsibility: he must not gloss over any aspect of the crime. He looked up at the clock above the reference desk. The library was filling with high-school students, milling about the periodicals section and leaning over the backs of cubicles, chattering in low voices. Did any of the carefree faces hide the barely suppressed impulse to kill? The quiet one in the corner, who occasionally eyed the more boisterous youths with what looked like contempt: was he busy compiling a list of all those who had slighted him?

The unforgiving plywood chair pressing against his lower back interrupted his musings. He spread his arms out to gather up his notes and sighed.

Wanted

'Sing, O barren woman, you who never bore a child . . .'

Detective Kendall, 2008

He turned over slowly, shifting his weight painfully from one hip to the other, threw back the blanket and placed a pillow between his knees. His pyjama shirt, wet with perspiration, clung to his skin.

A soft breeze moved the gauze curtain and fanned his face. Outside in the night a frog croaked. June had always said they were a sign of good luck. If he had any luck left at all, he thought, he would be joining her soon.

The pain in his left hip eased a little and Phillip Kendall drifted towards sleep, floating weightlessly down a warm red tunnel. As he touched the sides and swam effortlessly through a clear liquid that seemed to massage all the pain from his body, the phone rang.

Reaching across the bedside table to answer it, he overturned a tumbler of water and sent it crashing to the floor. The digital display on the clock radio read 11:49.

'Hello?'

'Mr Kendall?'

'Yes, hello . . .'

A light went on in the hall outside his room, bleeding through the gap beneath the door. 'Dad?'

'It's all right, Lauren. I've got it.'

'You okay, Dad?'

'Of course. I'm on the phone.'

'Detective Kendall?'

'Yes, who is this?'

'My name is Grant Oliver. You probably don't remember me but I was a constable at the time of the Allen case. I was involved in the search of the crime scene.'

'I remember you. It was your second week as a constable.'

'I'm a detective now, stationed at Observatory Hill. Something odd happened here tonight . . .'

Phillip Kendall swung his legs off the bed and sat upright in an effort to concentrate.

'I got your number from Vic Saunders at Central Division. I'm sorry to call so late, but I think I've seen one of them.'

'Seen one of who?'

'I think we've just had Daniel Simpson here in the station.'

Phillip Kendall got to his feet in the darkened room. He switched on the lamp and stood by the bed. 'What?'

'We were staking out a park toilet after a series of bashings. We busted two guys in a cubicle. The younger one turned out to have a fake ID – it looked like he was under age. We were holding the other one until we could check it out. Turns out the boy really was over sixteen, but the older one, there was something really familiar about him.'

Kendall fumbled in the bedside drawer for a pen. He clenched the phone under his chin and scrawled some notes on a paper napkin.

'While we were holding him, this guy seemed very nervous, almost agitated. After he was released I checked his prints on the database and came up with a match, but the file was blocked.'

The elderly detective stopped scrawling.

'I told my partner, who looked into it. An hour later he came back and told me the guy's prints were not a match to prints from the earlier attacks and to drop it. When I quizzed him he bit my head off.'

'Did you mention who you thought it was?'

'No, I hadn't made the connection then myself, but I couldn't stop thinking about where I'd seen him before and why his file would be protected.'

'You know how it works.'

'Even the ages add up.'

'What was he actually charged with?'

'Offensive behaviour.'

'The sex was consensual?'

'Apparently.'

'What is you want me to do? If it is him, his identity is protected, and for good reason.'

'He had a knife.'

'Did he threaten the boy?'

'No, the kid corroborated that.'

'Then I suppose it'll get dealt with by a magistrate. If it was Simpson his parole officer will get a full account.'

'You think so? Whoever he is, he's not accessible on the system.'

'People higher up will be taking care of it, Grant. He may be protected but he's also monitored. It may not even be him. I'll admit I've had moments myself where I second-guessed complete strangers of a certain age – I still have dreams about it, for Heaven's sake. The case left us all marked.'

'I just felt I knew him.'

'What makes you so sure?'

'While he was being fingerprinted I noticed his hands.'

'What about his hands?'

'They were sort of out of proportion, short heavy fingers, and the little finger was barely long enough to reach past the knuckle of the third finger.'

Phillip Kendall sat down on the edge of the mattress. Unconsciously he trailed his fingers along the shallow depression that had formed, over time, on his side of the double bed. 'Sometimes we just have to trust the system.' He picked up the pen and paper and slowly wrote a few more notes. He thanked Oliver for the information and restored the phone handset to its base, where it gave a series of beeps to show it was connected. Another of Lauren's 'improvements'.

He looked down at his upturned palms, remembering the hands of Danny Simpson, the small fat hands of a childish brute, hands that had obeyed their owner's command to inflict pain and kill. He remembered them all right.

Rachel, Friday, 3 September 1993

Rachel Allen slid across the sheets to make way for the little bundle of tawny brown arms and legs that had crawled under the quilt beside her. Benjamin squirmed into position, snuggling into his mother, bumping his head under her chin.

'Careful,' she whispered, stroking his sleep-matted hair and planting a soft kiss on his forehead. The smell of his head was always irresistible to her. Like a caramel-scented bird's nest, was the only way she could describe it. Mathew tugged at the quilt in an attempt to reclaim some. Rachel tucked her corner under her son; he was already fast asleep and softly snoring.

He did this every morning at five a.m., like clockwork. Mathew's mother said they should *set limits* but Rachel wasn't ready to give up the ritual. She enjoyed holding him close, feeling the warmth of his little body. She rested her cheek against his and drifted back to sleep.

An hour later the light touch of a finger tracing the contours of her face broke through the fog of her dreams. She opened her eyes to meet Benjamin's, big, wide and vivid blue. He deliberately fluttered his long black lashes against her cheek. She tickled his cheek with hers. He giggled and threw himself back onto the pillows.

'Daddy gone,' he said.

'Daddy's gone to work.' She tickled his ribs and little belly.

'Uh-oh!' His padded training pants felt damp. 'Did you wet your bed before you came in to Mummy?'

He stared innocently up at the ceiling.

'Never mind. Time to get up anyway.'

'No!' he squealed, crawling up the bed away from her.

His mother pulled on the patchwork quilt, slowly dragging him towards her. 'Got you now.' She scooped him up and carried him off to the bathroom.

Later, in the kitchen, Rachel made toast and tea. A shaft of sunlight cut through the amber liquid as she poured herself a cup. It was still only September. The nights had been cold, but mild days had stimulated the jasmine creeper outside the kitchen window into bloom. Perfume from a sprig of the tiny blue-pink and white flowers filled the room. When Rachel closed her eyes and took it in, she was reminded of long walks to school past the suburban gardens of this very street.

Benjamin appeared at the kitchen doorway in his singlet and underpants. He held out a pair of rust-brown corduroy trousers in one hand and a thick, apple-green roll-neck in the other. 'Cuppa tea,' he said, dropping the clothes onto a chair and climbing on top of them. He was fascinated by the tea-cosy his nana had made: yellow and black were the colours of his father's favourite football team, the Richmond Tigers. Benjamin liked to pat the fluffy pom-pom at the cosy's peak and to feel the warmth of the pot beneath.

'Be careful.' Rachel poured a small amount of tea into her son's little mug and filled it up with milk.

Benjamin knelt on the chair and rested his elbows on the table, holding the mug with both hands to drink his tea. 'Oooh, hot!' He pulled a face, then rubbed his hands up and down his exposed arms and shivered. 'Cold.'

Rachel laughed. 'Make up your mind.'

He was still shivering. 'Come here.' She opened the front of her fleecy dressing-gown. Benjamin scrambled across the chair beside him and climbed on board, hunkering down in her lap. She closed the robe around him and fastened it to his neck, so that only his little face protruded. He slipped his hands through the gap between the first and second buttons and reached for his mug.

He was such an easy child, Rachel thought, nearly always happy. She and Mathew had waited until she was twenty-eight to start the large family she had always planned. Mathew wanted to own their home so that Rachel could give up work for a few years at least. It had taken them more than five years to save the deposit for the cute cottage at the heart of the Terrace, a small warren of hilly streets lined with Victorian and Federation homes. The house was modest but it was a start. Mathew had completely renovated the kitchen, installing a dark green Aga he had bought from a demolition site. It had previously been used for storing old newspapers and magazines but was fully functional. Together they had done the place up, dedicating most of their weekends to stripping, sanding and painting. Mathew's house-painting partner Keith had helped him to build a third bedroom and a small deck at the back behind the kitchen.

Rachel had miscarried their first child after three months: a blighted ovum, the doctor had called it. She had been disappointed but not completely shattered. Her mother had given birth to four healthy children and her GP had told her there was nothing to prevent them from trying again.

Then Benjamin had come along, a perfect baby boy, after a wholly uneventful pregnancy. He would be three next month.

He took a bite from a slice of Vegemite toast, then wiped his hand on the front of his mother's dressing-gown.

'Okay, mister.' Rachel undid the buttons and her joey hopped out. 'Time to get dressed, Benji.' She stood behind him and held his trousers open for him to put them on, then stretched the skivvy over his head. 'Hands up.' She rolled the sleeves down over his extended arms.

Rachel Allen took Benjamin with her everywhere. Even though her mother, Barbara, lived in the next street and was quite willing to baby-sit, Rachel found it hard to leave him. All Benjamin had to do was slip an arm around her leg, look up with his enormous eyes and say, 'Mummy.'

Today they were going shopping in town with her sister Julia and her eighteen-month-old daughter, Lily. They had arranged to meet at the coffee shop near the fountain on the mezzanine level of the Regency Arcade Shopping Centre.

By the time Rachel Allen had found a convenient spot in the underground parking area, beneath the shopping centre, it was already eleven fifteen. She unclipped her seatbelt and got out, then opened the door to the back seat and reached in to release Benjamin. He swung his legs back and forth; one foot wore a sturdy shoe, the other only a blue sock, which had slipped down below the heel. '*Benjamin!* What happened to your shoe?'

Benjamin strained his neck to look down between the seats of the compact station-wagon as his mother stooped to find the shoe. 'Oh, for goodness' sake. We're already late.' She leant further in and ran her hand under the rear of the front seat, stretching as far as she could to grasp hold of an object she could feel with her fingertips.

'Bloody hell.'

'Rude, Mummy.'

'Got it.'

Once the shoe was on, she released him from the seat and stood him beside the car. As she pointed the remote at the car and locked it with a piercing beep, the toddler began to trot across the concrete landing towards the nearest entrance.

'Wait for Mummy!' She caught up to him and grabbed his hand. 'Put this on.' She draped a blue anorak around his shoulders and fed his arms into its sleeves. He set off again before she could take hold of the silver toggle and zip it.

His head was on a swivel as they rode the escalator to the upper floor, taking in the endless variety of shops, crammed with bicycles, toys, sports caps like Daddy's, the smell of doughnuts and hot chips, the lights reflected in the shining floor tiles, the brightly coloured words painted on windows and above doors, and the streams of people. Big fat mothers with prams and babies that cried, a little boy like him about to take the first lick of a blue ice cream. *Could ice cream be blue?* Pretty ladies reading magazines and drinking tea. Teenagers sitting on the benches outside the music shop smoking cigarettes.

'Ice cream, Mummy.'

'I scream, you scream, we all scream, "Ice cream!" Maybe later. Quick jump,' she said, lifting him up by the arm as they stepped off the vanishing escalator track.

She was anxious about being late: usually she would have picked up her sister, Julia, and they'd have come together in the one car, but Julia had to be home early to prepare for a lingerie party she was throwing that evening. Rachel might go along if Mathew wasn't too tired and felt up to bathing Benjamin and putting him to bed. Well, that was the fantasy. More likely she would come home to find Benjamin sleeping in his day clothes and an exhausted Mathew flaked out on the couch.

Julia and Lily weren't at the tables outside the coffee shop, or inside. Rachel was about to ask at the counter when Benjamin spotted them browsing in the discount clothing store opposite. 'Look . . . Uli!' He pointed in the direction of his favourite aunt. Across the busy mall, in the doorway of Best and Lest, Julia saw her sister and waved.

Lily was installed in a luxurious padded pushchair, a row of plump fairies strung in front of her. When she saw Benjamin she gurgled an approximation of his name.

Benjamin pushed Lily round the clothes racks while Julia and Rachel rummaged through a sale table of baby clothes: Julia was expecting her second child in six months.

In Ladies Wear the women attempted to try on some dresses but it was hopeless: Lily cried every time her mother disappeared behind the changing-room curtain and Benjamin rushed in and out of the cubicles, bursting in on strangers.

The children played well together in the toy corner of Marty's Hairbiz while the sisters had their long dark hair streaked – *4 foils, any colour, 12 dollars.*

As Rachel and Julia said goodbye to each other at the top of the escalators, Benjamin's attention was captured by the rhythmic bouncing of a large multi-coloured super ball. The dense acrylic sphere sprang high into the air as its downward momentum was checked by the hard terrazzo floor. He watched, mesmerized, as a boy in a yellow hooded jacket caught the ball on its upward trajectory, then sent it slamming back to the floor. Another boy sat on the bench beside the first, eating a burger and watching Benjamin intently as he chewed. *Boing, boing* . . . Up and down went the ball.

'Benjamin,' called his mother. He turned as she took his hand.

'Say goodbye to Lily.'

'Bye.' He opened and shut the fingers of one hand. He looked over his shoulder for the boys with the ball, but they had vanished.

Benjamin began to grow restless as they waited in line at the Medicare office. He played with the rope railings until two fell over. He was tired and bored now. He wanted to go home. Rachel didn't get angry with him: she could remember her frustration as a little girl on the long walk home from town with her mother. How desolate she was when her mother's hands were full of groceries and couldn't hold hers. 'Not long now,' her mother would say.

'Not long now,' she said stroking his head.

'Pusscat,' he said, referring to the cover of a picture book on a stand outside the newsagent's.

'Would you like that?' said his mother. She lifted it out of the slot and put it into his hands. He gripped it tightly and nodded. 'Just let me pay for it.' She took the book back from him and put it on the counter.

Benjamin watched the book disappear into adult hands. It was still a mystery to him how Mummy could pay for things and make them his. He didn't fully understand why, but he was beginning to realize that you had to be 'good' to get what you wanted.

'You can read it with Daddy tonight.'

In the fish shop Benjamin stood corralled behind his mother, carrying his new book. Between the legs of the customers around her, he saw the boy in the yellow jacket through the window, making funny faces with his nose pressed against the glass.

'Thirteen ninety,' said the fishmonger, wrapping some ice with the order.

Rachel Allen let go of her son's hand for just long enough to open her purse and collect the parcel from the countertop. The feel of Benjamin's little fingers slipping from hers would be her last memory of her son.

When she turned around he was gone. Only the picture book remained, discarded on the cold marble floor.

Danny and Graham, Friday, 3 September 1993, 6.30 p.m.

They were in a hurry now to get home, to place themselves elsewhere, away from the deed. To paint the lie. Suddenly Graham was an eleven-year-old boy again, acting like a six- or seven-year-old, tearful, panicked and anxious, blaming it all on Danny, as if Danny had lured him into yet another misdemeanour that might get him into trouble.

'What if somebody saw us in town with the baby?'

'Shut up! We never went to town.'

The deed was done and, unlike Graham, Danny was not about to give himself away by wetting his pants.

'What if they find out we were at the Regency?'

'Listen, you fuckhead,' said Danny, gripping Graham's arm. 'We never went to town. We bought some lollies at the shop near school, remember? And we hung around the football fields and smoked some cigarettes and went back to your house. Then we walked over to Westside to get a takeaway.'

'You won't tell them I did it, will you?' pleaded Graham.

Danny wanted to kill him, wished he had killed him instead of the boy.

Graham began to cry.

Danny stared him down. In Danny's universe, if you got copped for something, you didn't go crying like a baby, you toughed it out, no matter how scared you were, no matter what 'they' did to you. He stopped outside the take-away next door to the Westside bowling alley and emptied his pockets of coins. 'Four bucks. Give me what you got.'

Graham felt in his pockets and found another three dollars. Together they went inside and ordered two large portions of chips. The unsmiling proprietor watched impatiently as Danny counted out the change. The shop was getting busy and several people pushed past the two boys as they waited for their order. Graham sat nervously jiggling one leg up and down, while Danny made faces and played peekaboo with a little girl as she sat on the counter. She buried her face in her mother's shoulder, then peeked out again. The woman turned to see the boy in the red windcheater pulling funny faces.

Back outside, under a streetlight, Danny shoved a parcel of warm chips into Graham's chest. 'Take these and go home. Your mum'll be out lookin' for you if you don't hurry up.' Graham held the chips and stared mutely at Danny. 'Just keep your mouth shut. Don't say nothin' about nothin'.' He reached over and tore open the end of Graham's parcel. 'And fucken eat some on the way or she'll be wondering why you bought them.' He ripped open the other package, pulled out a steaming chip and put it into his mouth.

'She hates it when I ruin my dinner,' said Graham.

Danny studied him while he chewed cautiously – the chip was still hot. 'It'll give her something to go on about then, won't it?'

The two boys held each other's gaze briefly, then walked away in opposite directions.

Mathew, Friday, 3 September 1993, 10 p.m.

Oblivious to the sting of the frigid air on his skin, Mathew Allen walked steadily through the dark ahead of a team of searchers, who began to fan out along the grid of lanes that bordered the shopping precinct. He turned up an unlit alley, moving the beam of his torch along the perimeter, over the mildewed brickwork. The light travelled upwards crawling into recesses and crevices, bouncing off broken glass and spilling through cracked panes into the forbidding blackness of a fathomless warehouse.

'Benjamin!' called a chorus of voices behind him. He shone the torch down at the heavy grille of a storm drain and tested the size of the opening with the toe of his shoe before he was satisfied. Others created a beacon of light while he scaled the side of a skip, flooding its interior with illumination as he looked down, petrified, at the refuse bags and empty cartons.

On and on they trudged through the bitter night, across soccer fields, industrial parks and subdivisions, along riverbanks and railway lines, scouring bins, bus shelters, water tanks, toilet blocks and schoolyards, anywhere a toddler might be trapped or hidden.

'Hello!' he called, picking his way through a group of sleeping derelicts at the rear of the Salvation Army depot. 'Has anyone seen a small boy, a three-year-old?'

A man grunted and rolled over.

'No kids here this time of night,' said another, sitting up and watching the activity with interest.

'How long's he been missing?'

'Several hours,' offered a volunteer.

A taxi entered the depot to execute a U-turn. Hailed by one of the group, it came towards them. 'Can you get on your radio and ask around about a missing boy, three years old?'

'We heard, mate. Cabbies are on the lookout.'

'Someone should get a ride to the police station and come back to us with an update,' said Mathew.

'And coffee,' called Mathew's brother, Ewan.

'And more batteries,' added a voice.

The brothers separated from the others, covering the territory behind the enormous car park adjoining the City Stadium. Eerily lit by rows of overhead lights, the empty car park held few hiding places but every shadow needed to be eliminated. Mathew's torch was flickering – he loaded it with fresh batteries from his overall pocket, while he walked slowly towards the automated ticket dispenser. The stronger beam revealing nothing but asphalt and cement. He turned and looked back at the distant lights of the Regency Arcade Shopping Centre. Inside, Rachel would be searching with security guards and detectives in the desperate hope that Benjamin might still be found there, hiding in one of the closed stores or perhaps returned by someone who had found him wandering nearby. It was two a.m. He had been missing for nearly nine hours.

The stricken father stared up into the blackness, a mist of rain collecting on the hairs of his exposed forearms.

His son was out there somewhere, in the cold and the wet, terrified and lost, or worse. He couldn't bear to think of him lying hurt, calling for his parents. 'God! *Please* bring him back to us. Please, God, don't let anyone hurt him.'

Detective Kendall, Friday, 3 September 1993, 10.30 p.m.

The team of detectives huddled around the video console in the Regency Arcade's CCTV control room, where they had gathered to review all footage recorded that day throughout the centre. Starting with tapes that covered the hour surrounding Benjamin's disappearance, the officers scanned each passing frame, searching the jumpy footage for the Allens – or potential predators.

'*There!* Top right corner, just coming into the ground-floor level,' called a young man, touching his finger to the screen. The paused image shuddered as he traced the outline of a small child in a dark anorak, walking alongside a slender woman in jeans and a light pullover. The pair appeared throughout the subsequent footage at various points along the route Phillip Kendall had plotted earlier, in his walkthrough with the distraught mother. He circled the exact locations on the centre's floorplan and flipped the lid on his takeaway, wolfing down a few mouthfuls while another cassette was inserted.

Several minutes into the new tape, uploaded from a central camera point, Benjamin Allen finally reappeared.

'Hold it there.' Kendall noted the time signature: 4:41 p.m. 'Play it,' he said, folding his arms and leaning forward as he studied the ghost-like image. He found it hard to believe what he was seeing. There on the screen an indistinct little figure, wearing trousers and a jacket, with what looked like two older boys. One held the child's hand and led him forward, the other stood rear guard, off to one side – occasionally obscuring the toddler's outline.

At Kendall's request the footage was replayed. He watched closely as Benjamin was led towards the exit and out of video range. *Why would two children take another child?* His fellow officers shared his disbelief, silently floored as they realized they were not looking for an adult paedophile but for two young boys, mere children themselves.

Rachel and Mathew, Saturday, 4 September 1993

They sat motionless on the tartan settee in their modest living room, watching in numb disbelief as a headshot of their only child's smiling face filled the television screen. A crumpled copy of the *Herald* lay on the couch between them. Above a grainy enlargement of a squat figure in an Adidas pullover, and a taller child in a hooded jacket, who held the hand of a toddler, the headline screamed, 'WANTED.' Below the photo a second headline asked, 'DO YOU KNOW THESE BOYS?' The images were so indistinct that they might have featured almost any neighbourhood kids from eight to fourteen. The newsreader called for information from 'anyone who saw Benjamin Allen at the Regency Arcade Shopping Centre yesterday, or in the surrounding districts'. Overnight, pictures taken from the CCTV footage had been broadcast on all the local and national TV networks and ultimately beamed across the world.

By the time Phillip Kendall arrived at the Allen house, hundreds of phone calls had been logged: neighbours reporting troublesome kids, shopkeepers providing descriptions of regular truants, several mothers even suspecting their own sons. When Rachel's sister Julia ushered him into the room, the detective sat down opposite the couple. As he politely declined a cup of tea, Rachel searched his face for information, simultaneously willing him not to speak. She looked away.

'We don't know anything new,' he said.

Rachel began to sob.

'We've received dozens of calls, and we're taking them all seriously.'

Mathew reached over and held his wife's hand.

'Several people claim to have seen Benjamin in the network of streets between the Regency Arcade and Battery Cove. We have intensified our search. Dozens of officers are out interviewing residents in the area.'

'Was he all right? Did they say if he was hurt?' asked Mathew.

'Witnesses report seeing him in the company of two older boys. Descriptions vary, but there is no point reading too much into any one statement until we have carefully checked each one.'

'What about these boys? Doesn't anyone know them?'

Rachel wiped her eyes and waited for the answer to her husband's question.

'We've had hundreds of calls from people who believe they do. I'm waiting on a comprehensive list of absentees from all the schools in the greater Henswick area. We'll check every one.'

'We're going insane here!' cried Rachel.

Kendall nodded sympathetically. 'At this point we need you to stay at home. As difficult as it sounds, you should get some sleep.'

'We can't just wait here!'

'If you think of anything that might help or you need to talk to a member of my team at any time . . .' He handed Mathew a card listing phone numbers, the same card he had given the couple a few hours earlier when he had delivered them home. 'A direct appeal to the public is something you need to consider.'

Rachel Allen buried her head under her husband's arm and began to cry.

Phillip Kendall saw himself out and noted the collection of framed family snapshots that lined the canary-yellow hallway. As the hours passed it became less and less likely that the children who had taken Benjamin were acting alone. His heart felt heavy with dread at the prospects for a defenceless toddler who had been delivered into the hands of persons unknown.

Detective Kendall, Sunday, 5 September 1993

The Central District police station was buzzing with activity. In the austere conference room a long bank of tables flanked the wall. A battery of policemen and -women answered the incoming telephone calls, furiously recording information on the printed forms in front of them. Two detectives studied and correlated details from the constables' notes, then passed them to a typist for transcribing.

Out in the hallway Phillip Kendall spoke quietly to Rachel Allen about a televised appeal to the public. A fair-haired female detective handed him a lengthy faxed document. It was a list of absentees from every school in the district on Friday, 3 September. A male officer appeared at the doorway of the conference room and passed him a sheet of paper, an update of reports from the public. Phillip Kendall scanned the list of locations and sightings. He noted the names provided by callers who claimed to know the identity of the two boys in the pictures.

'What is it?' asked Rachel.

'More information from the public that needs verifying.' He turned to the blonde detective, who still waited patiently. 'Roslyn, if you could sit with Mrs Allen for a while and take her through what she should say in her appeal, I'll go and make a few phone calls. Maybe get her some lunch.'

'I don't want anything to eat.'

'Or a cup of tea.' A mobile phone rang. Kendall apologized as he reached inside his suit jacket and retrieved the bulky article from its holster. He excused himself with a nod and turned away to take the call.

Rachel looked off into the distance as Detective Roslyn Teagues began to repeat the likely procedure for any televised appeal. At the end of the hallway, near the head of the stairs, a knot of people had formed around three uniformed officers who had just entered the building.

'I'll be there in five minutes,' said Kendall, and returned his phone to his belt. He registered the scene at the end of the hallway immediately. He shot a look at his female colleague and gestured with an inclination of his head towards the doorway of a nearby room.

'Perhaps we can go in here and get a cup of tea,' suggested Roslyn.

Rachel glanced at her, then up the hall at the advancing contingent of police. 'What's going on?' she asked.

Kendall walked away from her towards the group, then ushered his team into his office and closed the door.

'What was all that about?' said Rachel, standing up.

'I don't know. It may not be about Benjamin.'

'They've found him!' she cried. 'They've found him.'

Several seconds passed before Phillip Kendall emerged from his office and walked back up the hall. His mind involuntarily counted off the steps: thirteen. It was one of the longest journeys of his life.

Christine Harris, Sunday, 5 September 1993, 5 p.m.

She peered again at the blurred photograph of the two boys on the news-stand. A draught chilled the back of her neck as she pumped several litres of petrol into her car. She had seen the same picture on the news last night. The more she looked at it, the more she became convinced that the Adidas windcheater was the same as one she had bought Graham a few months ago. He had lent it to Danny Simpson when he had stayed over and, typically, he had never given it back. There were probably lots of striped Adidas windcheaters out there, but Danny Simpson was a little shit for sure.

'Oh!' Christine stepped back to avoid the drops of petrol spilling out from the nozzle onto her new shoes. 'For God's sake.' A light drizzle irritated her face as she ran towards the petrol station's kiosk. Inside she picked up a copy of the *Evening Sun* and paid for it, along with her fuel. Thank God Graham wasn't hanging around with that Simpson kid any more – not since she had found cigarette butts in the backyard and Graham had confessed that Danny had tried to make him smoke one. She had soon put a stop to that.

She drove as far as the next set of traffic lights, then pulled over. Up ahead there was a small shopping plaza and a single payphone. She slipped the folded newspaper under her arm and stepped out into the downpour. In the booth her breath condensed on the cold glass. She turned the soggy front page of the paper and dialled the Benjamin Allen hotline number. 'The boy in the Adidas windcheater looks like Danny Simpson, a local trouble-maker if ever there was one.'

'Do you know his address?'

'He lives on the Sunnybank Housing Commission estate.' She hung up. It did not occur to her that the taller boy in the picture, hiding under his heavy jacket, was her own son.

Ewan Allen, Sunday, 5 September 1993, 8 p.m.

Clutching the cracked army-belt at the waistband of his work shorts, knees trembling, Ewan Allen stepped back from the mobile gurney as a sheet was reverently peeled away by a pale-faced officer. The shrouded form in front of him was barely recognizable as the body of his tiny nephew, or as that of any of other child, for that matter. It was the small feet, delicate and intact, one bare, the other still encased in its miniature shoe and bloodied sock that destroyed him: the contrast between the merciless cruelty that had rained down on the tiny body and the footwear placed where a loving mother had put them, never knowing she was dressing her child for the last time.

He could not fit the scene before him into his conscious mind. He concentrated only on the foot and the thought that Mathew and Rachel must never see the body, and prayed that one day he, too, might be able to remember Benjamin as he was before.

Danny, Monday, 6 September 1993, 9.02 a.m.

A thickening crowd gathered outside the Regency Arcade Shopping Centre where, overnight, an impromptu memorial had sprung up at the western entrance. Appalled residents had deposited bunches of flowers, soft toys and messages of grief and condolence. In an act of morbid curiosity, Danny had taken a ragged teddy bear from the wreckage in his toy box and brought it to place among the other tributes. It appeared that half of Henswick was wandering about in a state of shock. And there, among them, mingling with the crowd, was a pudgy-faced eleven-year-old boy on his roundabout way to school.

Rachel and Mathew, 16 September 1993

The broken couple stumbled through the arrangements for their son's funeral like sleepwalkers. The scale of their pain was so great they were almost beyond feeling it. Hundreds of people from the local community attended the service, many of whom they did not know. When his father and uncles carried Benjamin's tiny white coffin from the chapel, a featherweight on their shoulders, Rachel could barely stand. Mathew remained upright, stoical throughout.

Returning to the little house in the Terrace without him had been the moment of reckoning. The house was unbearably still and silent. A red plastic tricycle was parked where Benjamin had left it under the phone table in the hall. Recollections of joy, of what had been stolen from them, were nearly as cruel as the knowledge of what they had been unable to protect him from. Hardest of all was the abrupt severing of the future, the annihilation of every hope and dream they had once shared.

On the first night, after they had told Rachel her baby was dead, she had gone to his room, and curled up across his empty bed, cradling his pillow to her chest. As she breathed in his smell she had willed herself to imagine that it wasn't true, that the nightmare hadn't happened, that Benjamin had wandered off and given them all a terrible fright, but now he was safe in her arms, his head under her chin.

Now, as she moved about the house in a daze, every room held something of Benjamin, frozen moments of his life. His striped pyjama bottoms stuffed into the laundry hamper. An opened fruit yoghurt in the fridge, with the spoon sticking out. Everything reminded her that his life had stopped for ever. In the yard one of his red T-shirts flapped on a pole above the timber fort. Mathew had built the tree house last

Christmas, with Benjamin shadowing his every move. A tin of coloured markers still lay open on the play desk in the sunroom. The drawing next to it was a mass of circular orange scribbles above four furry black legs. And there was the orange marker, abandoned without its lid when Benjamin's attention had moved to something else. She picked it up. The tip was bone dry – he was always leaving the tops off. There it was, under the table. As she knelt down to retrieve it from the litter of picture books and toys, something gave way inside her and she clutched the pen to her breast and wept uncontrollably. The nightmare was the reality.

Names

'Whose names are not written'

Detective Kendall, 2008

Lauren tiptoed barefoot down the hall. When she quietly pushed open the door to her father's room, the bed was empty. She eventually found him sitting on a bench beside his vegetable patch in the back garden, staring into the distance, apparently meditating on the worn timber sleepers that edged the path. His face was drained of colour and his lips were almost blue.

'What's wrong, Dad?'

He coughed into his handkerchief. 'A rough night . . . I'm just a bit tired that's all.'

She returned a few minutes later with a tray holding a pot of tea and a copy of the *Sunday Globe*. She held out a cup.

'Not now, I just want to sit here for a while. I'll be in in a minute.' Reluctantly she left him alone.

A squadron of white moths appeared, flitting among the silver beet leaves and dropping their eggs onto the budding heads of the young broccoli. He hadn't dusted it for weeks and couldn't raise the enthusiasm to shoo them away now. He watched indifferently, feeling desperately useless, already gone from the world.

He looked at the newspaper on the tray beside him, unfolded it and scanned the headlines. 'MEDIA MAGNATE MOURNED'. He allowed himself a little laugh. 'RACE FIX EXPOSED'. In the features bar at the top of the page he saw the small printed image of a familiar face. 'IDENTITY THEFT. Is Cyberspace Safe? Part II by Alex Reiser.'

A flare of hope lit inside him as he remembered the bombastic journalist who had reported on the Allen case. Despite Kendall's deep-rooted professionalism, Reiser had become almost a friend after earning his respect with his incisive coverage of the case. With so much vitriol written about it, he had been the first to question the culpability of a society that had spawned a pair of children so desensitized that they could imagine, let alone carry out, such a brutal killing.

His investigation into the backgrounds of Harris and Simpson had pulled no punches. His arguments for social influences were persuasive, even to those involved with the case, but when Kendall had looked into the eyes of Danny Simpson, as his lips had formed the lies conceived to save him from punishment for his crime, he could not help but see a purer form of evil, one that took pleasure in causing harm and deceiving others. He could not find it in himself to compare the two psychologically deformed children with other socially deprived delinquents. He didn't want to: he had seen at first-hand exactly what they were capable of.

As his body began to fail and death drew nearer, it gave Kendall comfort to tie off the details of his life, signing his property over to his daughter, finalizing his will, and shredding years of case notes and papers. It was hard for Lauren to watch as he sat at his desk in the sunroom, using what energy he had left to jot farewell notes to friends, each including some memory or shared joke. He shook his wrist to revive the blood flow and finished off one last note. He added it to the top of his pile. Then, as an afterthought, he took another sheet of paper and copied down some names from his Teledex. He slipped the list inside one of the folded letters and put his pen aside.

'I have to go, Dad,' said Lauren, coming into the room. 'I'll be back at six.' She kissed his forehead. 'I've got the mobile.'

'Of course you have.'

'You should lie down.'

'I will.'

He observed her through the window, pulling the bins onto the street before getting into her car. He felt a trace of guilt that the prospect of leaving her alone in the world bothered him much less than he would once have imagined. She was strong and loving. She would always make the best of things, and financially she would never have to worry – he had seen to that. There were far worse things for a parent than to predecease his child.

Catherine, 2008

Standing at a bank of payphones outside the Avondale Street post office, Catherine addressed a bundle of stamped A4 envelopes: Glasgow and West Scotland Family History Society, Glasgow Genealogical Society, Glasgow City Archives, Births, Marriages and Deaths. That done, she turned her attention to the pile of regional phone directories stacked on the adjacent counter. She dug through the tattered pile, extracted one and let it flop open. She found the Ds and began searching for 'Douglass'. Her eyes followed her index finger as it travelled rapidly down the lists. There were hundreds of Douglases with one *s* but only fifty-odd with two. Five of those were J. Douglasses. Her finger stopped below 'Douglass, J. S., 3/12 Windsor Rd, Richmond'. She picked up the handset, her heartbeat accelerating as she dialled the number.

'Is that John Scott Douglass?'

'Who's this?'

'My name's Catherine Douglass. I'm trying to locate my husband's father.'

'I don't know who you're talking about, love.'

'I'm trying to locate John Douglass, John Scott Douglass. My husband's name is Liam.'

'You've got the wrong number.'

'Do you know of another John Douglass?'

'Double s?'

'Yeah, they lived in the Richmond area about ten years ago.'

'That's a while back. Look, I've never heard of a Liam Douglass, not in our family. It's a common enough name.'

'Thanks anyway. I'll keep looking. Sorry to have bothered you.'

Catherine felt suddenly silly. Liam's father could be anywhere, and if he was as big a no-hoper as Liam said he was, then he probably wouldn't welcome being found. For all she knew the unforthcoming John Douglass she had just spoken to might have been Liam's father. She only had his word for it that he wasn't. She looked at her watch. Her amateur-detective efforts had not only made her feel foolish but now she was in danger of being late for her doctor's appointment in the city.

She gathered up the labelled envelopes and took them to the bottom of the ramp, opened the drawer on the red mailbox and dropped them inside. With any luck she would soon know more about the Scottish side of the family.

A light rain began to fall as she drove across the Argyle Street bridge. She turned the wipers on and strained to see the car ahead through the grey-white slurry on the unwashed windscreen. She felt instantly irritated with Liam. Why didn't he take care of the little things any more? Since she'd fallen pregnant she'd felt that she was nursing his sensibilities rather than the other way around. She pulled the wiper lever forward and a jet of water squirted onto the windscreen. The wiper blades sloughed it away.

Traffic in Carlyle Street was thick. Cars crawled along through the now-heavy rain. She scanned the street for available parking but all the spaces were taken. She turned left towards the Macquarie Business Centre. The traffic came to a standstill as a stream of pedestrians entered the crossing. Catherine rubbed at the condensation now forming on the windscreen with the end of her sleeve. Through a clear patch of glass she thought she saw a familiar face. *Was that Liam?* He was seated near the window in the café opposite. The face turned away. She rubbed at the glass again. The man turned back. It was Liam all right, sipping coffee and talking to someone she couldn't see. Probably a client. She grabbed her mobile and fast-dialled his number, smiling at the joke she was about to play, but when she saw Liam pick up his phone, look at it and switch it off, the smile vanished. A car horn sounded behind her; she saw through the windscreen that the road ahead was clear. Reluctantly she pulled away.

A few minutes later, as the doctor palpated her abdomen, her mind was elsewhere. He wrote notes in her file and listened carefully to the foetal heartbeat. The stethoscope was cold as it pressed against her stomach. The baby gave a little kick of protest. 'Someone's getting plenty of exercise,' said the doctor.

She pulled up her maternity jeans and buttoned her cotton blouse. Liam had probably been in the middle of an important conversation, she told herself. But what was so important? They both constantly answered mobile enquiries while they did other business. He had seen her number come up and he had blocked her call. So what? He was in the middle of something. She would just have to stop being stupid and ask him.

In the busy food hall, she browsed the counters of fresh noodles, sushi and pressed meats, and picked out a selection of cheeses and antipasti. As she stowed the bags of food on the back seat of her car, she remembered Liam's dry-cleaning and rushed back into the shopping centre. The proprietor was reaching to pull down the shutters when Catherine appeared, waving her ticket. He cheerfully slid hangers across a long rack until his hand found a jacket with the corresponding number.

On the drive home the stale-chemical odour of the dry-cleaned jacket and the cloying smell of warm shallots rising from the back seat combined to make her feel mildly ill. When she pulled into the driveway at home, Liam's green BMW was already parked on the verge.

She got out of the car, opened the rear door, gathered the few bags and reached across for the jacket. As she pulled it towards her, holding it through the flimsy plastic, it slipped from its hanger. She gathered it up under her free arm and kicked the door shut. Inside she dumped the load on the kitchen bench. Liam's keys were in the fruit-bowl. Strains of the instrumental guitar music he liked so much wafted into the kitchen from the front room.

'Liam?' Catherine took hold of the crumpled jacket and flicked it out flat onto the counter. As she did so a tiny yellow square of paper fell out. She picked it up and carefully unfolded it. Written on the inside of the Post-it note was what looked like an email address. It had been scribbled out with several lines of dark blue ink. Hotmail. com could still be clearly seen, and she could easily make out @. She held the scrap of paper up to the light and was able to read 'She', preceded by xX. 'xXShe@hotmail. com': that was it. Puzzled, she refolded the paper and slipped it into the pocket of her jeans.

Carrying the jacket with her, she climbed the stairs to the first landing and opened the bedroom door. Liam sat in front of his computer with his back to the door, typing.

'Hi!'

He jumped. He hadn't heard her come in. 'Scared the hell out of me,' he said, recovering. 'I'm trying to get this paperwork out of the way before your parents get here.' He clicked a button and stood up.

Catherine's eyes involuntarily scanned the screen and saw only an innocuous set of property listings that he was apparently compiling. 'I called you this afternoon,' she blurted out.

'Yeah, I know.'

Catherine felt herself relax. For some reason she had been afraid he would deny having seen her number come up.

'I couldn't pick up because I was in the office with John and he was in full flight about the new advertorial deal he wants to run in the *Advocate*.'

She watched his lips move as he elaborated on the lie. The saliva in her mouth dried and acid trickled into her stomach. It already seemed too late to cry, 'But I saw you! Why would you lie?'

Something stopped her speaking. She wanted to know what had he really been writing on the computer when she came in.

'What are we feeding them?'

'Who?'

'Your parents.'

Catherine's hand slipped into her pocket and closed around the folded paper square. Who was 'xXShe'? 'I thought we'd just have a platter. I bought some cheeses and other stuff. Maybe you could go and get a good bottle of wine.'

In the time that it took Liam to drive to the nearest store and buy two bottles of decent Shiraz, Catherine arranged the cheeses, olives, stuffed vine leaves, marinated vegetables and salads on a large oval platter and covered it with plastic wrap. She then went to Liam's computer, which was still running, and clicked the space bar: the screensaver of flying shapes shattered like a pane of coloured glass to reveal the real-estate listings he had been working on. She wasn't sure what she was looking for, but she was convinced that Liam had been working on something else when she had come into the room. Maybe she was being an idiot. But why had he lied to her? She remembered the email address and took it out of her pocket.

She reduced Liam's document and clicked the internal email icon on the screen. She scanned the lists of received mail for 'xXShe' but found nothing; she checked the deleted files and file drafts. She closed the program, opened the Start menu and Search. She glanced at the paper and typed the letters into the search line. The computer began to sift through all the data in the hard drive, searching for documents that contained the same phrase. The search-in-progress meter flickered on the screen. 'Come on!' Liam would be back soon. A file listing 'xXShe' appeared in the results window. She double-clicked the listing. A Word document located in a sub-file of his 'My Documents' folder.

Dear M

Being able to talk to you helps. Baby changes everything – have to be so much more careful. Can never tell C. June meeting impossible. Get back to you when I can.

xYHim

Catherine tried to digest the message. 'Can never tell C'; 'be so much more careful'; 'Baby changes everything.' My God! No wonder he didn't want a baby. Catherine blinked away hot tears. She opened the file menu and checked the properties of the unfinished document. 'Created: 13 May 2008 4.02 p.m.' It was not what he had been writing before she had come in, but it was enough to confirm her growing suspicions.

A car door slammed outside. She closed the program, leaving only Liam's opened property listings on the screen.

When Liam came through the door carrying the wine, she was setting the table with four places. She watched him open a bottle, winding the screw all the way through the cork, concentrating as he pressed down on the little arms, and withdrawing it with a soft plop, then setting it aside to breathe, just like she had taught him. She was amazed at the charade, the way he appeared to stumble inconspicuously through life, following the map she had given him. Could Liam, unassuming, unworldly Liam, have a secret life? She couldn't quite wrap her head around it. Liam was supposed to be her creation.

'You want me to do that?' he asked, taking the cutlery from her.

She looked at the wine standing on the shelf above the fridge, its gold and maroon label, the florid copper-plate lettering 'Yalumba Family Reserve Shiraz'. 'That's a pretty good wine, isn't it?'

'It was on special for nineteen dollars.'

'How did you know it was any good?'

'You always ask for Merlot, Shiraz or Cabernet.'

'You've never tasted it yourself?'

He looked at her incredulously. 'I don't drink, remember?'

'No, of course you don't.'

'What? You think I have a few drinks on the side, do you?'

'No. I just wouldn't presume to know everything about you.'

Liam had no idea where any of this was coming from.

'You're such a quick study really, aren't you, Liam? I suppose anybody you know could have ordered that wine and you'd have filed it away as a recommendation.'

'Look, the bloke at the bottle shop said it was excellent. If you want something different I'll go and get another one. Just tell me.'

Catherine felt close to hysteria. She didn't want to reveal her hand but she couldn't stop herself pushing the issue. 'You were having coffee with someone in Macquarie Street today.'

'So what?' Despite the dismissive words, he looked alarmed.

'I called you from the car, on your mobile, Liam. I was driving past. I saw you pick it up and turn it off!'

'I was with a client.'

'You said you were with John. Remember? Why would you lie?'

Liam didn't speak. His mind was working hard, trying to untangle the threads.

'You lied because you had something to hide and you didn't know I saw you.'

'What? Are you following me now?'

'Who's the client, Liam?'

Liam sighed. 'Look, I wasn't with a client. I met my counsellor there.'

'Your counsellor? You expect me to believe that? Why would you meet your counsellor in a coffee shop?'

'I was having a bad day.'

'A bad day?' She opened her eyes wide and pulled a forced smile. 'Oh, and by the way, Liam . . .' She reached into her pocket and pulled out the yellow square. 'You left this in your jacket.'

Liam looked at the scrawl on the paper. His eyes narrowed as he tried to read the words.

'xXShe. Who's that, Liam?'

Liam shook his head. 'I don't know, it doesn't ring a bell, maybe a contact . . .'

Catherine threw the note at him and laughed. 'Surely you remember who "She" is? Talking to her makes you feel so much better. Of course, the baby changes everything, doesn't it?' Catherine's voice became high and thin. 'You'll never be able to tell Catherine now!' The blood drained from Liam's face. 'Tell me what, Liam? That you're a fucking fraud? A complete fucking impostor. Who were you with today?'

'I told you. I was with my counsellor.'

'What is it that you'll never be able to tell me, Liam?' she cried, striking him in the chest with her open hand.

He looked at her distorted face as she pleaded to know the answer. 'Tell me!'

'The counsellor and I, she . . .' Liam was groping for words. 'We've been s-s-seeing each other.'

'What?'

'I didn't want to tell you. I tried to end it today. That's who "She" is. That's who I was writing to.'

'What are you talking about?' Catherine grabbed hold of his shirt and began striking him with her fists. 'What are you fucking saying? You fucking bastard, Liam. What the hell are you talking about? I'm having a fucking baby, for God's sake.' She began to sob.

'I know, and that's why I was trying to end it – before things went too far . . . We never slept together – you have to believe me . . .'

'Believe you?' Catherine slumped into a chair at the table. 'I'll never believe a word you say again.' Liam tried to put a hand on her shoulder but she wrenched her body violently away.

'I'm sorry. I'll never see her again. I'll get another counsellor.'

Catherine turned and looked at him with wild eyes.

The phone rang. Liam went to the kitchen and answered it. Catherine pulled several paper towels in a row from a dispenser and wiped her face. 'All right, we'll see you soon.' He hung up. 'Your parents, they're going to be late.'

Catherine didn't answer or even look in his direction. She left the room and walked up the stairs to the bedroom. He followed as far as the landing and saw through the open door that she was packing a small suitcase. He watched as she folded a pair of white linen trousers and added them to an orderly pile. He wanted to take hold of her and tell her it was all a lie, that there was no one else, but how could he do that without offering her the truth? *The whole truth and nothing but the truth.* That he had spent the morning with his parole officer, as he was required to do once a month for the rest of his life. That 'She' was not his secret lover but the woman who had given birth to him, his real mother. That his whole life story was a pack of lies, lies told by the minute, every hour of every day, an elaborate invention of mundane fabrications, constructed to hide a single deed that would never be erased, no matter how deeply it was buried.

Catherine zipped the suitcase shut and heaved it off the bed. She carried it to the head of the stairs.

'Catherine?' He tried to take the suitcase from her. She stared at him for several moments before pushing past. 'Catherine,' he pleaded. 'What about your parents?'

She gave a hollow laugh. 'Where do you think I'm going?'

He sat on the steps as she opened the front door and disappeared.

Alex Reiser, 2008

The coffin lay at the front of the small Edwardian funeral chapel, raised on a grey and white marble platform. A single spray of wattle decorated the simple mahogany casket. An elderly Uniting Church minister stood behind a plain white lectern. He spoke in a quavering voice about God's higher purpose and how he beckoned some to a special calling. He read briefly from the Bible in his hands: '"I am the resurrection and the life. He who believes in me, though he may die, he shall live."'

The mourners in the packed chapel sat in respectful silence. Despite her firm promise to her father, Lauren Kendall began to cry. At last he was at rest, liberated from his pain-racked body, but in a world without his gently guiding light she felt suddenly bereft.

Alex Reiser sat to her left, his long legs uncomfortably folded under the narrow wooden pew. He touched her shoulder. The stoical but sympathetic look on his unshaven face reminded her that her father would not want her to weep for him any more than he had wanted the police funeral he was entitled to. She had dutifully fulfilled this last request but it hadn't stopped them coming. The front row of the chapel was full of dark-suited men who bent their heads low in honour of their calm, compassionate colleague.

Outside in the street a group of uniformed men and women, hats off, were clustered around the chapel's entrance. As the coffin was carried outside, by steady hands, into the harsh sunlight and lifted into the back of the waiting hearse, the voice of Maria Callas singing 'La Mamma Morta' floated out to them from the chapel.

Lauren held her head high, determined not to cry again. It was her father's favourite piece of music, sung by his favourite singer.

Alex Reiser held a ridiculously small triangular sandwich between his thumb and forefinger. What was it about funerals? Someone might be dead, but did it really mean that the survivors should be put on rations? He lunged for another morsel as a tray floated by at eye level.

He recognized many faces in the crowd, the cream of the state's police force. Even the hard-boiled and the corrupt had had real respect for Kendall: his incorruptibility, the part he had played in the state's biggest ever 'man' hunt and most notorious crime. Not one of them doubted that the case had eventually killed him.

'Alex?' Lauren Kendall touched his sleeve. 'Thank you for coming. My father had a great deal of affection for you and he admired your work.'

'I had the utmost respect for him. He was a good man.' The adjective seemed to Reiser wholly inadequate. 'An outstanding man,' he added. Then, 'Look at me. I've turned into some sort of American – a fate worse than death. *Sorry.*' He pulled a face.

Lauren laughed. 'It's all right. I know exactly what you mean.'

'What I really mean is that he was a colossus of integrity, and that's what I'll write. I admired his certainty.'

'Good. He would have liked that.' She reached into her handbag and drew out a folded wad of paper. 'He wanted me to get this to you several weeks back but events took over. He said you would know what to do with it.'

Reiser took the paper from her and slid it into his pocket.

'Thanks again for coming.' She shook his hand.

He watched her make her way around the room, acknowledging her father's peers and accepting their condolences. It was then that he noticed Mathew Allen, hovering near the back of the room, sipping tea from a cup held in a shaky hand. The man was barely recognizable. A faint shadow of himself, grey, washed-out, eyes sunken in hollow cheeks. He shook his head and felt a momentary flash of irritation that today, of all days, Allen should be there as a living reminder. Then again why should he not pay his respects? It wasn't *his* fault. He considered crossing the room to speak to him but couldn't face it. Instead, taking one more excuse for a sandwich from a nearby tray, he slipped quietly away.

A yellow ticket fluttered on his bonnet as he approached his shining hire-car. 'Charming.' He lifted it from behind the rubber wiper. Two car spaces away there was a marked police car; he walked over to it and wedged the ticket into the driver's side mirror. 'Rude not to,' he declared, to the empty, tree-lined street.

Once inside his car he opened the folded pages, revealing a short list of names and telephone numbers. Two were current police officers and one was an ex-detective whose name he knew; the others were unfamiliar. Beneath the names was written: 'Re: Whereabouts of Simpson and Harris.' He spread the page across his thigh and looked out of the windscreen to the world beyond, comfortably occupied with its own business. 'Even to the grave,' he said.

He looked back at the sheet of paper, thumbed his chin and carefully reconsidered the information printed there.

Reiser deposited another file carton on the low Javanese-teak coffee-table at the centre of the brilliant red Afghan rug that covered half of the living-room floor.

'Can't you do that in your office for once?' asked Ruth, then stuck a slice of buttered sourdough toast into her mouth and grabbed her car keys from the kitchen counter.

He sighed irritably. '*Ruth.*'

'Well, what's the point of having an office, then?'

'You won't even be here,' he said, scattering a row of grey file-folders across the carpet in front of him. His blue and white pyjama pants barely covered the crack of his buttocks as he leant forward to arrange them in chronological order. He lifted a heavy green soapstone toad from a nearby occasional table and plonked it down on a pile of loose papers. 'I'm sure there's room in here for one more artefact.'

'Okay, forget I spoke. Bye.'

'Bye.' He waved a hand behind his head without looking at her.

He heard her car start in the drive as he opened the first file, marked '1993, Allen. Abduction/Murder'. He browsed quickly through his notes, press clippings and newspaper reportage of the case. He sipped tepid coffee and opened a second folder, 'Interviews'. This contained sheaves of handwritten notes about the victim and his family, police interview transcripts and interviews with the killers' families. Every word of the material was instantly familiar to him; it stimulated and exhausted him to exhume it. He would need to review it all to write the book he imagined, to tell the story from the inside, from every angle. To do that he needed to talk to *them*, he needed interviews, and what he was looking for among all these words was anything that would give him a lead on finding Harris and Simpson.

He flipped the wings on a second carton and extracted several plastic folio boxes. In the first, 'Parole Hearing', there was a yellowed newspaper clipping: a photograph of an embattled Deborah Simpson attempting to hide her face as she was surrounded by a mob of media, behind her a row of brown-brick council houses. 'KILLER'S MUM EXPOSED'. The story reported an attack on a corner store where she had briefly worked before being exposed again at the time of the parole hearing. He turned the clipping over to reveal a street address: the last-known residence of Debbie Simpson. He noted it down and continued through the files.

A svelte grey cat appeared beside him and nuzzled his arm.

'Hello, Sammy.' He rubbed its head with the back of his hand. It rolled over onto the scattered paperwork. Reiser swatted the floor next to it and the cat leapt onto the coffee-table, spoiling a near perfect landing by losing its footing on a sheet of paper and toppling his mug. A pool of coffee began to soak into the carton below. He pulled the Indian-cotton runner off the coffee-table and dabbed at the liquid in an attempt to save his papers. He held up the stained runner. 'She's gonna love that . . .' He folded it into a small square, then lifted a stack of papers from the box to bury the evidence at the bottom.

As he did so a small blue diary caught his eye. He recognized it as one of several he had used when writing a long feature about the possible early release of the killers. He turned to a page of notes, a list of figures calculating the cost of the perpetrators' incarceration. Wedged into the spine of the book between two pages was a slip of lined rice paper. Written on it in neat capitals was the name Christine Harris and a phone number. He copied the number into his current work diary and looked around him at the expanding circle of papers. He got to his feet but could not immediately straighten his knees, his left foot had gone to sleep. He stood on one leg and rubbed his bare belly before reaching for the phone. He remembered a desperate Christine Harris calling him before the parole hearing, pleading her son's remorse, hoping to influence his coverage of the case. That was nearly ten years ago. He rang the number and held his hand over the mouthpiece.

'Hello?' There followed a lengthy silence. 'Who is this?'

It was her, all right. The engaged tone sounded rudely in his ear as the call was terminated.

He rummaged about in the bottom of the carton until he found an address book, page after page scrawled with the names of contacts he no longer recognized. Incapable of writing between the lines or conforming to the imposed format, he found it difficult to decipher his shorthand as he scanned the pages. Scribbled randomly across the space for two entries were the words 'Harris née Buttrose – 48 Magellan Road, Northcote'. It was the address she had provided along with the phone number several years earlier. He keyed the information into the contact list on his mobile. If the gods were with him, she would still be living at the same address.

Liam, 2008

Catherine sat waiting at a table in the rear of the Ocean Pearl restaurant, pretending to read the menu. She glanced up, registered Liam's arrival, then turned away again. He made his way awkwardly through the rows of tables, now filling with other couples, and pulled out his chair. His shirt was untucked and he looked as if he hadn't slept for several days. She watched him sit, already affronted by his presence. He attempted to smile. Catherine picked up her mineral water and sipped.

They sat in silence. Catherine wanted him to say something that would make it possible for her to consider forgiving him, anything that would rewrite the situation so she could drop her pride. Instead he seemed to be waiting for her to make some pronouncement.

'Have you ordered?' he asked.

'No, Liam, I haven't ordered.'

It was as if they were already strangers; she wondered what she had ever seen in him.

*

Liam watched her face as she wrapped a folded paper napkin round and round the end of her thumb. Even her features had altered, swollen with the hormones of pregnancy.

A waiter appeared.

'What will you have?' asked Liam.

'Just another mineral water, thanks. I'm not eating.' She dropped the napkin onto her bread plate.

'I'll have the soup. Are you sure you don't want something?'

She turned her head slowly from side to side. 'No, thanks.'

Liam fiddled with his cutlery as the gulf between them widened. 'How are you doing?'

'I'm fine. The baby's fine. How would you expect me to be?'

'Upset.'

'Why are we here?'

'I'm hoping we can find a way to be together for the baby . . .'

'Yes. Wouldn't that be nice? For the baby.'

Liam pushed on, ignoring the hostility in her voice. 'I should have been more honest with you from the beginning. I should have talked to you.'

She wasn't listening. 'You know what hurt me most, Liam? It wasn't just that you lied to me and deceived me but that I had no idea you were even capable of it.' She laughed bitterly. 'I actually thought you loved me.'

'I'm sorry . . . *I do.*'

'I realize you're not who I thought you were.'

'Catherine, I did a terrible thing.'

'Yes, you did. You betrayed me. I won't put up with any more secrets or lies if you want to be part of this baby's life, in any way . . .'

'Will you come home?'

'No.'

'You won't change your mind?'

She shook her head again. 'I won't stop you seeing the baby. I want my child to have a father, but I don't think I can ever trust you again.'

Liam understood. It was too late. There was nothing more to say.

Apart from his sadness at the distance between them, he felt an overwhelming sense of relief.

After Liam had paid the bill Catherine waited until she saw him cross the street and get into his car. Only then did she allow herself to wipe her eyes with the crumpled napkin.

Alex Reiser, 2008

Number eight Magellan Road was a smart Californian-style bungalow with a leafy cottage garden. Through the windscreen Alex Reiser had a clear view to the front door. The house was in a lower-middle-class suburban neighbourhood, quiet and anonymous. The buzz of a motorbike announced the arrival of the postman as he crossed the journalist's field of vision, travelling a well-worn groove in the nature strip. Holding his bike upright with one hip, he tugged a cluster of envelopes from a wad and fed them into the mailbox, then went on his way.

Reiser allowed a few minutes to pass, then collected the mail and made a beeline for the house. His loud, confident knock produced an instant response from inside.

'Coming,'

The door was opened by a woman in her mid-fifties. The confusion on her face told Reiser she had been expecting someone else. She stared at him, then at the mail in his hand. She looked again at his face trying to place it.

'Christine. Christine Harris?' He extended his hand. 'Alex Reiser. Do you remember me?'

Her face slackened as she stepped back inside and held out her hand for the mail. 'Please don't print this address,' she whispered. 'Please.'

'I have no intention of creating trouble for you. Let me come inside where we can talk in private.'

'What about?'

'I'm writing a book and I want to tell all sides of the story. I'd like to talk to Graham.'

She looked at him for several seconds as though he were insane. 'I'm begging you not to give anyone this address. We moved at least six times after the . . . This place, my garden, it's the only peace I have.'

'I wouldn't do that, Christine. I just want to talk, if not to Graham then to you.'

Her eyes widened. 'I don't have contact with Graham. I wish I did.'

'No contact at all? That must be very painful.'

'It would be too risky. I can't think what more there is to say that hasn't been said.'

'I want to write about the impact on all the families. I know this didn't just destroy the Allens. I saw the agony on your face at the trial, as you stood by Graham.'

The woman looked at him, then up at the street. Seeming to choose between two equally undesirable options, she opened the door wider and ushered him inside. 'No one here knows about my past. I'd like it to stay that way.'

'I understand. I mean no harm.'

'And I haven't heard from him,' she said, throwing her hands up for emphasis.

'I believe you.'

Looking around the neat room he noted, among the ceramic statuettes and dried flower arrangements, a set of brass-framed photographs of cute grandchildren. There was no sign of Graham or the nightmare of the past. 'Are you and Denis still together?'

Christine Harris flushed. 'No. He hasn't coped well. He has Alzheimer's . . . Please don't disturb him, he needs to be left alone.' She vigorously twisted the gold ring on her middle finger.

Reiser still stood in the doorway, his satchel draped over his shoulder.

'You may as well sit down,' said Christine, lowering herself stiffly into an armchair. 'Look, none of us will ever get over what happened. There's just no point in dragging it all up again.'

Reiser nodded. 'It's never really gone away, though, has it? Mathew Allen still lives and breathes it, the public still wonders where the boys are. There's a story in the paper every other week speculating on *who* they are . . .'

Christine's composure began to crumble. Her mouth turned down, and her eyes were moist with tears. 'I wrote to the mother countless times, and every letter came back unopened, as if they wanted me to know they hadn't read them.' She tilted her chin. 'The police told me not to write to her again. I only ever did it through her solicitors. I never wanted to bother the woman, but she had to know how sorry Graham was and is . . . He's not the same person. It's selfish, I know . . . It's so awful, everything is awful . . . The world forgets, but I still live with it every day.' She patted her cheeks dry with both hands. 'I've lost the right to be happy on any level.' She gave a little smile. 'Do you know what that's like?'

Reiser shook his head.

She laughed. 'I was so sure he hadn't done it. So sure that it was down to Danny Simpson . . . but they were both as bad as each other.' She looked at him for silent confirmation; this last realization had been a long time coming. 'I did something wrong, I know. Somehow something I did . . . It was my fault.'

'Well, you didn't kill anyone,' he offered.

She shook her head. 'I wasn't a good mother, I was angry all the time. I've had a lot of counselling over the years, but how many times can you talk about the same thing? How does a *child* do something like that? Finally I faced up to it. I was awful to Graham, I didn't cope. Denis was useless. It's true what they wrote – what you wrote . . . There were so many signs that we just ignored or closed our eyes to. He'd lashed out violently before . . . I was just *so angry* with him. I had too much to deal with. Graham's behavioural problems were the last straw. At times I hated him. A child knows that.' She wiped her face again and looked down at the carpet. 'On more than one occasion I lost control and hit him . . . hard.' She straightened up and looked the journalist in the eye. 'I was so good with the others, especially little Claire, but Graham just brought out the worst in me. And all the rage he visited on that baby boy? I know it came from me. The only thing I hang onto is that Graham has a new chance at life . . .'

A door closed somewhere in the rear of the house. Christine Harris looked up. A tall man in his early thirties appeared in the doorway. He looked first at the stranger, then at his mother. What hairs were left on the back of Alex Reiser's neck stood to involuntary attention. The man's resemblance to the recent computer-generated photograph of his younger brother was unnerving. Here before him stood a living facsimile of the adult Graham Harris. 'Joel,' said his mother, 'this is Alex Reiser.'

'I know who he is. Are you right in the head?'

'It's OK,' began Reiser. 'I have no intention of revealing anything about –'

'You people never have any intention but to feed on the misery of others.'

A dark-haired girl ran into the room carrying a pink backpack.

'Hello, my lovely,' said Christine, kissing her cheek. 'Nanny's just talking to a man.'

'Sarah, make yourself a sandwich in the kitchen.'

The girl looked disappointed but followed her father's instruction.

'I was just telling Mr Reiser that we don't have any contact with your brother and we don't know any more than he does, that everyone concerned just wants to be left alone and that even Graham deserves to be left in peace.'

This was too much for Joel. 'Peace,' he said bitterly. 'That he's paid the price . . . We all have.'

'If you're going to talk to this parasite, Mum, why don't you tell him the truth?'

She stared at her son.

'Did she tell you she's been writing to him?'

'Joel.' The woman's face became a stony mask. 'That's not true, you know it's not.' She stood up and held the gold confirmation medal that hung at her throat. 'I swear to you I don't know anything about my son since his release. I have nothing more to tell you.'

'What were you *thinking*?' demanded Joel.

Reiser saw the hunted expression on her face as she tried desperately to transmit a silent plea for mercy to her elder son.

'I didn't come here to ruin your lives. Anything I write will be fiction . . .'

Joel laughed.

'I won't share my sources or any information about you.'

'Very reassuring.'

'I'm hoping to meet with Graham and talk with him, to tell his side of the story.'

Joel raised his hand. 'I don't give a shit about Graham. My brother forfeited his life the day he decided to kill a kid. *I don't care how old he was.* The kid was three, my sister was eight, I was fourteen. The kid's still dead, as far as I know, and his parents are still in hell.'

'He was a very troubled boy. I blame myself,' Christine repeated.

Joel's face reddened and he looked with disgust at the weeping woman. 'When will you stop making excuses for him? For God's sake! Tell the truth for once in your fucking life. You've been writing to him for months.'

'Mr Reiser, this conversation is over. I'm sorry, please leave —'

'You *blame yourself*,' mocked Joel. 'And yet you invite that poison back into our lives?'

'I swear to you I don't know where he lives.' She turned to Reiser.

A timid knock sounded on the living-room door. 'Daddy?'

'I'll be out in a minute.' Joel put his hands in his pockets. He looked first at Reiser, then at his mother. 'You'd better make up your mind, Mum,' he said flatly, and turned to leave. As he reached the door he looked back at Reiser. 'And as for you, you're kidding yourself. You want to profit from this story, no matter how much it costs other people.'

Voices

'Blessed are the Dead'

Liam, 2008

Alone in the empty bedroom, Liam sat staring at the words on his computer screen: Stay away from us. Papers littered the unmade bed behind him. The dressing-table and lowboy opposite had been stripped of everything but his medications. He looked down at the clutch of papers on his lap: You fucked us all. For what you did God has reserved a special punishment.

The one-line emails had been coming for the past two days. He silently reread them. The initial message, I know who you are and I know what you did, had come on the first Tuesday of the month to his Hotmail account. It had left him reeling. The address, known only to him and his mother, had been infiltrated by someone calling themselves Vengeance-mine. He had written to his mother for an explanation but six and a half hours later he was still waiting for a reply. He repeatedly refreshed the inbox but there was nothing new.

He lit another cigarette, took the child-proof top off a plastic pharmaceutical bottle and tipped two small yellow tablets into his hand. He swallowed them without water and studied the label. He shook the container: the pills inside rattled loudly. He stared again at the screen. The Valium did not stop the stream of paranoid thoughts forming in his mind. It merely acted as a mental lubricant, allowing each thought to slip away before it could coagulate with a thousand others and choke him in a paroxysm of terror.

He refreshed the in-box and there it was, not a reply from his mother's address but a new mail from vengeance-mine. His gut contracted violently as he read:

Fuck you, Liam. I'll make sure you never speak to our mother again. You have ruined enough lives. Other people are still serving your time for you, you twisted fuck. I don't care how old you were then or how pathetic your remorse is now. As far as I am concerned, you are already dead, and if you don't stay dead, I'll pass everything I know onto those who will make sure you are dead.

Joel

His mind could barely grasp the reality of what he was reading. His brother's hatred flamed in every word. He had seen him only once during a family visit since he had been taken into custody. Joel, then fourteen, had been cordial to him, but Liam, entirely preoccupied with his own grief and survival, had barely registered his presence, let alone been aware of Joel's own trauma.

In recent months Liam's mother had provided him with updates, via a primitive code, on Joel and his sister Claire's progress in life.

He knew little of the aftermath of his crime or his notoriety and their crushing impact on the rest of his family. Since the death of Benjamin Allen, his journey through incarceration and rehabilitation had been cloistered and self-absorbed. From the moment he had been bundled into the back of a police van with his head shrouded in a towel and driven through the gates, past a screaming mob, his former life with his family had ceased to exist, buried under an avalanche of thumping hands that had landed like a spray of machine-gun fire against the blacked-out windows.

'How do you feel now, you little bastards?'

'Mongrels!'

'Rot in hell!'

Rigid with terror, he had clung tightly to the hand of the policewoman seated beside him.

The drive to nowhere, the introduction to the facility, stripped of every familiar thing, the sudden absence of his guilt-ridden parents had been felt as a terrible strain. Now dependent upon people he could not control with his fragile moods, emotional outbursts and hysterical fears. Surrounded by experts, themselves governed by a code of conduct. Meals at regular times, schedules, expectations and rules. Tortured by daily therapy sessions and forced to readmit reality after nights of escapist dreaming or draining nightmares, a dreadful remorse had overtaken him.

Parental visits were a painful reminder of a life that continued outside while he struggled to survive the ever-present catatonic dread and the terror of violent flashbacks, afraid of ghosts and shadowy figures that walked the hallways at night. He had dreamed repeatedly of being drowned in the canal by a mass of hands that pushed him down and held him under the water. His high-pitched crying night after night affected all who heard it.

'The boy's mum, please tell her I'm sorry.'

All the intensive counselling and rehabilitation by experts, compassionate carers and a few steady repre-sentatives of a forgiving God had not moved the giant stone that weighed down on his sad, lonely heart. He had never been able to disassociate himself from the horror movies in his head. He'd wished then to forget every-thing, trying in vain to rebuild himself for a 'normal life'.

Every other week the unit received calls threatening his life. Tabloid headlines described him as 'born evil'.

As the years passed, sites dedicated to hunting him down and killing him proliferated on the internet. While such hurtful knowledge was vigilantly kept from his unbalanced young mind, his brother Joel had run the gauntlet in the world outside. Now Liam reread the hate-filled missive: You are dead. The enmity rocked him. He had known he was hated, but not by his family.

Alex Reiser, 2008

He blew the froth off the top of his flat-white coffee and sipped as he gazed across the paved foyer of the district courthouse to where a group of lawyers stood, pivoting from heel to toe on their Italian wingtip shoes. *A murder of crows.* If he was a parasite, Reiser's reverie continued, then what were they? Certainly the only benefactors of this whole sorry mess and countless other untold miseries.

Despite his well-honed cynicism, Joel Harris's comments about him had got under his skin. He was well used to justifying the value of the work he did but that remark had pricked his conscience: his ego *was* invested in every story he took on; he was ambitious; and there was no way to come up completely clean, not when *the work* involved using people's real lives as fodder for his word count. He was a good journalist, driven by the need to understand. It was part of the job description to dig into people's lives and extract meaning from their pain, to dissect the human story and confront the shadows. Sometimes there was a cost, a price often paid by those who could least afford it; a sacrifice for the greater good.

A lean, bespectacled dandy gave a wry smile as he approached his colleagues at the top of the landing; behind him, hovering nervously beside the reinforced-steel public seating, was a clean-shaven youth, wearing what appeared to be his Sunday best. A court attendant came out onto the landing and called a name. The lawyer turned and motioned for his client to follow.

The remaining lawyers nodded, closed the circle, and continued their smug repartee. These shiny black insects clubbed together, drank together, cut deals over lunch and in the back of cabs. They shook hands over their clients' heads and carved up the spoils. No matter what the human outcome, they were still handsomely paid.

Reiser gouged a glazed cherry from his muffin and ordered another coffee from the young waitress. He looked irritably at his stainless-steel Seiko. Mathew Allen had agreed to meet him here at two thirty – fifteen minutes ago.

A grey-haired suit at the next table was in deep conversation with a severely dressed woman. She glanced in Reiser's direction, recognized him and gave him a polite wave. He smiled back. Melody Davenport was a family-law solicitor with a fearsome reputation, a prematurely dowdy spinster with a fetish for high heels. Known in court circles as the tit-bull terrier, once she had hold of a client she didn't let go until every available cent had been extracted from the opposite party. Even spouses who went to her with a fair settlement in mind soon ended up convinced they deserved the lion's share of everything. She was a university chum of his wife, Ruth, and Reiser regarded her with respect and awe, and had often thought that his only recourse, if his marriage were to disintegrate, would be to engage the tit-bull before Ruth did.

Several more lawyers entered the coffee shop and ordered at the counter.

Melody Davenport's table companion, a senior partner of a prominent local law firm, looked past Reiser towards the rear terrace, then away again, shifting in his seat with some discomfort. As he turned to follow the line of the man's gaze, a dishevelled Mathew Allen pulled out a chair and sat down. 'Sorry I'm late.'

'Never mind.'

'I was in the bookstore using the internet. I don't usually come here,' he added.

'No?'

'I make people feel uncomfortable.' He looked around the room at the clientele.

'We can go somewhere else, if you like.'

Allen shrugged his indifference. 'What did you want to talk to me about?'

The waitress deposited a mug of coffee next to him. He put the Manila folder he had been carrying onto the table. His hands were flecked with powder-blue house paint.

'Did you want anything to eat?' said Reiser, hoping to insert a few niceties into the conversation before he answered the question.

'No.'

'I really just wanted to tell you face to face that I'm writing a book . . . about a case similar to Benjamin's . . .'

Allen listened impassively, holding his gaze.

'It's a novel and I'll be writing under a pseudonym. I just didn't want you to read it one day and be blindsided.'

'I won't need to read it.'

'No, of course you won't.' Reiser hid his embarrassment.

'Just don't go making excuses for those bastards.'

'I'll try not to fall into that trap.'

Allen swallowed a mouthful of coffee and opened a folder full of documents.

'What is all that?' asked Reiser, happy to change the subject

'Papers I need to lodge at the courthouse. I'm defending myself.'

'Against what?'

He held up a letter. 'My most recent lawyer is now refusing to act for me in regard to an Apprehended Violence Order . . .'

'An AVO?' Reiser took the letter and began reading.

'Yeah, a barrister who acted for the Harris family, during the parole hearing, took out an AVO against me. And this . . .' he handed Reiser a second sheet of paper '. . . is a bill from my original lawyer in the contempt case.'

Reiser scanned the page. The letter suggested none too subtly that Mathew Allen find new representation and hinted at legal action if the outstanding amount of three thousand dollars was not paid. 'I'm confused,' said Reiser. He was beginning to feel oppressed by the weight of Allen's multiplied woes. 'The parole hearing was years ago. Why did the barrister . . .' He looked again at the page in front of him. 'Why did Tony Cross take out an AVO against you?'

'I went to see him, we argued and he threw me out of his office.'

'You must have given him some cause.'

'Yeah, well.'

Reiser sighed and leaned forward. This was the third lawyer Allen had engaged in as many months. To finance his legal battles he had so far lost his house, spent an inheritance from his mother and had begged and borrowed at least eighty thousand dollars. 'So now you're representing yourself?'

'Yeah. It's claimed that I breached the AVO.'

'Did you?'

'I took some pictures from the opposite side of the street.'

Reiser smoothed his hand over the dome of his head. He resented the guilt and discomfort Mathew Allen's presence made him feel, that the man's tragedy somehow exempted him from listening to reason. 'Why would you even go near him?'

'I wanted some information, that's all'

'Tony Cross is a barrister, for Christ's sake. He's hardly going to aid and abet vigilantes. What were you expecting?'

Allen waved a dismissive hand.

'I guess I'd probably do some stupid things if I were in your position,' said Reiser, hating himself for the lie. *Look, man, give it up, for fuck's sake,* he wanted to say. *Your son has been gone for fifteen years. Stop this shit! Bury your dead, cut your losses. Decamp, rebuild. Find God. Do something other than walk around as a half-dead living reminder of your own tragedy.*

Mathew Allen stirred three sugars into his coffee. 'Today is Benjamin's birthday. He would have been eighteen.'

Reiser looked away, ashamed of his thoughts. Suddenly he felt himself on the verge of tears. What right did he have to judge a man who had endured all that Allen had lived through?

'It must be very hard, Mathew. I can only imagine what it's like to walk around in your shoes.'

'I have nothing else to live for,' Allen said.

Reiser nodded soberly. Despite his compassion, he felt trapped and wondered how soon he could politely take his leave. Allen riffled through his paperwork and withdrew a handwritten list of names. 'Do you recognize any of these?'

Reiser picked at his teeth with a matchstick. 'What are they?'

'Names people send me.'

'Oh, for God's sake. Come on, what are you going to do if you find them?' He pulled the list towards him and gave it a cursory glance.

'Don't I have just as much right to look for them as you?'

'I'm a journalist, Mathew, armed with a pen.' Reiser's eyes stopped halfway down the list as one of the names jumped out at him.

'I'm only asking you to take a look.'

Reiser pulled his own list out of his wallet.

'What's that?'

'Kendall's daughter gave it to me at the funeral.' He put Allen's list beside his and compared them.

'Let me see,' said Allen, leaning in for a closer look at the unfamiliar names.

'Nothing stands out,' said Reiser.

'I just thought you might recognize something.'

'Listen, Mathew, I write stories about awful things that happen to decent people like you. That's my job.' He handed Allen's list back to him. 'You're a father, you did your best. Maybe it's time to let this go and move on.'

The frail man with the weary eyes gave the list one last look before crumpling it slowly in his fist.

Mathew, 2008

Fluorescent lamplight gave a blue cast to Mathew Allen's pale face as he pored over a list of entries in a large journal; he damped his thumb on his bottom lip before he turned each page. Every now and then he referred to a notepad on the desk beside him. Roughly printed on the pad were the names he had memorized from Alex Reiser's list that he had seen at the café. A circle of dark blue ink outlined one: Geoffrey Roland Wickham.

He flipped backwards through the journal until he came to the page headed 2001. Here, in a list of names, was almost an exact match; 'Geoffrey Wickham. Mayfield. RTA.' He considered the entry thoughtfully, but he had long since forgotten the significance of the name. He got up from his desk and began to pace quietly around the room. A row of cartons was stacked against the wall beneath the window and he lifted several onto the floor.

The first was full of Manila sleeves marked with the year of their collection. He leafed through until he located one labelled '2001'. He lifted the flap and tipped a small pile of mail onto the floor. He examined the postmarks and looked closely at a blue-and-red-trimmed airmail envelope. He could just make out the letters 'LD' on the tail end of the faded postmark.

He pulled out the thin blue sheet within and scanned the typed letter until his eyes locked on 'Geoffrey Wickham'. The author, like several dozen others, claimed to have uncovered Danny Simpson's new identity: a colleague had recently issued a driver's licence to an eighteen-year-old youth who, according to the correspondent's source, was attended by a 'minder' and 'appeared petrified' after passing his driving test. The boy was 'a dead ringer' for Simpson. The authority of this identification was based on the fact that the author's colleague had owned a shop in Battery Cove at the time of the murder and had had the 'misfortune' to know all of the Simpson children.

He examined the enclosed photocopy, a copy of a copy of a laminated licence. He could just make out the shape of a pudgy face buried among the ink shadows.

Several lines identifying the location of the RTA and the licence number had been struck out. The address line '29 Innes Street, Mayfield' was clear. The birthdate of the licence-holder was 18 January 1982. On seeing this he remembered why he had been sceptical about this 'sighting'. Danny Simpson had been born a year earlier, on 21 April. The letter itself was unsigned, as most such missives were – yet here was the same name on a list compiled by Phillip Kendall.

The white Nissan Bluebird station-wagon was parked at the edge of a freeway rest stop. A human toe traced a line in the condensation as it slid down the inside of the front passenger-side window. A grey wallaby emerged from the surrounding scrub to nibble at scraps of food littered around a bank of Sulo bins. A male voice sounded from inside the car and the animal froze, then jumped away.

Mathew Allen gave a muffled scream followed by a deep groan. He opened his eyes and stared ahead in terror, looking wildly around the darkened interior of the car. He wrenched the glovebox open and closed his hand around the heel of the Kimber .38 pistol, safely stowed where he had placed it after pulling over to sleep the night before. He began to breathe normally again, replaced the gun and shut the glovebox.

His feet were cold. He pulled them up under the open sleeping bag that was wrapped around him and attempted to go back to sleep, shifting his weight repeatedly to avoid the hump of the gear shift. Eventually he gave up, pulled on his coat and struggled into a second pair of track pants. The back of the station-wagon was loaded with paint cans, several buckets and boxes. He groped among the items, found a pair of runners and put them on.

He opened the car door, stepped outside, walked to the edge of the truck stop and relieved himself on the surrounding bushes. Slivers of dawn light illuminated the horizon. He laid a map on the bonnet of his car with shaky hands and reached into his coat pocket to produce a small vial of pills. He studied the map, opened the bottle and dropped a collection of tablets into his palm. He went to the rear of the car, took out a large container of water and swallowed the pills.

The freeway was almost empty save for the few long-haul trucks and road trains that passed him. His bloodshot eyes processed the information on the large green directional signs. Various chemical compounds from his pharmaceutical cocktail flooded his bloodstream, cancelling his fatigue and pain, and numbing his reason.

The road sign read, 'Kingston, Mayfield'. He moved into the exit lane and braked, crossing the newly built overpass with its fresh white concrete windbreak. The road to Mayfield followed the river and was flanked by grass and reeds; rusted machinery and scaffolding bore evidence to a previous era when the river had been the site of local industry. A foul stench filled the car and Allen wound up his window. Mayfield's current economy was heavily reliant on the local abattoir and meat-processing works located just outside the town.

In Mayfield he parked outside the Chick Inn. He put his hand on the door and remembered the gun; he took it out and slid it into the inside pocket of his coat before leaving the car.

On his way to the rest-room he passed several groups of people eating breakfast at the red Laminex tables. He washed his hands and studied his face in the mirror, the tangled black hair flecked with grey, the sadness in the faded blue eyes. *What the hell was he doing here?* He wetted a paper towel and applied it to his face, then held it against his eyelids.

Revived, he went to the counter, ordered an egg burger and took it to a nearby booth. Staring out of the window he noted the nondescript town: a Woolworths supermarket parking lot directly opposite, a cramped Tandy electronics storefront to its right. It appeared no different from any other town, the whole world now apparently carved up into market shares of one brand or another.

He ate without appetite.

A small boy at the next table began to cry. On the floor beside him lay the contents of his breakfast box, a half-eaten burger bun and a small heap of French fries.

'It's all right,' said the child's mother, picking up some of the mess. 'We can get you another one.' She patted his head and smiled. A waitress delivered another burger; the child unwrapped it and took a bite.

Mathew felt tears welling in his eyes and blinked them away. He was so tired of pain and hate and tears.

Innes Street was in an older part of the town where rows of original worker's cottages were now being renovated. Number twenty-nine was a hybrid of brick and Colourbond cladding. A huge satellite dish was suspended above the front awning.

Mathew Allen drove past several times, circling the streets in the surrounding grid. Almost directly behind number twenty-nine there was a closed community hall and a vacant block; the adjoining house shared a small part of the boundary. He parked the car in a nearby cross-street and walked back to the block. Behind the hall he climbed onto a brick incinerator to gain a view into the yard of number twenty-nine.

A tattered trampoline stood on its side, leaning against the rear of the house. Several pairs of men's work overalls hung on the rotary clothes line. He straddled the fence, stepped onto the roof of a low potting shed and jumped quietly down. As he crossed purposefully, without hesitation, to the back door of the house, he could hear a television, or people talking inside. Looking through what appeared to be a laundry window, he turned the adjacent door knob slowly. It was locked.

He padded across the veranda, inching along with his back to the wall. The voices grew louder. Dropping to his knees as he encountered a row of windows, he paused to listen. A man's voice could be heard over the sound of the TV. Raising himself up, he peered through a gap between the curtains. He could make out at least two figures seated at a table, off to the side of the main room.

The man spoke again: 'Because I said so.'

Then a smaller voice complained, A child or a woman.

'Shush,' said the man. The volume of the television went up.

At the next window he caught sight of the man's back and square skull. A small child fumbled with something on the table. A woman began clearing items away, picked the child up and moved further inside the building, beyond his line of sight. The figure at the table remained seated.

Mathew tapped several times against the glass. The head turned. He hung back alongside the front door. Gripping the pistol inside his coat, he knocked with his free hand. The door opened and a slightly built Asian woman peered out. 'Yes?'

'Mrs Wickham?'

'Sorry . . .'

'Who is it?' called the man.

'I'm looking for Geoffrey.'

'Nobody here called that name.' Allen pushed past her.

313

'Hey!' The woman shouted something excitedly in rapid-fire Chinese.

'What the fuck?' The man's chair crashed to the floor as he stood up.

A dishevelled Mathew Allen stopped, paralysed, at the centre of the room. The astonished man at the table was well into his forties. 'Sorry. I just had to see . . . I thought you were someone else.' He backed away.

'Sorry?' repeated the man.

The child began to cry and the woman ran to it.

Allen registered the details of the interrupted family scene: the Disney bowl half full of pumpkin mash on the high-chair tray, an overturned box of Weetabix on the floor, cereal flakes littered around it.

What the hell was he doing here?

'Call the cops!' the man shouted.

Allen was sprinting now, out of the door, then scrambling over fences, through several yards and across an empty oval. When he was in sight of his car he forced himself to slow to a walking pace and get in. He drove for several hours, the picture of the terrified family filling his mind. The bulk of the pistol inside his coat pressed against his chest. *What had he become?* What if he had found Danny Simpson, or someone who looked like him? Was he really going to gun a man down in front of his family? What then? 'For the love of God, this has to stop,' he said out loud.

Ahead of him to the left was a turn-off where the old coast road crossed a railway bridge over the river. He took it and stopped near the embankment. He stepped across the broken and missing sleepers until he reached the middle of the bridge. There he knelt down and took the gun out. He looked between his knees, through a gap in the planks, to the brown-green water below. He let the weapon slip from his fingers: the small black object hit the surface of the water and disappeared.

Alex Reiser, 2008

He nursed the laptop on his belly, dragging himself up against the arm of the couch, stuffing an extra cushion behind his coccyx. A point in the lumbar region of his back nagged at him. The pain was dull and grinding, persisting even after two fingers of Scotch. He lifted the cat off the couch with his feet and stretched out his legs. Every surface within touching distance was covered with stacks of paper, clippings and open books. Dozens of screwed-up pages lay scattered on the floor.

Even with the pain in his back it was sheer luxury to be at home with the entire house to himself in the middle of the afternoon. He'd been cobbling together an outline of his novel for months now. All he needed was a few days to himself with no distractions and he'd be able to get on top of it.

Referring to the notes beside him, he typed furiously, endeavouring to keep up with the flow of ideas that bubbled into his mind, stopping for a moment to jot something in his notebook before it was lost. The pen travelled at the speed of his thoughts, albeit almost illegibly. The typing lagged behind it, forcing him to pause and make choices. Folders full of longhand notes were relentlessly reduced to one meaningful paragraph, as more crumpled pages joined the others on the carpet.

Wearily, he closed the screen and slid the laptop onto the floor. He fingered through his crowded research summaries, highlighting sentences and phrases in streaks of fluorescent lime until his eyes closed and the marker dropped from his hand.

A phone vibrated on a hard surface and gave a soft ping.

'Is that your mobile?'

Reiser opened one eye, his wire-framed bifocals on his forehead. An empty whisky tumbler was wedged between his thighs. Ruth stood over him, picking up sheaves of papers, shuffling them into some sort of order and stacking them on the coffee-table.

Reiser put out his hand. 'Leave those on the bean-bag. I haven't got to them yet.'

She was reading one of the pages.

'It's pretty grim,' he warned.

'I'm sure it'll make for a brilliant essay.'

'It's not another fucking essay. It's the background for the novel. I've already pitched it to Vanessa over at ALM and she can't wait to read it.'

Ruth looked sceptical. She shook out the cotton throw, folded it over and rolled it into a neat log.

'What?' said Reiser standing up.

'I just don't want to see you disappointed again.'

'There it goes – the most insidious sentence of dream-slayers throughout the ages.' He gathered up the piles of documents and held them to his chest. 'I'll be in my office wasting my time.'

'Your mother called.'

'What did she say?' he said, stopping in his tracks.

'She thought you could bring Jakko with you next time you visit.'

'It would be funny if it wasn't so bloody tragic. What did you tell her?'

'I asked her to look at the picture by her bed and reminded her that he had a new home on a farm.'

'Bloody dog's been dead for twelve years.'

'Maybe we should pop in on Saturday. It's been ages.'

'I can't stand that place on weekends.'

'Fine. I'll go then.'

'For God's sake, Ruth, she's my mother. I'll call in one day next week.'

Christine Harris had remained emphatic in her denial of having any ongoing contact with her son. Without her cooperation Reiser had drawn a blank on Graham's whereabouts. From what he could discover, the Simpson family had since scattered across the state, their ongoing criminality the only thing they still had in common. Their records, copied for him by a friend in the police department, made interesting but predictable reading. Daniel Simpson's eldest brother, Damien, had been in and out of jail for small-time drug-related offences since he was seventeen. He had several charges recorded before that as a juvenile, one for 'aggravated violence', involving a glassing during a bout of underage drinking. Surprisingly he had been out of jail for five years without so much as a parking fine.

Adam Simpson's passage through the criminal justice system had been more tragic. He had died in custody, aged thirty-one, while doing a five-year stretch for break-and-enter.

Their half-sister, Olivia Parry Simpson, had committed only one offence but had been known to police as a drug addict and part-time prostitute. Information on their mother, Deborah, had proven much harder to find. Her old address had yielded nothing and she had stayed clear of the law for twelve years. The latest information on Damien was accompanied by two addresses. He had been using one with the Department of Social Security and the other was the home of a woman who had stood bail for him on two occasions – the words 'de facto' were printed next to it.

The social-security address had turned out to be that of a disused factory. The woman's home was in a semi-residential street in the next suburb. At first sight the peeling weatherboard house looked uninhabited. Remnants of open-weave nylon curtaining shrouded most of the facing windows. The carport was empty.

Reiser mounted the steps to the front door and knocked hard on the frame of the ugly, steel-grille security screen. The metal absorbed most of the sound and hurt his knuckles. The inner door was opened quickly by a stocky man in a stained singlet that barely covered his stomach; his meaty arms were crudely tattooed.

'Damien Simpson?' asked Reiser.

'Who wants to know?' he countered, sucking hard on a mangled cigarette.

'Alex Reiser. I'm a journalist.'

'Fuck me, you got a nerve.' Damien looked the intruder up and down, making no attempt to open the grille.

'I'm looking for your mother.'

319

'Good luck.' He laughed, exposing a gap where his upper left canine had once been. 'What do you want with her?' A black utility vehicle pulled up in the street below. 'Look, I'm a busy man. I haven't seen the old girl for years . . . which suits me.'

Reiser noticed his red eyes and dilated pupils.

'Unless you're here to score,' Damien added. 'In which case I don't do that shit any more.'

'I don't care about any of that.'

The driver of the utility sounded his horn.

'If you don't mind, I got some business to take care of.' Damien disappeared for several moments then reappeared wearing a bulky cargo vest. He began unlatching a series of locks. 'The last time I saw Mum, for want of a better word, was when I was dealing shit. She came over a few times to score. That was three years back, maybe more. Last I heard,' he added, relocking the chains on the door from the outside, 'she got custody of Olivia's baby.' He gave a caustic laugh and smiled strangely as some new realization struck him. 'You don't wanna talk to her. You want Danny.'

Reiser made what he hoped was an inscrutable face, as he followed Damien down the steps.

'Even if I did know where he was I wouldn't tell you.'

The passenger door of the utility gaped open.

Damien tossed the end of his cigarette onto the bitumen and put one hand on the roof of the waiting car. He paused to spit a shred of tobacco from his lip and gave the burly journalist a final look. 'If you do find him, you can tell him there's nothing to come back here for.'

Jacaranda Gardens Retirement Village

Sitting with her legs crossed in a pair of black Chinese pyjamas, the diminutive old woman at the end of the hallway could have been any well-kept eccentric waiting for a train or bus. She looked up from her crossword puzzle as he approached. 'Alex.'

'What are you doing out here in the hallway at this time of night?'

'The light's good,' she said, as he bent to hug her.

He sat down next to her and took a look at the half-finished puzzle. 'Two across, like beasts.'

'Yes, I knew that one.'

'Oh, for what it's worth . . .' Reiser offered her the copy of *Vanity Fair* he had been carrying under his arm.

His mother looked unimpressed. 'Thank you.'

'Ruth thought you'd like it for the articles.' He stooped to lift something out of a sisal bag. 'And a cantaloupe.'

Her eyes lit up.

'I know they don't let you have it in here.'

'They let me have it all right. The kitchen witches just won't give it to me.'

He pulled a nearby chair over and lifted his feet onto it.

'You look sad.'

'I'm not sad, Mum, just tired.'

'I know it's hard, but the term will be over soon.'

He raised his eyebrows and smiled kindly. 'That's a relief.' How was it possible for someone so apparently lucid to imagine that her balding forty-eight-year-old son was still sequestered in a boarding school somewhere? He looked across at the collection of memorabilia and photographs that the nursing-home staff had helped her assemble for display in the sealed window-box outside the door to her room.

The woman beside him, craning her head over her Latin crossword book, with a pen to her mouth was still recognizable as the vivacious woman in the snapshots.

'*Mens rea*, ten letters,' she said tapping the top of the pen against her lip.

'Guilty mind,' he volunteered. 'Listen, Mum, there's something I've been meaning to say.'

She looked up attentively.

'I hope you know that whatever we went through over the years, with your health, you were all I had, and you were a wonderful mother.'

Her cheeks reddened. 'Oh, Alex, I know we had some awful times. Let's face it, I was bat-shit crazy.'

'Nevertheless, you were a wonderful and inspiring mother and I knew I was loved . . . That's all I wanted to say.'

She smiled. 'It was never boring, was it?'

'No, Mum, never boring.' He clasped her hand and kissed it.

Liam, 2008

The light was just breaking when he crossed the foot-bridge over the swollen river and stepped onto the gravel path that passed through the children's playground. The ground was sodden from days of rain and the equipment was still wet. He wiped the base of the tubular slippery-dip with his palm and sat down. He remembered being small enough to fit through a slide like this, his brother Joel watching over him while his mother lifted Claire onto a swing. Joel had always been the good one, his mother's little helper.

The sight of a child's sandal, discarded among the pine chips at the base of the flying fox ladder, brought him back to the present with a sickening jolt. Joel was right: he had caused more than enough harm in the world already. Every lungful of air he took was surely an insult to the universe. In the days since his brother's emails, any remaining confidence Liam had about his ability to live a normal life had been demolished.

Along the riverbank near the closed kiosk a dog began to bark insistently. As he walked towards it, he could see it running in small, frantic circles. In the water below, an elderly man was struggling to wade up the bank. He repeatedly lost his footing and was lifted away by the swirling water, his long gabardine coat washed around him. Liam picked up a stick and held it out to him. After several attempts he was able to take hold of the other end, drag himself up and regain his footing on the rocks. The little dog ran around his legs shaking itself off and licking its master's face when he sat down to catch his breath.

'I wasn't quite done for yet, but if you hadn't come along . . . Thank you.'

'What happened?'

'This silly animal,' he said, rubbing his dog's head, 'followed a stick in and got taken along by the current. I stepped in to reach her and lost my footing. She practically climbed over my head to get herself out.' He stood up, took off his sodden coat and wrung it out, draped it over his shoulder and held out a hand. 'Thanks again.'

As he stood and watched the man walk away Liam became aware of the morning's chill. He briskly retraced his steps.

Climbing the stairs to his flat he contemplated his brother's words and saw the futility of attempting to reply. A single envelope lay across the threshold; he stooped to retrieve it. The letter had no stamp. He ventured a look out of the open door; the street was Sunday quiet.

Tearing the flap open, he rifled through the documents inside. A photocopied birth certificate of some sort for a Brenda Halliwell, a death certificate, a page from a type-written letter stapled to some handwritten notes: 'died 1979 aged twenty, never married, one stillbirth recorded. No previous issue.' He looked again at each page for some message or sign that would identify the sender.

The notes were written on a compliments slip from Ancestors Regained, Professional Genealogists, Glasgow. A single line was scrawled across the back: 'Every word you ever uttered was a lie – I don't even know who you are.' The handwriting was Catherine's.

Apart from a sickening dread and the old fear of being found out and exposed, he felt a fatalistic sense of release. With his new identity under attack from all sides, he could finally let go of the hopes and dreams he had been encouraged to form. He saw with blinding clarity the impossibility of a life constructed from a network of lies. He looked again at the empty street then shut the door against the light.

Whatever Joel or Catherine did now didn't really mat-ter. He needed to talk to his mother one last time and, one way or another, to disappear. He calculated how much money he had on hand and how quickly he could get access to it. The deposit he had been saving for the house with Catherine was more than twenty thousand dollars.

In the bedroom he opened the file-drawer in his desk and flipped through the alphabet. At M, he slipped his hand down the back of a file and pulled out a takeaway menu. A telephone number was written on it.

He sat on the unmade bed, then opened his mobile phone and keyed it in. He heard the number ringing. A woman answered: 'Hello . . . hello?'

The sound of his mother's voice immediately paralysed him.

'Hello?'

Unable to speak, he closed the phone and ended the call.

Daylight mocked him through the high dormer windows. Who was he kidding? There was no one he could safely reveal himself to and there never would be. He was dead already. He got up, opened the wardrobe and took down a green canvas duffel bag. He pulled a few items of clothing out at random and stowed them in it.

At the top of the linen cupboard he found a small box filled with his papers and placed it on the bed. He fingered through the few pages, his entire 'identity'. He removed his wedding ring and watch. He observed the initials 'L.D.' on the back, then placed both items inside the box. He lifted the bag onto his shoulders and walked out the door, leaving Liam Douglass in the room behind him.

Truth

'Wide is the gate'

Alex Reiser, 2008

The afternoon sun was obscured by a screen of white cloud. Pine needles covered the ground beneath Alex Reiser's feet as he walked across the Queen's Park reserve towards the Gumnuts playground. He could make out a fair-haired man sitting on the bench beside the sandpit. Detective Grant Oliver had agreed to meet him here and he had driven straight from the airport, after a two-hour flight.

A plump four-year-old left the sandpit, ran to the bench and pulled on the man's trouser leg. He looked at the large, bald figure walking towards him. 'Grant?' asked Reiser, once he was in earshot.

The detective lifted the boy onto his hip and stood up. The two men shook hands.

'Sorry to be so cloak-and-dagger.' Oliver deposited the boy on the ground. 'You go and play in the sandpit while Daddy talks.' He patted him on the rear as he bounded off. 'It's my access visit with Sean and I didn't want to meet anywhere near the station.'

'I'm just grateful you're willing to talk to me.'

They sat down, facing the playground.

'I don't know for sure if the guy we arrested was your guy. I had a pretty strong sense that he was . . . and when I asked about accessing his file I was told in no uncertain terms to leave it alone.'

'Look, Daddy.' Sean held up a handful of sand and dropped it into a red plastic bucket.

'Good work, mate. Make a castle for Daddy . . . I was part of the search team who found Benjamin Allen's body. Some things you don't forget. Even now I can close my eyes and see that baby's face.'

Reiser nodded. He had read all the transcripts.

'And those two freaks who did it . . . The Harris kid was hysterical, screaming and crying, a real fruitcake, shaking and begging his parents to save him. Simpson was a different story, a callous little liar. Even though we were looking at a kid, quite a few of us had a hard time staying neutral, not dishing something out to the little bastard . . . I don't think I could forget him, not even fifteen years later in an adult body.' He reached under his coat. 'This is the address he gave at the police station.' He handed Reiser a yellow race-guide with an address written at the top of the page. 'I've been tempted to go round there and put the wind up him myself, but it's not worth my job.'

'I never reveal a source,' said Reiser. 'Cheers.'

Reiser popped the ring-pull on a can of gin and tonic, and sat down on the bed in his room at the airport Best Western. He leant back and contemplated his game plan. The address of one Geoffrey Roland Wickham was tucked into his trouser pocket. He pulled it out and located the corresponding map reference in the local directory. Less than a ten-minute drive across town from the hotel. After a decent meal and a good night's sleep he would be ready to begin.

He opened the bottom drawer of the bedside table and smiled to see the near-new Gideon's Bible, a reassuring idiosyncrasy of motel rooms. On a whim he took it out and opened it at random: 'You shall know the truth and the truth shall set you free.'

'Amen.' He closed the Bible and opened the room service menu.

Fruits

Geoffrey, 2008

Feathers of dark auburn hair were scattered in a semi-circle on the bathroom floor. Geoffrey Wickham turned on the shower and stepped into the hot stream. He slid a bar of soap over his naked chest and shoulders, rubbed it over his bare scalp, turned his face into the water and rinsed off the foam. He surveyed his newly bald head in the bathroom mirror as he rubbed himself dry.

He pulled on a pair of jeans and a black T-shirt, then slipped his arms into the sleeves of his leather jacket. A horn tooted outside. Through the venetian blinds he saw the waiting taxi. At the bottom of the stairs he stopped to extract a wad of mail from his letterbox, a sushi menu, a local newspaper and one white envelope addressed to Geoffrey R. Wickham.

He climbed into the back seat of the taxi and glanced at the photo ID of the turbaned driver. Ignoring the Sikh's attempts at conversation, he opened the letter. It offered him a place on the computer programming course his counsellor had urged him to apply for in preparation for his impending relocation. He studied the attached enrolment form and allowed himself a little smile.

After his recent arrest and a warning from his parole officer, he had been in a constant state of anxiety, forever looking over his shoulder, convinced he was being followed. Smithfield Institute of Technology not only offered an opportunity to retrain but, better yet, it was thousands of miles away on the other side of the country.

The cab stopped outside a crowded nightclub hung with glowing red lanterns. Geoffrey took his place in line as a huge Samoan bouncer let patrons in and out of the building. The man looked at him for a moment, then gave an amiable nod.

Dr Zoo's Monkey Bar was a madhouse of sound and light. A central floating bar was surrounded by sections of dance-floor and seating. A live band played on a mounted stage; video graphics were projected on several screens. A mezzanine level supported couches and private booths. Geoffrey bought himself a beer and a vodka chaser from the bar and sat down on a red banquette. Three young women stood nearby, shouting into each other's faces, attempting to communicate above the noise. One, a slender redhead in a skimpy green dress, looked in his direction as she spoke. Then she leant towards him: 'Lissa's lost her mobile. She was sitting in that chair.' He shook his head, unable to hear above the noise. The girl repeated what she had said.

Geoffrey stood up and the girl ran her hand around the back of the seat but found nothing. He skulled his vodka and watched the three walk back to the far side of the bar. He felt a core of warmth building inside him, filling his body, momentarily pushing the static out of his mind. He waded through the tangled mass of youth on the dance-floor and began to throw his body loosely about, lurching to the music, just another rhythmically challenged, white male dancer. Occasionally he opened his eyes and registered the strobed faces and flailing limbs around him.

When the techno beat intensified, his movements became more frenetic. He pivoted his arms in the air and threw his gleaming head back and forth. As his movements expanded, he began to encroach on the other dancers: a small circle opened around him as they retreated.

'Look out,' said a female voice above the noise.

He opened his eyes. It was the girl in the green dress, her expression hostile. He ignored her and spun around. He closed his eyes again and tried to get lost in the music but it was no good: his mind was now alert for trouble.

'Hey, mate,' called the bouncer, as he left the bar. Geoffrey stopped. 'Do you know anything about a girl's phone left on a red couch?'

'No, I don't,' he said angrily.

'Hey, pal, I'm only asking.' The bouncer stepped into Geoffrey's body space.

For a full second he fought the urge to slam his skull against the fat Samoan's forehead. He visualized the impact and saw the bloodied nose, the big man dropping to the ground. He willed himself to walk away.

He took the escalator to the Underground and bought some cigarettes at a kiosk. He sat on the platform and smoked several in quick succession. A few feet away, wrapped in an overcoat, a man lay on the cold cement. Geoffrey looked at the bloated red face of the sleeping drunk and thought idly of how easy it would be to roll him off the platform under the oncoming train, now shunting into the station with a screeching of brakes. The compartments flashed by, blank faces staring out. He boarded the train and stood between carriages. The thought of returning so soon to the empty flat was almost unbearable.

He got off at the next stop and walked a block and a half to the Astor Cinema. The video games arcade attached to the complex was full of teenage boys and younger children. A few die-hard gamers in their early twenties drew a small crowd as they hogged some of the more popular machines. Geoffrey found a chair-console with a gun-sight that pointed to an animated screen. He dropped a coin into the slot and began eliminating the human targets that leapt continuously into the frame.

The incessant gunfire soon drew a group of young spectators, who loitered around him. A boy placed a coin on the dashboard to reserve the next game. He draped his arm over the canopy, as the highest-score display flashed a row of digits, awarding a free game, then sat on the side of the console.

Geoffrey zeroed in through the gun-sight and took out the oncoming opponent. He offered the gun to the boy and vacated the seat for him, then watched for several minutes. When the game ended he bought himself a hot-dog and walked the last few blocks home. Sauce from the bun ran down the side of his hand as he shovelled the remaining quarter into his mouth. He wiped it on the back of his trousers and he rounded the corner to his street.

He immediately noted the outline of a late-model hatchback parked opposite his apartment block, and was unnerved to see the silhouette of a man behind the wheel. He accelerated his pace, and only when he was inside the gate did he dare to glance over his shoulder. The car was still there.

He let himself into the flat and locked the door. Through the window, his view of the street was partially blocked by a neighbouring gum tree. Tired now, he dropped onto the dilapidated couch and pulled a quilt over himself. The TV remote lay on the floor in front of him. He picked it up and turned the set on. A group of unshaven, hungover musicians thrashed about wildly, screaming, 'Hold you down and dirty, baby, I know you want it, baby . . . baby, baby.' He changed the channel. An advertorial extolled the compact roll-away virtues of the Gym Master Mark II. Geoffrey's eyes closed.

Liam, 2008

Blood trickled off the knuckle of his right thumb. Liam sucked it, then tightly wound a handkerchief around it. He reached through the shattered glass of the small window-pane and grappled with the inside latch of the door in front of him. He heard a distinct click as the lock opened.

A large round stone lay on the black-and-white-tiled floor surrounded by segments of glass. He pushed aside the debris with the toe of his boot and walked along the passageway to the kitchen. He placed a half-empty container labelled 'Berridale Emporium Pet Milk' on the stainless-steel counter. He carried a green canvas bag into the empty living room and dropped it. He unlatched the French windows, walked out onto the timber deck and surveyed the surrounding countryside. Most of the ridgeline was already in shadow. The landscape that had once inspired hopeful dreams now underlined his isolation.

He sat there for more than an hour, watching the darkness fall, then went inside and climbed the stairs to the attic.

White gravel crunched under the wheels of a silver Jaguar as it turned into the driveway of the farmhouse and pulled up outside. Colin Holmes stepped out into the sharp morning air; he opened the rear door for one of his passengers, a well-dressed woman in her fifties. A slightly older man emerged from the front and joined them.

The couple looked up at the house, and Colin stepped back. He loosened the knot of his pink tie, put his hands into his pockets and smiled smugly. 'Impressive, huh?'

'Very,' conceded the man.

Colin led the way past the Creighton and Davis for-sale sign, up the stairs to the front door, with its tarnished brass knocker, and turned the key in the lock. Inside, he made way for the couple and allowed them to wander through the lower rooms. 'Quality inclusions, full country kitchen, marble tiles, two bedrooms down here and the attic has already been converted.' He waited at the bottom of the stairs for the couple to join him. 'The staircase is Huon pine.'

The woman looked at the yellow-blond grain of the timber step beneath her suede boots.

'I handled this property before the previous owners renovated. They've done a great —' Colin stopped abruptly. A pair of feet was suspended at eye level in front of him. A man hung by his neck from a blue-and-white nylon rope tied to the heavy rafter above.

'Oh, Christ,' said the man behind him, grabbing his wife's arm.

The woman let out a little wail. 'Oh, my God!'

'Jesus,' whispered Colin.

Under Liam's hanging body, off to the right, lay an overturned tea-chest.

Geoffrey, 2008

The knocking continued for several seconds before it penetrated his dream: it became a volley of shots from a gun he was firing into a vacant building . . .

The knocking sounded again. He opened his eyes and sat up.

The TV was still on: a woman blew a bubble through a large wire hoop while a man in a bear suit mimed actions to a children's rhyme.

Geoffrey sat immobile on the couch as the knocking sounded for the third time. It was polite but insistent. Finally it stopped. He held his breath. After what seemed like eternity he slowly eased himself off the couch and inched his way to the wall until he was almost close enough to see out of the window.

A scratching sound at the base of the door stopped him dead. A small square of paper slid into view from beneath it.

He knelt down and extended his body across the floor until his outstretched hand reached a business card: 'Alex Reiser, Writer/Journalist'. Geoffrey's mind was spinning as he turned the card over: *Danny, it's in your best interests to speak with me.*

Adrenalin flooded his chest and his extremities tingled painfully. He jumped up and went to the window. Through the foliage he could discern the outline of the same car he had seen the night before. A siren wailed insistently in the distance.

'Danny,' said a low voice, outside the door. 'Danny.'

He dropped back to his knees and put his hand over his mouth.

'Danny,' said the voice more loudly.

'Fuck!' Someone was in the hallway of his apartment building, using his real name. He pressed himself to the inside of the door and hissed, '*What do you want?*'

'I need to talk to you, Danny.'

'That's not my name.'

'Okay – Geoffrey. That's what you go by now, isn't it?'

Geoffrey was devastated. Whoever was on the other side of the door knew everything.

'How do I know you aren't here to kill me?'

'I haven't come to hurt you. I want to write your story. No one else knows I'm here so let's keep it that way.'

Silently he considered the implied threat.

'Geoffrey?'

He unlatched the door and threw it open. 'Keep your voice down,' he snarled.

An unshaven Alex Reiser stood outside, his large frame shrouded in an oilskin coat. Geoffrey let the journalist in and searched the hallway for signs of his fellow residents before he closed the door.

Reiser was already seated on the couch with his coat off. 'It is Danny, isn't it? I know a few people in the Police Department. The word is that you've been in a spot of trouble and you'll be moving to another town or state.'

Danny's rattled mind began to focus. He was listening now.

'Starting over can be tough.'

'What do you care?'

'Maybe we can help each other out.' Reiser turned back the flap on his satchel and took out his notepad. 'I'm writing a book, Danny, a novel, about what happened. I'd like you to tell me your side of the story.'

'I'm not allowed to talk to the press. I'd go straight back to prison.'

'Like I said, it's a novel. It's not about you or the Allens, it's just a story . . . I want to get it right.'

'And I get what?'

'You get to set the record straight after all these years.'

Danny gave the journalist an embittered look, unable to imagine anyone interested in anything he had to say.

'You're right, it would be illegal for you to profit from your story, but I could pay you for your time. I think that's only fair.'

'How much?' said Danny, cutting to the chase.

Alex sighed. 'Say, one hundred and fifty an hour?'

Danny was unnerved by the proposal. It was chicken shit — and what good would money do in his predicament? On the other hand, it was a very long time since anyone had offered him anything at all. 'What would I have to do?'

'Just talk about what happened and about what's happened to you since. I want to understand.'

'No one will know you're writing about me?'

'You'll be a character in a work of fiction.'

'And you won't tell anyone about me.'

'You have my word on that, Danny.'

Over the next hour they struck an arrangement to meet for a series of interviews. They shook on the deal, which meant little to Danny — he had only Reiser's word on any of it, and the man had him firmly over a barrel. During the subsequent days they met for the three five-hour sessions that would serve as an outline for Alex's eager editor.

At the final session Danny sat facing Reiser, sizing up the journalist as he fumbled with his recorder. He set the device between them and paused it. His turn now to sit back and examine his subject.

Danny's hair had grown back to a stubble and he was sporting the beginnings of a neat beard. He chewed the nail on his thumb.

'Ready?'

Danny nodded.

During the previous sessions, as they had worked their way circuitously through the events of that long-ago day, Reiser had observed Danny to be, at times, cunning and calculated in the way he ordered information, sometimes leaving out key facts. Facts that were well established and already on record. The unshaven adult sitting before him held a tight rein on the flow of communication, hesitated before he spoke, betrayed little emotion, and stopped short of discussing certain details. But every now and then, when the memories took hold or when he was ambushed by an unexpected question, Reiser witnessed a shift as Danny the boy within looked out from his hiding place.

'Why did you take the child?'

Danny broke eye contact and fiddled with the leather loop attached to the Dictaphone.

Reiser pulled the machine aside. The question had the effect of putting Danny immediately on guard. His account always began with Benjamin's long walk away from the safety of his mother and never with the boys' motive for taking him in the first place. Circling warily around the bigger question.

'Graham was the one . . . It was his idea. It was kind of a joke that we'd take a kid and get him lost – and all these things we were gonna do to him, like in the movie the lawyer told us to say we never watched. I didn't think he'd really do it 'cause he was all talk.' Danny looked at Reiser. 'I was the one that *did* things, not Graham. Graham was a wimp . . . but he had a psycho temper.' He bit at the jagged nail again. 'When the kid came over to him and took his hand . . . We just kept walking. We walked for hours.' He began to recount the seemingly endless details of the meandering journey the three children had taken, away from the safety of the shopping precinct to the docklands.

The story was interrupted as the recorder stopped. Reiser slid the mini-cassette into his shirt pocket and peeled the cellophane off another. Danny rotated a glass of water on the table between his two thumbs as the fresh tape was inserted with a click.

'All the time you were walking around, what were you thinking?' Reiser was tiring of going over the same story without getting any closer to the truth inside Danny's head.

'We just wanted to get him somewhere away from people . . . where no one could see us.' Danny fell silent, staring into the distance as though remembering.

Goosebumps appeared on Alex Reiser's flesh as he looked at the hunted face opposite him, searching the eyes for the presence of remorse, empathy – even consciousness. The person he saw was malformed, stunted. Born of a long line of violent drunkards and malingerers stung by society's inequalities, dropped on his head into their grubby world of drama and shame. Neglected and brutalized, what hope was there for him?

Thinking of the many injuries the defenceless victim had sustained in the attack, Reiser pushed on for an answer to the obvious question: 'Why would you want to hurt a helpless baby?'

It was a question, even now, that Danny could not answer. How could he explain the depth of his hatred for any goodness or softness, his rage and hostility, his desire to inflict pain, the relief of doing what was done to him? The power and the thrill of taking a child from a mother, and life from the child. He did not understand it himself. How was it possible to express that, from the moment they had clapped eyes on him, Benjamin – small, vulnerable and protected – represented all that he and Graham were denied?

343

He shrugged his shoulders, a recalcitrant eleven-year-old again. 'I don't know. It was just something to do.'

Something to do. To even the score with life by taking from it. A long moment outside time to exact vengeance on an innocent baby, an unwitting family, a whole community and an indifferent world. An arbitrary death sentence handed down long before the perpetrators were even born.

Reiser's palms were sticky with sweat; the hand with the pen had stopped writing. He contemplated the narrowing spool on the tiny recorder and hung his head, filled with revulsion and sorrow. After all his digging, what had he expected? Some detail or revelation that would make sense of atrocity? A satisfying explanation of cause and effect? It made no sense – it never would – but it was the dark and ugly truth that he had asked for.

'Do you ever think about the parents?'

Danny shook his head unconvincingly. 'Whatever, they have to live with it, I have to live with this.' He looked from wall to wall of the tiny flat that represented the cage of his life.

Uncomfortable with the comparison, the journalist crossed his arms and studied Danny for a long moment.

'I don't let those thoughts in.'

Reiser tried again. 'Do you think if your home life had been . . .' He paused, searching for the right word.

'If my father hadn't been an arsehole drunk and my mother wasn't a useless whore?' Danny didn't wait for the rhetorical question to be answered. 'I didn't choose to be born. You don't have to be a head doctor to know that if I'd grown up in a normal family that kid would still be here.'

'Do you ever wonder who you might have become if you hadn't gone to the Regency Arcade that day?'

'That's easy,' he said, without a moment's hesitation. 'I'd be in a real prison right now.'

Reiser nodded. Although the insight surprised him, it was an ironic twist of Fate that Danny had been lucky to escape his family at the age of eleven. He'd had a more stable upbringing and a better education in custody than he could have imagined back in the Simpson household.

'Sooner or later I was going to do something,' he said flatly. 'I had it in me.'

345

Living

'Valley of the shadow'

Mathew, 2009

The incline that led down from the overpass was now a bare slope. The gorse bushes had been levelled and an attempt made to plant it with native shrubs. The few that survived were low to the ground; nothing seemed to want to grow there. Well-intentioned locals had made plans to erect a humble monument but the Allens had intervened: this was not a place they wanted commemorated. People still came to see where it had happened; some left tributes anyway.

The other side of the hill overlooked a different universe, one of reclaimed docklands and open parkland. Battery Cove was now a gentrified development of factory conversions and desirable apartments.

Dead flowers crunched under his shoes as he walked steadily downhill, carrying a bunch of scarlet carnations. He had never been able to bring himself to visit this place of death. Every inch of it was known to him: a map of carnage and agony. His eyes went immediately to the exact spot where his son had been found. How many times had he steeled himself to come here? Each time feeling himself a coward not to face up to it and stand where Benjamin had stood alone and fallen. With the anniversary of his son's murder approaching, he finally felt ready to shoulder his last responsibility as a father.

By not setting foot here he had been able to keep the awful details of Benjamin's last hours, read in court and told to him by detectives, in separate compartments in his head. He had been forced to confront each of these facts, had needed to know exactly what had happened to his son, but without coming here he had avoided joining all the dots together. Kneeling in that place, the scene he had held down for so long came to life around him. He heard the plaintive cries of his baby son, his high voice pleading. Cries for mercy that were met with the mocking laughter of his attackers.

'I want my daddy.'

'I'm here, Benji!' he cried, running along the slope, slipping on stones, scrambling to his feet.

'Daddy?'

'Your daddy isn't here.'

'Don't listen to them, Benjamin. They can't hurt you now. You're safe.'

'I knew you'd come.' The toddler giggled in the old infectious way. 'Daddy, you look tired.'

'I am, son. I had to stay awake. I had to find you . . .'

'I'm not here any more.'

He blinked back tears. 'I know, love. You're with the angels now.'

Benjamin smiled as his father laid the carnations carefully on the ground and let the tears roll freely down his face, able at last to forgive himself for not being there when his child had needed him most.

He sat for a long time afterwards in the open playing fields above the dockside. Two toddlers in Kelly green shirts ran about, shrieking with delight while their young father chased and tackled them, then threw them into the air, allowing them to chase him in turn, letting them slap him gleefully and pull him to the ground. They were tireless. Their father was their moon and stars, the arbiter of all justice and protection, safety and adventure in perfect measure. When one boy inevitably fell hard and burst into tears, the father lifted him up and held him. Ever so gently, he soothed the child, while playfully dragging along his sibling, who was wrapped around his ankle.

Joy, comfort and love. Mathew Allen had had all those with Benjamin, and for that he would be eternally grateful.

Rachel, 2009

A young girl sat huddled on her father's lap observing the uniformed bus driver as he emptied the luggage hold. She wriggled down onto the cold concrete and skipped beyond the shadows of the bus to the next bay, climbing up onto the cement rockery to pick the tiny flowers off a pink baronia, crushing the petals between her fingers and bringing the scent to her nose. The girl's father tracked her movements out of the corner of his eye.

Rachel McKenna watched her too, through the windscreen of her car. She pressed her head back into the passenger seat and closed her eyes. David reached across and touched her hand. 'You'll be fine.'

A small group of teenagers stood by the doors to the terminal. More arrived in a steady stream and soon the platform was full of teens toting bags and pairs of hovering parents. Boys in caps, earplugs tethered to their iPods. Coltish girls in patterned leggings, who jiggled from foot to foot in an effort to stamp out the cold.

A Greyhound bus slid into view and pulled up in the crowded bay. 'Here it is,' called Thomas, from the back seat of the Land Rover.

Martin threw open his door and jumped out. 'I'll get my bags.'

Thomas made to follow.

'Hang on,' said his father.

Rachel's eyes were locked on the bus. David leant over and undid her seatbelt. 'You can do this.' He stepped out of the car, walked to her side and opened the door.

Martin took out his backpack and slipped it on, pulled his bag from the hatch and wheeled it across the cement.

Rachel finally stepped out and stood in front of him, taking hold of both his shoulders. 'You're going to have a wonderful trip, and you're not going to worry about me. Okay?'

Martin smiled broadly. 'Okay.'

She kissed his forehead and held him close.

'I'll be getting *Dragon Ball Z*.' Thomas commandeered the suitcase and dragged it behind him.

'We haven't forgotten. Do your jacket up, Martin.' Rachel pulled the hood from his collar.

'This is it, then.' David marshalled his tribe and ushered them across the car park.

Light from the early-morning sun backlit the terminal, creating the effect of a halo above the roof of the bus. Rachel reached down and took her son's hand. The four-teen-year-old made no protest. He squeezed hers and pulled it to his side.

Beside the charter bus, a tall, athletic man held a clip-board to his chest, ticking off the names of his charges as they surrendered their luggage. 'Hey, Martin. Good morning, folks.' He pointed to the front of the cargo hold. 'Pop that straight in here, buddy.'

Thomas upended the fat rectangle and hoisted it in with the other kids' bags.

'That's the way.'

The teacher turned again to Martin. 'All ready?'

'Yep.'

'And don't you worry,' he said, winking at Rachel. 'I'll take good care of this one.'

'You've got all our numbers,' said David.

Rachel was looking at her son. 'I expect a phone call every single day,' she said, smiling hard. 'I want a picture of you standing in front of that bloody lake at sunset, okay?'

'Sure, Mum.'

She ruffled his hair and let go of his hand.

'I'll be fine,' he called over his shoulder, bounding up the steps and forging his way to the back of the bus.

Alex Reiser, 2009

Inside the air-conditioned taxi, Reiser thumbed the dog-eared pages of his *Lonely Planet Guide to Indonesia*.

'Which terminal?' The driver's dark eyes were framed in the rear-view mirror.

'Virgin,' said Reiser, replacing his bookmark.

'You go?'

'Bali.'

The driver pouted, then nodded. These fat Australians were always headed off to Bali. Some of them never came back.

Reiser knew exactly what he was thinking but his interest in Bali had nothing to do with sweaty nights of

Bintang passion. This was no holiday. He was returning to a squalid jail near Denpasar to interview the inmates, chasing down a story about the fate of foreign nationals in custody. His flight was being met by the mother of a young drug trafficker awaiting execution.

The taxi squeezed into the drop-off lane outside the teeming airport, nosing into a gap between two minibuses. A horn sounded. Reiser heaved his bag onto the roadway, slammed the boot and waved the driver on.

After queuing at the check-in desk, he headed straight through security, keen to find his boarding gate. He held his big hands out from his sides as he walked through the metal detector, keeping pace with his bags as they got a free ride to the other side. For good measure, an inscrutable security officer beckoned him over for another pass with her scanner. In his creased white linen jacket and baggy trousers, he was an unlikely drug mule.

He quickly moved away from the crowded hub of the fast-food hall, with its stink of stale oil. Halfway along the tunnel of overpriced designer clothing outlets and day spas that led to his boarding gate, he stopped to adjust his grip on his luggage. As he heaved the heavy laptop satchel back to his shoulder, his attention was caught by a stack of paperbacks, front and centre, in the airport bookstore. His eyes locked on the cover of a facing book standing on top of the pyramid. A broken white picket fence, beneath an overcast, but breaking sky.

Across the foreboding image, in black type, loomed the title *THE WRONG HAND*.

Epilogue

'Don't ask, don't tell'

Geoffrey, 2010

A bell sounded as the doors opened onto the first-floor lobby of Bell and Pearson Software Systems. A small boy let go of his mother's hand and rushed into the elevator. He reached up to the control panel.

'Where to?' asked the auburn-haired man, who was the lift's only other occupant.

'Fourth,' answered the boy's mother.

'I wanted to push it.'

'Never mind.'

At the third floor the lift stopped again and the man alighted. He carried a leather bag slung over his shoulder. The corridor was lined with frosted-glass panels, interrupted at intervals by heavy doors engraved with a single lotus and the slogan 'Ideas First'.

The pretty receptionist looked up from her station opposite the lift. 'Can I help?'

He handed her a card. 'I'm here to see Gabriel Lowe.'

'A Mr Anderson to see you,' she said, into the mouth-piece of her headset. 'I'll send him through.'

Gabe Lowe's desk was at the centre of an open-plan office that covered half the floor space of a large, light-filled atrium. 'Hey!' He stood up and shook the incomer's hand. 'You're early. I like that.' He waved in the direction of one of his co-workers. 'Brian! Come meet Anderson. This is the guy I told you about, our new systems-installation administrator.'

'Good to meet you, Anderson.'

'Brian looks after our brains trust, so to speak. He makes sure everyone stays up to speed and keeps doing what they do best.'

Anderson nodded awkwardly.

'Sit, sit. First the paperwork.' Lowe pulled out several sheets from a ring binder. 'The usual stuff . . . Tax forms, Superfund, personal details, salary sacrifice.' He laid the forms down one by one.

Anderson began writing, furiously replicating his details across the top of the pages.

'First aid. Don't worry if it's not current. The firm runs a refresher every quarter. Police background check.'

Anderson paused, halfway through a word.

'That's a legal due diligence, given that some of our clients are libraries and educational institutes.'

He put the pen back to the paper and continued writing *Geoffrey Wade Anderson*.

'Welcome on board, Anderson – or do you prefer Geoffrey?'

'Anderson is just fine,' he replied, without looking up.

Acknowledgements

Heartfelt thanks to my agent Piers Blofeld, for his conviction and enthusiasm in championing this book.

To the entire team at Penguin MJ. Louise Moore, Maxine Hitchcock. My Editor Clare Bowron for her insight, patience and sensitivity. Copy-editor Hazel Orme for all her help. Hana Osman for hers.

To loved ones, parents, family, friends, and readers past and present, who have offered encouragement along the way; you know who you are.

Thanks to my son Martin for his love and support.

To my son Hari for his love and support, and for his editorial input, creative feedback and counsel throughout the project.

To Lauren for the love, laughter and guidance. To Bill for the letters and the words, RIP.

To past mentors: NRWC, QWR, Hachette, AFC, Mark Malatesta, Bernadette Foley, Marele Day, Annette Barlow, Sarah Armstrong, Rebecca Sparrow, Angela Slatter, and Peter Bishop.

And God, who sent them.

Reading Group Discussion Questions

1. Has your response to the plight of the three families involved in this tragedy surprised you at all?

2. Do you feel Danny and Graham were too young to be 'capable of malice'? How does this affect your views on the nature/nurture debate?

3. Many would say the perpetrators of a crime like this were 'born evil', but this book disputes that in a very thought-provoking way. What do you think?

4. Alex Reiser finds a surprising number of precedent cases in his research, and the public and legal responses are all quite different. What did you make of the Norwegian case and the decision not to report it as a crime but as a tragedy?

5. Rachel and Matthew grieve in conflicting ways for Benjamin and it seems that all too often after loss or trauma a marriage fails. Do you think it would ever be possible for a marriage to survive something like this?

6. The author shows how greatly the lives of the perpetrators and their families were destroyed as well as those of the Allen family. Do you think this is

appropriate punishment for such a heinous crime? Or a further tragedy in itself.

7. And what does this make you feel about the penal system and the responsibilities of the press?

8. Rachel Allen talks very movingly about how much harder her grieving process was, due to the press intrusion and Benjamin being 'public property'. Do you think this was inevitable given the nature of the crime or do you think the press had an unsavoury role that would benefit from being addressed going forwards?